Angels in Your Beer

Angels in Your Beer

Jeremy Scott

W. H. ALLEN · LONDON
A Howard & Wyndham Company
1979

To PMS, and Roger and Jill Marshall,
with thanks

Printed and bound in Great Britain by
Butler & Tanner Ltd, Frome and London
for the Publishers, W. H. Allen & Co. Ltd,
44 Hill Street, London W1X 8LB

ISBN 0 491 02238 7

In Paris Henry Miller has been going through a lousy time, cold, penniless and unemployed. Suddenly he gets a job and a place to live; fortune smiles on him and money fills his pocket. This makes him apprehensive. He writes that at times like these he is most fearful, for it is always at such moments that the angels choose to piss in his beer.

One

That morning they took the autoroute from Paris, getting up and starting later than he had planned. Grey cloud lay low over the highway in Auxerre turning to slow drizzle which streaked the flanks of the white Ferrari with mud and painted the road to the same slick blackness as the tyres.

There was little traffic at this season and the man held the car at a steady 170 kilometres an hour as the motorway curved southward through the rain-drenched rolling farmland, Vivaldi on the radio, the swell and sob of violins above the snarl of the motor and hiss and snap of the wipers flickering across his vision.

The man drove with his arms and legs stretched out straight in front of him and the seat set back to its limit. He was tall and thin. His face was drawn and tired and there was a pallor around his mouth and jaw as though the skin there had been denied sunlight. He wore sunglasses with mirrored reflecting lenses which hid the swollen purple bruises around his eyes but the rest of his features were good. His hair was full and well cut and turning white. For the last five years women had described him as distinguished. It was not a word which pleased him particularly but he reckoned that if you had to grow old it was better than some.

A tall sign flashed past, BEAUNE SUD, white line curving off to the side. Another sign, CHALON 17. He reached into the glove compartment and passed a red Michelin guide to the girl in the passenger seat.

'Read for lunch.'

She had eaten boiled eggs and three croissants with butter and cherry jam for breakfast in the Crillon and now she was starving. He liked that.

The girl wore a white shirt with grey culottes and a straw boater decorated with a green ribbon. Her blonde hair was escaping from its pins and drooped softly over the nape of her neck. It needed to be washed and as she opened the Michelin he saw that her fingernails were dirty.

According to her passport which he carried in his jacket she was eighteen years of age and had been christened Marianne Gladys Brent. Beside it, the other passport in his pocket described its owner as forty-seven years old, born in Hampstead, London, and was issued in the name of Michael Phillip Law. It contained a photograph which was an excellent likeness of the man, the mouth set down a little at the corners in the ironic suggestion of a smile as he faced the photographer. But the passport itself was a forgery.

She was reading aloud.

'The Chateau de Vernegues, in red print, telephone, garage, crossed knives and forks ...'

'Stars?'

'Two.'

'Go on.'

'Specialities, *terrine de canard truffe*, *écrevisses a la creme* ... what's that?'

'Crayfish.'

'*Poulet au bour ... bour ...*' she stumbled on the word.

'*Au Bourgogne*. Sounds promising. We'll eat there.'

He glanced at his watch and minutely adjusted his foot's pressure on the accelerator. The red needle on the accelerator flickered to 200 KPH.

The Chateau de Vernegues had stood undisturbed for five centuries in thirty hectares of private park before the autoroute had sliced a broad and profitable furrow fifty metres from the double sweep of steps which mounted to its lordly entrance.

Inside was cool and resonant, with a lofty hall, stone walls, a stairway curving upwards into shadow. The man led the way to the reception desk across a vast floor paved with flagstones.

'*On peut manger?*'

'*Mais bien sûr, monsieur.*'

There was a certain authority to his manner. He was accustomed to being well received in hotels and restaurants. He wore a light grey flannel suit and brown shoes, thin as slippers, whose buckles chinked faintly as he walked. There was the ease and assurance of wealth in the way he moved. She followed him into the dining room.

They were shown to a table by the window. Outside, beyond the balustrade of a flower-hung terrace, lush pasture stretched to the treeline. Enclosed by a picket fence horses grazed in the rain. There was neither sight nor sound of the autoroute.

The waiter spread open the leather-bound menu and laid it in the man's hands. He placed the wine list upon the table.

'*Si vous me permettez de vous conseiller ...*'

'How are the *quenelles de brochet*?' the man asked.

'They are one of our specialities.'

The girl had lit a cigarette and was reading from a booklet she had found upon the table.

'The Chateau de Vernegues belonged through marriage to the Marquis de Sade ...'

She looked up.

'I never thought the Marquis de Sade was a real person.'

'Who then?'

'I thought he was someone in a film, like Count Dracula. You know what I mean.'

'He was real enough,' said the man with a smile. 'What do you want to eat?'

She studied the unintelligible menu recognising only omelette and not what was in that.

'What's *cass . . . cassoulet*?'

'Goose. I'm sure delicious but very heavy. Why don't you have fish?'

'You choose.'

He did it well, ordering for both of them a lobster soufflé and grilled turbot. His accent was good and the waiter made no attempt to talk back in English.

The girl looked about her with unaffected pleasure. The room was elegant and airy, the tables well spaced, laid with starched white linen, silver and forests of wine-glasses. A half-dozen tables were occupied, mostly by local people with one other couple who were clearly travellers. A pale youth in apron of floor-length white stood by an elaborate chariot of *hors d'œuvres*.

'Pretty classy place he lived in, the Marquis.'

'Not always. He spent a certain amount of time . . . away.'

'Inside? What did they nick him for?'

'Please,' said the man, his tone exaggeratedly pained. 'Do you mind if we talk about something else?'

The girl laughed.

The waiter poured the wine and she sniffed and tasted it as she had been taught before she drank.

'Montrachet,' she pronounced, reading the label. 'A white burgundy, a bottle with no shoulders.'

'You're learning.'

'Am I ever,' she said and laughed again. Her teeth were very white. She had the face of a *gamine*, both bold and sly, and her mouth was too big. He studied her with pride. She was very pretty. She looked less than eighteen, the daring ringleader in some schoolgirl magazine, a fearless heroine of spirited adventure.

She ate ravenously, the man more slowly but with great pleasure. Throughout that morning, with every mile added to the distance between him and England, he had felt better. The tense clamp on the back of his neck had slackened its grip, the muscles loosened in his shoulders. For the first time in months he felt at ease. He could afford to relax now. Paris had been the last cut-out. From here on the sun was shining.

They spent two hours over lunch. The rain cleared while they ate. The clouds rolled away.

He ordered coffee, and a brandy for himself. He did not feel like driving. He chose a cigar while the waiter hovered attentively with a cutter.

'We could take rooms here,' he suggested. 'Have a siesta, dine, go on in the morning. One last night of luxury.'

She shook her head with childish vehemence.

'No! I want to see the Mill. You promised!'

He let a rich cloud of smoke float toward the moulded ceiling and smiled indulgently. 'As you will.'

It was she who had found the advertisement in *The Times*:

'FOR RENT. SOUTH OF FRANCE. CONVERTED MILL. SECLUDED. THIRTY POUNDS WEEKLY.'

At the time she had read it he had had other problems on his mind, bad ones. He had consented only to humour her, knowing at that season it would be easy to find something else better and a great deal more expensive. Price was of no importance now.

'I'll drive,' she proposed.

He felt indulgent, but not that indulgent.

'Too alarming. Like swimming after lunch, at my age it could be fatal.'

She grinned.

'Get off!' she said.

The bill was served on a silver tray. The girl craned her head to see it and her forehead knotted as she made the calculation. She said incredulously, 'But that's fifty quid.'

'It's a good restaurant.'

'Cripes!' she said.

He paid from a plump bundle of 500-franc notes. He always liked to have a lot of money in cash with him. In the old days of the white five-pound notes he had carried a fat wad of which only the outside two or three were real and the rest tissue paper cut to size. But that was a long time ago now.

By four they were past Aix. At Avignon the season had changed, sun on the wide turgid river ripening vines first planted by the Romans. A warm, rich gentle land. Now the motorway cut through hills of pine, gorse, outbreaks of rock; rough country, empty of houses. The sun was lower and the afternoon air smelled of herbs and resin.

The girl paid little attention to the passing scene. Her interest was quickly satisfied. She fiddled with the radio.

He asked, 'What are you thinking?'

'Nothing.'

Her eyes met his guilelessly. Liar, he thought. The hills pressed closer, steeper here, the foothills of the Alps. Then the highway climbed in a long straight sweep and, as the car dipped over the ridge, the ground fell away and the whole bay of Cannes was revealed beneath them, the sea a deep dark blue and the town white and tiny. In the far distance the mountains were covered in snow, icy and brilliant in the sinking sun.

His heart lifted at the sight and he glanced at the girl to see her reaction, but the smooth child's face was inscrutable.

At Cannes they left the autoroute and turned inland. They began to climb immediately. The road followed up the valley. Away from the coast the houses were fewer and less opulent. They passed a perched village over to the left, set upon the crest of the further slope. The hills grew steeper. Ahead of them the glittering wall of snow-capped peaks was constantly in view.

A hundred yards beyond a crossroads he stopped to study a map. He turned the car and took the lesser road. A mile further and they reached a village.

'Do you have those instructions?'

'The place is not easy to find . . .' she read from a letter written on thin blue paper by a wavering and infirm hand. The directions corresponded poorly with the map. Poppies grew thick along the verges of the narrow road beyond the village. They drove for a mile without seeing a house. He drew in to the side so a car might pass, a battered *deux chevaux* driven by a florid man in worker's overalls who stared at them curiously as he went by.

At once the road began to descend steeply, twisting and looping down the valley. To one side was a high bank tangled with bramble and wild flowers, the other fell precipitously to the valley floor where a river gleamed in the gathering gloom. The hillside was uncultivated and overgrown, creepers hanging from the trees.

He stopped.

'Read it to me again.'

He studied the map helplessly; there was no correspondence.

'Well . . .'

He shrugged, and slipped the car into gear. Its hard suspension jolted them over the potholes.

'Lost in the boon docks. And you a city child,' he said.

He turned onto a dirt track which led down toward the river.

It was dusk here. The sun had gone from the valley floor but above them reared a spike of rock, a thousand-foot-high vertical crag which blazed in the last rays of the setting sun.

'Look!'

At the bottom of the gorge was a house, grey, stark and square, unadorned and angular as a drawing done by a child. A classic millhouse, built for utility, its row of tiny prison-like windows and stern façade in this lush pastoral setting beside the river was disconcertingly forbidding. As he switched off the motor the roar of water washed over them.

She opened the door and ran from the car, disappearing up the overgrown path which led toward the unlighted house. He swung his legs to the ground with reluctance. The accumulated fatigue of all he had gone through emptied his limbs. He felt suddenly drained and old. No longer a man in the freedom of transit, he had arrived.

He straightened up. It was no time to become fanciful. Anyway, this was a stopping place, not a destination. But he shivered as he moved toward the house. Here with the sun gone, the place was chill. A blank stone wall confronted him, a single door.

'Down here! Come quick!'

Her excited voice came from somewhere below him. Steps led down, turning at the angle of the wall, weeds grown high between their stones. He followed carefully in the failing light.

Around the corner he halted in astonishment.

The river rushed ten yards below the house, cascading over a waterfall into a broad rockpool, a millpond confined by the sides of the gorge and stoppered by gigantic tumbled rocks jammed into a natural dam, polished white and smooth as bone by the torrent. Wild figtrees grew in cracks between the rocks, their lower branches brushing the surface, tugged at by the current. The place was hidden and secret, a miniature perfection.

The walls of the ravine cut off much of the sky. Behind him reared the dark bulk of the house. In no direction was the view longer than forty yards except above the roof where, two miles distant, the very summit of that single spire of rock still flared in the sun. Even as he watched, the engulfing shadow raced up the final peak and swallowed it into darkness.

'Look at me!'

She had stripped off her clothes and stood naked upon one of those polished boulders which formed the dam. As he turned she dived, her lithe body arching forward as a white flash in the dull light. She disappeared into the churning water without a splash.

He ran down the remaining steps in alarm but by the time he reached the water's edge she was already there, pulling herself out and gasping from the cold. Catching up her shirt, she used it to towel herself dry.

'I didn't know you could swim like that.'

Her teeth were chattering. He knelt to feel the water, icy from the melting snows which fed the river.

'Come. You'll freeze to death.'

He took off his jacket and laid it around her shoulders. On bare feet she scampered up the stairs ahead of him. Pearls of water beaded the firm calves, glistening on her lean hard thighs.

The door of the mill was unlocked. He pushed it open and found impenetrable blackness. He felt over the rough wall for a lightswitch, found it and pressed it down.

They stood on a raised platform which formed one end of a long, beamed room on three levels, the entire lower floor of the mill, the old machine room converted to human habitation. Converted badly and inadequately, the man's eye noted in passing, moving from the naked flex which trailed the ceiling to the Victorian sideboard and a pair of collapsed armchairs which, together with a massive wardrobe, were the only furniture. Yet such details seemed irrelevant beside the heavy beams, the vast open fireplace and the flagstone floor. The overall effect of the place was nothing less than stunning.

The girl stood naked in the doorway. She had forgotten how cold she was.

'Too fucking much,' she said.

He found a bathroom, a makeshift affair, and handed her the single skimpy towel. She dried herself while he climbed a winding staircase and prowled upstairs. Two bedrooms, hardboard partitioned, one big one small. His and hers. In the second, one leg was missing from the bed which sagged forlorn, its corner resting upon a deck of tiles. A folded deck-chair leaned against the wall, BOGNOR CORPORATION stencilled on its canvas.

The floors were of painted concrete embellished by two threadbare mats. But by the bed stood a chair the man recognised as Chippendale, in poor repair. The place had been converted in the cheapest possible manner, with the barest concessions to modernity, by someone with no conception of comfort. He noticed with dismay that the only heating in this bedroom was provided by a dismal two-bar electric fire, an infirm antique with blackened wires crusted with ancient crumbs of toast. He went downstairs again. The girl had left the bathroom and was standing on the farther platform, separated from him by the sunken section of the room. She had tucked the towel around her waist like a man and stood with her head thrown back, gazing up into the smoke-blackened rafters, her expression rapt.

'Mindblowing,' she said.

'Never expected it would be as great as *this*.' She scampered down the steps and bounced up to him impetuously.

'Congratulate me! I found it. Go on, admit it, it blows your mind too. Admit it! Congratulate me!'

He gazed at her fondly. His misgivings about the place, its damp chill and discomfort, those spoiled ease-ridden considerations of a middle-aged adult, left him before such childish joy. Her face glowed. She was as excited as a puppy.

'It's astonishing,' he said.

At that second all the lights went out.

In total blackness the man's reaction was unseen by the girl but it was immediate and instinctive. He had spun about to face the door which he knew to be behind him and was crouched with arms still and fingers splayed to grapple with the terror which was about to spring on him from the night. His mouth was dry and his heart raced. He was deadly afraid and he was ready to kill. The girl giggled in the dark.

'Cor! Industrial stoppage.'

He relaxed, straightened up, glad not to have been seen.

'Where's your lighter?'

'In the bathroom.'

'Go for it slowly.'

He heard her bare feet shuffling on the stone, then padding

carefully down the stairs. He could distinguish nothing at all. The blackness was absolute.

'More probably a fuse,' he said.

'What are we going to do?' Her voice came from the other side of the room.

'Drive, find a hotel. Deal with it tomorrow.'

'Maybe we could find a candle.'

The creak of a door, a wink of light, and her face appeared distant and high, suspended in limbo.

She dressed quickly while he waited. Raising her arms to put on the tunic, the pool of light flickered across the pink buds of her nipples.

Outside, the sky was clear and starlit. The night was cold and windless and a sickle moon hung low over the icy line of the mountains.

From this side of the mill the river was invisible, its roar muted. The forested hillside stretched away dark and lifeless.

He started as the girl touched his arm. She pointed. Above them, a single light glimmered through the trees. He saw that the steps from the pool continued uphill.

She started out before him.

Briars caught at his ankles. Still wearing his sunglasses he saw badly. Once the stone crumbled beneath his feet and he fell, tearing his hand. He swore softly and sucked the gash, tasting blood.

'Butterfoot. It's easier here.'

He could distinguish her above him against the sky. He scrambled up the slope.

Many years ago the trees had been cut back here to form a garden, now long overgrown. Sealed in by the encroaching forest, in the clearing stood the dark bulk of a house, its sagging roofline a black curve below the moon.

They approached. At ground level the building contained no windows, no door. The wall rose sheer and blind to that single light. Searching the stone, his hand met air – a low arch, a hole. He flicked the lighter and held the flame above his head, glimpsed a vaulted tunnel slick with damp, the far-down sheen and gurgle of water.

'How do we get in?'

Knee high in undergrowth and roses run wild they felt their way around the corner of the building. Here was a flight of stairs with a hand-rail. A gust of foetid air breathed in his face. He took the lead.

Abruptly the staircase terminated in a closed door, light spilling from its ill-fitting surround and through its cracks. After a moment's pause he knocked sharply. The door swung open with surprising speed. A dark figure stood outlined in the frame of light.

Next day he would try to recall exactly that first impression but, by then, subsequent observation had enriched it with details which surely, in that first frozen moment before the gowned figure leaned toward them from the light and spoke, it would have been impossible for him to distinguish.

Dimly illuminated by a single lamp, the enormous room was austere and bleak. It could have been magnificent; instead it was forbidding. At one end, inadequately partitioned, was a wretched kitchen, the stove and tiny icebox visibly antiques. Such furniture as existed was in deplorable condition. The veneer was peeling from the bureau, the leg of the sideboard had been crudely splinted with unpainted wood. Yet the place was spotlessly neat and clean and the close air smelled of furniture polish.

'My name's Law,' the man said after a moment. 'We ...'

He was not allowed to finish. The old woman threw wide the door with a cry of welcome and stepped back into the light.

In the dingy yellow gloom he saw a gaunt, once pretty, face devoid of makeup, the hair gathered into a bun. The clothes were twinset and tweed skirt, decent, drab and worn out; but the voice was hearty and unabashed. She shrilled in the fierce accents of the English uppercrust, that exaggerated tone which pierces like a jagged blade.

'We know, my dear man, we know. Come in, do, both of you. We *know* who you are. We've been *expecting* you.'

So they were greeted, and thus it was that the man and the girl first entered the upper mill.

Two

The girl was gone when he awoke, but from the window he saw her already down by the rockpool.

In the primitive bathroom the hot tap thudded and shook then delivered a tepid trickle. He cleaned the basin, refilled it and shaved carefully. The girl's worn toothbrush stood in a cracked glass, sole sign of her occupation, her only article of toilet.

He studied his face attentively in the mirror. Massive bruising encircled the eyes, the flesh there puffed and purple though already the swelling was less than yesterday, he thought. He replaced his sunglasses before leaving the bathroom.

He had unpacked the night before and hung up his clothes on a rod set across the corner of the room which, covered by a thin curtain, did duty as a wardrobe. He had three suits, a selection of good casual clothes and a couple of dozen silk shirts. Every item that he owned was new and bought in Paris.

He dressed slowly, finding enjoyment in the process. Clothes had always been important to him and it was over two years since he had had the pleasure of dressing well.

The kitchen was bare. He searched for coffee without conviction. A cabinet contained only crockery, none too clean. The refrigerator was empty, disconnected or not working, filmed in green mould. It did not matter. They were not going to stay. He had decided that. The mill was not the only secluded place available for rent. Certainly it was picturesque. The romantic idyll is all very well but he was used to central heating. He was cold. It was uncomfortable.

Leaving the house he took the steps which led down toward the river. At the angle of the wall where they turned and the rockpool came into view he stopped again as he had last night.

By day the place was still an enchantment, the morning light striking upon the polished boulders but not yet on the sliding water, its sleek passage across the pool reflecting the overhanging sunlit branches of the wild figtrees clawed into the rockface.

He saw that the way divided where he stood, the steps continuing down toward the water, and an overgrown but paved path branching to follow the base of the house to a ruined structure which once had stood beside it.

Unable to distinguish what this might have been, he approached closer, and saw a series of drainage basins on descending levels, each the size of a small room, built to catch the spill of water which once had powered the mill.

Walking along the choked path and pressing aside the nettles with his unsuitably light shoes he made his way to the ruin. Three of the supporting columns still stood but the roof itself was long gone, collapsed in debris into the dry reservoirs. The remains of the building were buried beneath an impenetrable covering of thorn and ivy.

He stepped up onto the crumbling concrete which lined the floor of the lowest basin and found himself on a level platform set upon the cliff's edge fifteen feet above the surface of the rockpool which it overlooked. He was in a roofless, low-walled, three-sided room, the front open upon the pool and dominating it in the same fashion as a box in a theatre dominates the stage. The girl was down there. Outstretched upon the boulders below, she had not seen him. Wearing the same pants as the day before and nothing else, her slender body curved across the polished stone, eyes closed and face turned up toward the sun, flowerlike in shameless innocence.

In their separate positions man and girl stayed immobile for several minutes. At last he stooped, picked up a pebble, and tossed it into the water by her feet. She sat up instantly with a start. He saw there was no movement at all in her small breasts, no change of shape in those firm mounds with their sharp and rosy points.

'Where are you?'

She wriggled impatiently and looked about her.

He flipped another stone into the water. She raised her head, saw him and grinned.

'Isn't this just the most *fabulous* place you've ever seen?' she shouted excitedly above the noise of the waterfall.

'Outta-sight!' he called back, mimicking her speech, and she laughed for the outdated word in English accent sounded odd from him as he stood above her in his elegant expensive clothes, rich and old.

'Come,' he said, 'I'll take you to breakfast.'

'What?'

'Coffee, croissants. Black cherry jam.'

'Fried eggs?'

'Your every wish.'

'Yummee!'

She leaped up and sprang across the rocks, her legs like pale stalks.

He met her at the junction of the steps.

'Did you bathe?'

'It isn't half cold.'

'Later I'll take you to a hotel pool where we can swim.'

Ahead of him on the stairs she spun around, her face amazed.

'Are you crazy? This is just the most funky place I've *ever* seen.'

He waited below while she scampered up to her room, her head reappearing at the top of the spiral staircase.

'Do I have to wear the culottes or can I put on my jeans?'

'Anything,' he said, 'this is your day.'

'All super day?'

'All day,' he confirmed gravely.

‘Till sunset or midnight?’

‘Get dressed,’ he ordered.

When she rejoined him he was outside by the car. The back was open and he stood at the exposed engine listening to its noise.

‘Something wrong?’

‘Get in and rev the motor a bit.’

She squirmed into the driver’s seat and gripped the wheel. The engine roared into an explosion of sound.

‘Steady!’

He bent over, hands clean, making no attempt to touch the machinery. Normally he was careless with his possessions but the Ferrari was a new toy, bought in Paris. He slammed the cover shut.

‘Move over!’

She flung her leg across the gearbox and hitched her agile rump into the other seat, a movement impossibly awkward for an adult which she performed with coltish grace.

He had studied the map and in fifteen minutes of country roads they were in Lezat, a thriving market town eight miles inland from the coast. Its medieval centre was much enlarged by a surrounding development of apartment buildings and modern shops and, though he had been there years before, the man remembered it not at all.

He stopped at a garage to fill up with petrol.

‘If I accelerate the engine will you listen to the motor for an instant?’ he asked the attendant.

‘*Il y a quelque chose qui va pas?*’

‘There is a certain noise.’

The attendant studied the car with doubt, pump nozzle in hand.

‘The oil pressure, it is normal?’

‘Yes, but under power the sound is different.’

The mechanic’s expression suggested that he was not the best person to ask for counsel.

‘A car like that ... *c’est un peu specialisé.*’

He regarded the exposed engine with some awe.

'In truth, a car like this . . . you should go to Nice.'

'I just want to know that I can drive it. That there's nothing seriously wrong.'

The mechanic sucked the breath in between his teeth. He began to shake his head but the man persisted.

'Look, we have some things to do in town. If I leave it with you for an hour, will you look it over?'

'*Si vous insistez.*'

The prospect did not excite him but he accepted.

In the main avenue of the town they stopped at a stationers where he bought the *Daily Express* and *The Times.*

'You don't yet have today's edition?'

'Later, monsieur. This afternoon.'

He glanced attentively over the front pages of both before leaving the shop. Nothing there, he saw.

At a boutique he bought the girl two bikinis, and despite her protests, three pairs of underpants. He proposed shirts but, 'I've got shirts,' she objected.

'More jeans?'

She picked through the rack.

'These aren't so great really.'

He knew better than to press. There would come a time.

Cafés with awnings and pavement tables flanked the main square, once a garden, now a parking lot, the meters set amongst plane trees, drastically pruned, their amputated stumps feathered in tiny shoots of green. He ordered croissants and coffee. Eggs were impossible but she had a ham sandwich.

The man drank only coffee while he scanned the newspapers as though looking for a particular story. Not finding it, he laid them upon the table.

The girl lit up a cigarette.

'What now?' she asked.

He leaned forward, napkin in hand, and wiped a crumb from her cheek.

'I thought we might visit a few agents and look for a place to live.'

Her face collapsed comically.

'Oh no!' she wailed.

He said gently, 'It's not really very comfortable you know.'

'I *love* it! It's great!'

Her voice was hot and angry. Her face had flushed and she looked close to tears.

'It's awfully primitive,' he said.

'It's so *real*.'

Without knowing exactly what she meant he had to agree.

She said, 'It's the most beautiful place I've ever seen.'

'Yes, it is beautiful.'

'But you don't like it?'

'I do. But I'm old and soft and ease-loving and I'm terribly dependent on central heating and hot water and electric light and all that civilised rubbish.'

'But the light works now.'

'Yes.'

'It was only a fuse. That's nothing. Old Yvonne showed me how to fix it.'

Her eyes grew big with amazement at the memory.

'Hey, what about those two,' she demanded. 'Aren't they the living end? I mean they must be about a million years old or something.'

'You don't like them?'

She shrugged.

'They're all right, I suppose. But that room, it's like they were living in the Middle Ages. What's wrong with them?'

'They're old,' he said. 'And they're skint. That does things to people. It sours and twists you. It makes you bitter and a little crazy. I should know,' he said.

* * *

The old woman's face had composed into exaggerated welcome as she threw wide the door and stepped back into the room crying.

'Come in, do. We *know* who you are. You're Mr Law, we had your letter. And Miss . . . ?'

'This,' he explained, 'is Marianne.'

'Hello, dear. Welcome to the mill. I'm Yvonne and over there, that's Henry.'

In the gloomy light neither had noticed the other figure shrunk into an armchair. Older than she, he was seventy-five or more with the fragile body and delicate face of an ascetic, marked by age and wisdom, humility and pain. He had made a token effort to rise, straining forward courteously with arm outstretched.

The man touched the dry and bony hand.

'Please,' he said, 'you must forgive us this intrusion. The lights . . .'

Yvonne interrupted with a shriek.

'Oh no! The utter wretch. He *mended* them.'

The girl was staring at the pair in open-mouthed astonishment. She had never met their like. Born into the '60s, a child of prosperity, such genteel poverty was outside her experience. Certainly, after her companion's description of the South of France as a playground of the super rich, these two were, to say the least of it, unexpected, startling even; this combination of abject penury with the graciousness, the accents and formal mannerisms from another era.

The man, too, found the couple incongruous. Here they were sheltered from the march of time, he supposed, or else, finding so much of the modern world disagreeable, they had chosen to ignore it. They reminded him of his distant childhood, of maiden aunts and schoolmasters long ago, patient and kind and irredeemably out of touch. He said, 'It's probably just a fuse. If you'd explain . . .'

'Plunged into darkness just as you arrive. How perfectly vile for you! You *would* like a glass of sherry?'

But it was not a question and she ignored his answer, turning to the girl and continuing loudly, 'And you, my dear, an orange squash. Someone brought us a bottle out from England. Idris. Quite the best, we find.'

A tray displayed a pathetic selection of bottles and four glasses.

The man said, 'I'm sorry to bother you ... but if you have a torch ... if you know where the fuse box is ...'

From the depths of his chair Henry murmured, 'Rotten luck. Poor show, but we'll fix it in a jiffy. Hopeless workmen, the French, hopeless. Got to do everything yourself. Speak the language, do you?'

'A little,' the man admitted.

'So do I. Used to teach it, actually.'

'I don't,' Yvonne announced with pride, pouring the drinks. 'Totally unnecessary. They understand English if you talk slowly and loud enough.'

The man's eyes explored the room as he listened, splendid in scale and space, mean and poor in its arrangement. One wall was entirely of shelves, cheaply and badly made, their thin planks sagging beneath the weight of books, neat stacks of newspapers and magazines, bric-a-brac. Here life was lived too close to the bone for anything to be thrown away.

Three cats, crouched on the threadbare rug, regarded the visitors balefully. It was claustrophobic, depressing. He felt an overpowering desire to escape but a glass was already in his hand. The two had lived here for fifteen years, they heard. They loved it, *loved* it, they assured him, though Yvonne couldn't stand the French. The couple owned both mills, this and the one below, living in one, renting out the other.

'Isn't it just the most divine place?' they asked.

'... and the *pool*!'

For the first time the girl came alive.

'It's the most beautiful place I've ever seen,' she told them.

He swallowed the warm sweet sherry and old Yvonne found a flashlight and, surprisingly sure-footed, led them down the path to the lower mill and indicated the fuse box where, after a little time, it was the girl who finally fixed the lights.

They parted the firmest friends and Yvonne went off up the hill uttering shrill cries of joy and goodnight, her light bobbing away through the trees and her voice piercing through the night.

'How nice to get nice people,' she carolled, 'So very *very* nice. Too, too super! We've been *dying* for you to come.'

When he had finished his coffee the man told Marianne he had to make a telephone call.

'I won't be long.'

She kicked off her shoes, drew her feet up onto the seat of her chair and picked up the *Daily Express*.

'Do they sell English cigarettes here?' she asked.

'I'll get you some.'

He found the post office in the modern section of the town.

'I have to make a call to Zurich,' he told the girl behind the guichet.

He might dial direct, she said, giving him the code. He changed two bills of ten into five-franc pieces and entered the booth she indicated.

He dialled 19 and heard the tone change as he joined the international circuit, then the tumblers clicking down the line as the connection went through and the telephone rang on the desktop switchboard at 15 Paradplatz.

'*Hallo. Wer ist dort?*'

'Good morning, this is Mr Law. I'd like to speak to Dr Liebel.'

The girl changed immediately into perfect English,

'Of course, Mr Law. He is on a call just now but will not be long I think. Will you hold on, please.'

Dr Liebel only had one telephone on his ample desk.

'But I speak only to one person at a time,' he had explained when once the man asked him why. 'And here we do not really believe in these showy American ways. We are a dull nation, the Swiss. Punctual and dull. It is our character.'

His voice came on the line, flat and Germanic.

'Good day, Mr Law. You are well?'

'Thank you. And you? Your family?'

'We are all well, Mr Law. What can I do for you?'

'Tell me how we stand.'

'The guilder advanced a point on Tuesday and I sold for you at 2.38. As of today you hold 605,000 dollars in the Cayman Islands.'

'As of *today*?'

The man's voice expressed surprise.

'I explained to you it would take time, Mr Law. There are formalities which must be observed.'

'When will it go to Curaçao?'

'Huh! When will it move, in one week; when it will *be* there, maybe three.'

'Surely it can be telexed?'

'Of course. A telex transfer is done in two hours, a rapid and simple transaction which will take three weeks. You know why, Mr Law? Because the banks steal your money. Money is expensive now and they steal it and use it and profit. And then, when they have robbed and inconvenienced you and you have spent a fortune on communications, finally they are gracious enough to pay it into your account.'

The man laughed.

'But you'll stay after them?'

'Do not worry. Also, buying between currencies, with that amount it is valuable to wait for the best spot rate. You have immediate funds?'

'Yes. But I'll call you next week to keep you honest.'

'Please?'

Dr Liebel seemed not to know the phrase.

'Goodbye,' said the man. 'Till next week.'

While he had been in the Post Office Marianne had bought groceries. Two heaped bags stood on the pavement beside the café table.

'How did you manage?'

'Easy. Supermarket. Fabulous things.'

She would always manage, he reflected as they walked to the garage; lack of a language was no disadvantage. She would manage anywhere, in any place or situation, would always get by, sail through untouched. A survivor plus. A victor.

He had intended to take her for a drive and to lunch in a restaurant but she pleaded they return to the mill. She fetched down the Bognor Corporation deck-chair and set it up in that protected basin which overlooked the pool, installed him and insisted that he sit there taking the sun while she served him a glass of wine from the bottle she had bought, then went back inside to prepare lunch.

Half an hour later she brought out a tray. Bacon and cheese toasted sandwiches. Wine for him, coke for her. Mars bars for two.

He watched her fondly as she set out the meal, laid the places; a juvenile delinquent playing little mother. She leaned forward to refill his glass, her adorable face only inches from his own, the tip of her tongue bit between her sharp little teeth. She felt him stir and skipped back, out of reach.

'Eat up,' she ordered. 'No messing about.'

He did as he was told, finishing every morsel of two leathery sandwiches with the keenest pleasure, drinking the rough three-franc wine from a plastic bottle, listening to her prattle. He was ideally happy. He had escaped. No one knew where he was. There was nothing more he wanted, nowhere else he wanted

He ran his fingertips across the stretched material, the swollen little mound and the damp feel of her beneath.

She swayed toward him, her head drooping forward so he smelled the warmth of her hair before she straightened up with a dreamy lost expression on her face of private pleasure and shame, eyes shut and mouth open and wanton in a gasp.

The fabric was wet under his fingers now, the rims of the valley separate and distinct to his touch as a tiny sopping cleft.

She moaned as a spasm shook her. Her thighs clutched at his hand, imprisoning it. He felt her quiver and an answering leap in his own nerves, a thud in the groin and the sweet wetness drenching his fingers. Her body shook and a convulsion arched her forward over his chair.

She stumbled and would have fallen but he caught her. She collapsed limply across him as all strength drained from her trembling limbs. Her knees sagged toward the ground, head coming to rest in his lap. She sighed. A sleeper's sigh of exhaustion and peace. Beneath his hands her blonde hair tumbled and hid her face.

So he held her while she slept, his hands and his need and his eyes upon her, himself never more alive than at this moment, the blood in his veins flowing again thick and rich and sure with joy and delight of her and time ahead endlessly for everything. A state of perfect happiness.

Isolated in time and place, his eyes were only upon the girl. There was room in him for no other awareness and no consciousness except of her. But, had he turned his head and looked behind him up the hill above the tangled overgrowth of creeper and thorn, briar and nettle which enveloped the ruined basins, he would have seen the roof and corner of the old couple's house whose rest was hidden by the trees. And, had he turned and looked at that instant, he would have seen in that window a flash of light.

Suspicious and wary though the man was by nature, even had he observed it, the significance of that flare might have gone unremarked; explained and dismissed from mind as a windowpane catching the sun and not the reflective sparkle from the lens of an optical instrument aimed down in his direction. But, as it was, the man's back was to the hill. His eyes were fixed upon the girl, and that single warning flash of light went unseen.

Three

Ten days later they were still living at the mill. It was morning, ten-thirty o'clock, and the man was already dressed and installed in his deck-chair overlooking the pool, a book in hand, the girl sunning herself on the rocks below.

Both of them looked different. The girl was already lightly tanned and the man appeared healthier, his face tighter and younger with the skin around his mouth and jaw no longer blanched to that dead revealing pallor. Though he wore sunglasses to read he had no more need of them to conceal the bruises around his eyes. The swelling had subsided.

Except to buy food they had not left the house, apart from one afternoon when they had driven to the English bookshop in Nice. After clothes, books were the man's most essential requirement. Even during the bad times he had never gone without them.

He glanced up from the page to look across the river. The torrent flowed now with marginally less force. The overhanging branches of the figtrees were more advanced in leaf. Though the girl spent every day stretched out upon the rocks, for the man in the lightweight suit it was not yet hot enough to sunbathe. In his deck-chair in the ruined basin set over the pool he was at peace, at ease and free from the exterior and the interior compulsion, that consuming hunger for possession and show which had informed his previous life. Hidden in this secluded spot with this delicious wanton, he felt the need for nothing more.

On the boulders below suddenly the girl sat up.

'Hey! Know what?'

Her voice carried to him clearly above the noise of the waterfall.

'What?'

'We have an invitation.'

Impossible. They had met no one.

'Who?'

'The old couple. Yvonne came down this morning. I forgot.'

'Today?'

'For dinner.'

'What did you say?'

'Yes.'

'Impossible,' he told her.

'Why? We're not doing anything.'

'It would be ghastly. Can you imagine?'

'Maybe funny.'

'Not funny at all. Out of the question.'

'Why do you dislike them?'

'I don't. But I don't like them either. I don't want to go to dinner.'

'*I'd* like to. *Please*, Bob!' she called and then, realising instantly her mistake, a crimson wave flooded to her face. Suddenly she looked stricken and in terror.

The man's reaction was precise. He laid down his book and stood up. He walked the path to its junction with the steps then down to the river's edge. He stepped carefully to a small rock then up to the place where the girl lay. He kneeled beside her.

'*Never* call me that! Remember. *Never*. Even when we are alone together. Never. This is very important. My name is Michael Law.'

She babbled, 'I'm sorry. I'm so sorry. I forgot.'

His voice was harsh. 'Then *think*. Remember!'

'I'll make it up to you,' she said.

He smiled at that.

'What then?' he demanded.

'I'll wear the gymslip tonight.'

'And . . . ?' he prompted.

'I'll wear the gymslip and no knickers and you can do whatever you like to me.'

He reached out his hand and slid it beneath that mass of hair and gripped the vulnerable nape and forced her head forward, downcast, contrite. She knew it was all right then and that she was forgiven. But it was not easy for her to remember that he was Michael Law. She had always called him Bob.

And it was not easy for the man either to think of himself as anyone except Robert Just, the name he had been known by since birth.

Seven years ago, at the age of forty, Just had achieved his heart's desire and lived in bliss inhabiting the garden of earthly delights. Bliss was Belida, a tropical island, volcanic, lush, beautiful and over-ripe.

He part owned and entirely ruled a corner of it, a bay and peninsula, a development of luxury houses, yacht anchorage and clubhouse. A gilded hideaway for the super rich. A quarter of it was already built. His future was subscribed, all right with the world. On the corporation he ran a house and servants, a light aircraft, a Pontiac convertible, a matched pair of rosy-creviced chocolate adolescents and a yacht.

His way there had followed a winding route. He had gone through strange shifts to reach this sunkissed, shore by twilit paths whose memory evoked no pride.

But he had made it, and had lived there for five years.

Happiness makes blind. Good fortune thickens the keen instinct, blunts and makes clumsy. He should have sensed danger a long time before. He saw it all so clearly now. He remembered exactly when it first got to him, that first sign, no, not the first – surely the eighth, the tenth – but the first to make the sweat sting in the armpits and the first pinch of dread. And the sharp smell in the air, both fearful and thrilling, the scent of trouble. Marvin Le Roy. He had gone into town to see Marvin Le Roy.

It had begun as a bad day, he remembered. The only good part had been swimming out to the reef before breakfast as he always did. Then, after coffee, he had driven over to the construction site.

Only three men had been in evidence, Julian the foreman and two hopeless idiots he had employed to clear the mangroves. Passing a bottle between them they were seated on the ground with their backs against a foundation which they had poured yesterday, three weeks behind schedule.

He descended from the Pontiac with careful slowness and strolled over to where they sat.

'Where's the crew, Julian?'

Squatted in the dirt, the black man beamed.

'No work today, Mr Just.'

'No?'

'No work. Nothing to do.'

''cept build a house maybe?' he said.

'No sir. No way. De children of Israel dey can't make bricks without straw and Julian he can't build a house without blocks. No sir.'

Julian glanced over the desolate site.

'The truck's delivering material this morning from the harbour,' he said.

'No sir. No way. Truck's on strike. Harbour's on strike.'

Just smiled coldly at the grinning black. Irritation surged through him. Momentarily he yearned to live a century ago when this insolent nigger might be flogged to death.

'I want the crew here within an hour, Julian, or you're out of a job.'

He turned on his heel and walked back to the car. The last he saw of them through the dust in his rear-view mirror they had not moved but still sat against the wall, the bottle passing.

He controlled his fury. It was eight miles to the capital and he drove slowly. Stoned-out donkey drivers imperilled the jungle road; livestock and children littered the shanty villages along the way.

Port Belida was picturesque and smelly, a perfect natural harbour. The Geest banana boats came in to load every fourteen days. During the winter the cruise ships anchored off in the deep water outside the bay and launches ferried the passengers ashore. For an afternoon the town swarmed with camera-slung tourists in colourful clothes who returned aboard with woven baskets, shells and curios carved from wood, and mixed impressions, sometimes minus their wallets.

The cruise ships never stayed the night. Tourist development was in its infancy here. There were two locally owned hotels serving brown windsor soup and a few nightclubs where whites were not made welcome.

Backed by a teeming shanty town, the waterfront had character and charm. Once-elegant colonial wooden houses with screened verandas were painted in all colours, bleached and flaking. Shops, warehouses, deep-freeze stores and the offices of merchants jammed up against each other. The crowds and the uproar and heat were overpowering. The pavement was a market where women crouched in the dust behind mats piled with fruit and vegetables, trussed chickens, gory lumps of flyblown meat. Music was everywhere, the pounding yammer of steelbands and reggae blaring at full volume from transistor radios.

Everything of importance that happened on the island took place at the waterfront and it was here that Marvin Le Roy had his office.

He was Just's lawyer and obligatory local partner, a requirement imposed two years before on foreign businesses. There were seventeen lawyers practising on Belida. Just had interviewed all of them for the role and concluded that Marvin was the best that money could buy.

He was a rhiney negro with academic pretensions who had studied at the London School of Economics and qualified at the

Inns of Court. When Just came in the lawyer was standing in his outer office where three clerks worked in sub-Dickensian conditions, a room without air-conditioning whose windows opened on the bedlam of the port.

'Hello, Bob, what brings you? A cup of tea?'

'No. Come with me, will you?'

'What gives?'

'I don't know but I want you to sort it out. I've no crew on site and all my materials are stuck on the dock waiting to be trucked.'

They forced their way along the crowded waterfront. The shirt clung to Just's back. Heat and noise were a physical assault.

The gate to the quay was locked. On the other side of the chain-link fence he could see his consignment of stacked blocks and pallets of cement. The place was deserted. He swore viciously a bitter racist curse and Marvin winced.

'It's a strike, Bob. Nothing to do.'

'Pay someone. Get the stuff out.'

'Can't do that, Bob.'

'This is the last time,' he said furiously, 'you can tell them that, the last time. This afternoon I'm flying to Trinidad to charter a freighter. I'll ship material in direct to the site.'

'You can't do that,' Marvin told him.

'Like hell I can't. I'll bring it into the deep water anchorage and lighter it ashore.'

'You can't bypass the port. The unions wouldn't have it. Be cutting your own throat.'

The two men walked back to the office.

'Speak to the Minister and fix it,' Just ordered, 'we pay him, don't we?'

'For permissions. He won't fight the unions. Can't afford to. Not with Maxwell blowing up a storm.'

'This is a five-million-dollar investment,' raged Just. 'I've got seventy men on payroll. What are they going to do if we pull out? Go back to living in trees?'

Marvin looked pained. He said, 'You've got nine houses up and the land cleared and the club-house built. They know you won't pull out now.'

'Has Maxwell been stirring up my men?'

'Of course. For five dollars US a day? In the States you'd pay them seventy-five. He's the most powerful union man on the island and the government don't dare to jail him.'

They were passing through the outer office. Just said, 'If I catch him on my land I'll shoot him and hang him by his heels. Let it be known.'

The lawyer closed the door.

'Careful, Bob,' he warned. 'You're not exactly loved round here.'

'No? Because I pay the wages of seventy worthless niggers? Because I give them a dollar above scale and a bonus for attendance?'

'Because you're white and you're rich. And because people talk and you've a powerful taste for jailbait, my friend.'

Just blinked with surprise. After a moment he said, 'None of my little playmates has been complaining, I'll bet you that.'

Marvin was about to speak but the other gave no pause.

'Bullshit!' he continued furiously, 'I'm not taking this. I'm shipping my stuff in direct from now on. Just let them try to stop me. Not only that but I'll ship in labour too. I'm flying to Trinidad today.'

The lawyer carefully realigned the papers on his desk.

'That's not a good idea,' he said.

The words were spoken with such authority that again Just looked at him with surprise.

'Why?' he asked.

'Because you won't get there. Five years ago when you came to this island I told you to stay away from politics and minors and you'd be all right. But you didn't take my advice and you've meddled with both, my friend. Fly to Trinidad today and you'll drop down stone dead in the ocean. Last night someone put sugar in your petrol tank. They want your white ass you see. Maxwell wants you dead and he's out to get you.'

It was evening in the upper mill.

The kitchen where Yvonne and Henry were preparing dinner for their new tenants was sadly short on modern convenience. Still, they were accustomed to the three-ringed cooker which worked on bottled gas, and the other disadvantages. They had learned to manage very well. The geyser had packed in nearly a year ago but Henry considered that to use hot water for washing up was needless extravagance anyway. Rather unfair of him Yvonne thought occasionally to herself, for he only dried.

She had straightened the loose covers and gone over the room with a duster though it was already spotless. For the first ten years they had lived here a woman from the village had come in daily to do the cleaning. Then the expense had proved too much for them. This luxury – as so many others – they were obliged to let go.

No one suspected they were without help. Though visitors to the house were few, the look of the place was always impeccable.

Deprivation and making-do had not daunted the old couple's spirit. The remorseless passage of the years had not subdued them though theirs was a life sadly lacking in incident or event. Tonight, to have guests for dinner, this was a big occasion. They had even squandered five francs on two bottles of wine. As Yvonne laboured at the stove and Henry wiped the best silver with a special cloth and laid the table, they discussed the evening-to-come with lively anticipation.

'I must say,' Yvonne remarked, 'he's a remarkably handsome man, and very charming.'

'Very well dressed,' Henry agreed, 'even flashy. A bit of a show-off I shouldn't be surprised, but nice-mannered. That's unusual these days. What do you think he does?'

'Business, I expect. Seems to have pots of money. Saw them in the market, shopping. He took a whole roll of it out of his pocket, 1000-franc notes.'

Henry set a fish knife precisely into place.

'How do you think he made it?' he asked.

'Goodness knows, everyone seems to be rich these days. Except us,' she added with a little laugh.

Henry removed the plastic stoppers from the wine bottles and stood them on the table to 'breathe'.

'What do you make of the girl?' he asked. 'I've never heard her speak.'

'They don't these days,' his wife told him. 'She's young.'

'Very young,' agreed Henry. 'She could be his daughter. How old would you say he is?'

'Forty something.'

'Hard to tell when he always wears dark glasses. I think there must be something wrong with his eyes.'

Yvonne laughed lightly.

'To run around with that little trollop there'd have to be,' she said.

'You don't like her?'

'Like?' She sounded surprised by the question. 'Goodness knows, I haven't an opinion, couldn't begin to judge. She's simply not what one's used to.'

'Not . . .?'

'No, not our sort at all. My dear, she's got an accent you could cut with a knife. I know you like young people, Henry, but I'm afraid you won't find her interesting. It's common to say "common", I know, but she is, common as dirt.'

Punctually at seven, Just and Marianne climbed to the upper mill. The door was flung open even as he raised his hand to knock.

He accepted a glass of sherry. The girl was given orange juice. There was a toast of welcome and, shortly after, they sat down to dine.

Two trout are not adequate for four people. The fish forks and the doilies, the silver napkin rings of toilet paper did not transform the meal into a banquet though the *vin ordinaire* was ceremoniously sniffed and sampled and all the rites were formally observed.

The old couple graciously played host and hostess but mostly it was Yvonne who talked, her pale face growing flushed as the meal progressed. She was starved of conversation. As at the British Consul's cocktail at Christmas, the thrill of company and a little wine quite carried her away. She required no feedback or participation from the guests. Their captive presence at the table was enough. As she described their lifestyle on this millionaires' Riviera coast, an incongruous picture began to take shape.

They had lived here for fifteen years ...

His wine-glass empty, the man who had come to dinner listened to their story and felt a tug of unwelcome pity and a mounting irritation. He did not wish to hear of pluck and sadness, of chin-up bravery in the face of odds, yet he was trapped and obliged to listen.

Unashamed, Yvonne revealed all with a devastating candour. Poverty-struck expatriates, they were not alone in the manner of their lives. There were others here, as they, who borrowed yesterday's discarded *Times* to check the exchange rate against sterling with trepidation, who could afford neither to accept hospitality nor to return it, who had moved here in the early 'sixties on fixed retirement incomes when the franc was fourteen to the pound. Apart from their pensions and the summer rental of the lower mill the old couple had nothing, it seemed. The last of their capital – a word spoken in hushed religious tones – had gone in death duties, taxes and, most recently, in galloping inflation.

Yvonne's father had bought this property when she was a girl. They had used it for holidays before the war. They had been quite rich then. When Mother died at the age of ninety Henry and she had moved here permanently. England had changed beyond all recognition; the Labour Government had started the rot, of course. They simply could not afford to stay there. Here – at first – it had been different. Now, well....

They lived on a rigid budget of one hundred and fifty francs a week, plus stamps – an important item for both were conscientious letter-writers. Perhaps they did not receive *quite* as many letters as they sent, but they *stayed in touch*.

Just listened attentively to all that was being said. He showed sympathetic interest in their predicament but internally he seethed with anger. He had resolved in his new existence to do only those things which he wanted to do. Yet here he was at dinner eating poor food and being bored to death. Even the selfish life is not lived simply.

'Must cost a fortune to feed those cats,' the girl observed.

'But no,' Yvonne said. 'Not at *all*. We get free fish from the trout farm, you see. He gives us the ones that die.'

For a moment Just felt queasy. He suppressed the thought.

'But have you thought of selling?' he enquired.

'Of course, and it's worth a lot now, this place. But it's not so easy. The two houses form one single property, you see, and can't be divided. We can't sell the lower mill without our own.'

'And if you sold both ...?'

'*Leave*? Oh no!'

Both of them exclaimed in horror. Never. They just loved this place, adored it.

'We could *never* go back to England,' Henry explained, 'not now.'

This was their home, a beautiful, valuable property. In the desert of their lives this was the one certain thing they had. The only thing.

And ... well, they *managed*, they explained.

They kept their chins up and the flag flying. In summer they rented the lower mill. That brought in a little money though it was not always a happy experience.

'So rarely you get nice people,' Yvonne explained, and smiled fondly at them both.

It was after dinner now. Just had had the main share of the wine and the girl had been allowed a couple of glasses. He felt blessed in comparison to the lives of others.

'But surely,' he said tentatively, 'surely there must be some way to capitalise on the lower building. If you leased it with the tenant responsible for the upkeep ... Perhaps with some option to purchase eventually ... Perhaps something worked out along those lines ...'

The girl glanced at him sharply, then away.

'Oh that would be *so* nice,' said Yvonne, 'so very nice. At least the money would be sure and regular. What a thrilling idea. But how ... but who ...?'

Marianne said, 'Perhaps Michael would.'

Henry and Yvonne looked at each other in wild surmise.

'What we might ...' she began.

'What we could ...' he interrupted.

'Is sell it to you ...'

'With us in residence up here ...'

'Like sitting tenants ...'

'Sell it, that is ...'

'*En viager!*' they said together and, on the word, fell silent.

What it meant, Just had no idea. He waited for them to continue but they did not.

'*En viager?*' he questioned at last.

Yvonne said, 'Yes, like old Madame Contenti sold her farm.'

Henry explained: It was a method which existed in France since the Middle Ages to enable childless peasants, too old to work the land themselves, to sell their farms for a monthly sum for the remainder of their lives, themselves continuing to live on the property as protected tenants until that day when they had no more need of earthly residence. At which date it belonged clear and outright to the purchasers. A sort of gamble on the longevity of the sellers, but a gamble also on the lives of the buyers, for if it should be *they* who were the first to die then the property reverted to its original owners.

What a strange arrangement, a curious idea. Just pondered.

But it was late now. For the old couple who had fetched the shopping and prepared the dinner it had been a strenuous day, a thrilling but exhausting evening.

Yvonne cleared away the dishes. Henry's grey head had begun to nod. It was time for the guests to take their cue and leave.

The girl and the man who now was known as Michael Law said goodnight and went home to bed.

But the seed had been sown which was to alter everything.

Four

'Well, why not?' Marianne demanded. It was morning and they were driving into Lezat. Hands upon the wheel of the Ferrari, the man only smiled.

'You said yourself it is a good deal.'

'Spotting a good deal and wanting to go into it are two different things,' he told her.

'It's a fantastic place.'

He parked in the main square. He bought the English papers at the tabac and glanced carefully over their front pages before tucking them under his arm. There was nothing mentioned about him.

In the supermarket she took a trolley and pushed ahead confidently down the aisles. She wore one of his shirts knotted at the waist, jeans, no socks and scuffed sneakers. She had resisted all his efforts to buy her clothes. He followed, watching with delight her progress along the shelves, the impulsive grabs, hesitation with pouting mouth and furrowed brow, her curiosity for the new and childish greed for the tried and sure, a dozen Mars bars and a kilo of ice cream. Once she swung around to appeal for his translation, looseshirted in unbuttoned careless innocence and his heart turned over. Afterwards they took coffee outside the café on the square.

She fidgeted in silence while he leafed through the papers, still finding nothing. 'Well, why not?' she demanded again.

He folded the papers and laid them neatly on the table.

She continued excitedly, 'You could make the place we're in

into something really fabulous. I know exactly how I'd do it up, just huge cushions everywhere and candles on those long stands like in church. And knock a big hole in the wall for a window so you always looked out on the pool. It would be really nice.'

'It's the first house you've stayed in here in France – maybe there are other places you'd like better.'

She said with certainty, 'Not as good as this. And in time you'd have the upper mill as well. It's gruesome now but just think what you could do there when they die. That won't be long either. I mean they must be like a hundred years old already.'

He smiled fondly at her enthusiasm.

'We'll see. Order yourself another coffee, I must make a telephone call.'

In the Post Office the girl behind the grille recognised him. This was the fourth time he had come here. From the booth he dialled Dr Liebel's office in Zurich.

'Yes, good morning, Mr Law. The Doctor is not here just now.' Can I help you?'

In the pause he heard the whisper of dismay. With that flat Swiss accent who could tell if she were lying.

'No. Tell him I called, please.'

He could see the café terrace from fifty yards away as he came into the square. The girl sat at the table, her face turned up to the waiter – the swarthy young one who spoke no English. She was deep in conversation, vivid with animation, and, as he watched, her hand strayed out to touch the hem of his white jacket. He walked slowly, his gaze discreetly concentrated upon shop windows. When he reached the café she was alone.

'Have you still got those travellers' cheques?' he asked as he sat down.

He had bought three hundred pounds in England in her name.

She looked surprised.

'You need money?'

'I have some stashed away in the mill but we could use some running cash.'

She tugged a dirty handkerchief from her pocket, two ten-franc bills, the crumpled wallet of cheques. He paid for the coffees. The waiter swept up the coins with studied nonchalance, no sign of recognition passing with the girl.

They walked across the square to the Banque de Paris et des Pays Bas.

She asked, 'You've got my passport?'

She spread open the wallet of cheques upon the counter and took the pen from its plastic pyramid.

'What's the date?' she asked.

He looked up. Beyond the teller's grille a calendar hung upon the wall. He saw the day with a tap of memory on the heart, an involuntary clench of the stomach in recall.

'The thirtieth,' he said, 'thirtieth of April.'

On this day, two years ago, he had lain in jail, imprisoned in a room six feet by eight whose floor ran liquid with blood and the stinking slime of his own faeces....

Five

There had been no servants in the house when he woke that morning in Belida exactly two years ago.

He lay in bed thinking it must be early for there were no kitchen noises from below and no sound outside of the gardeners putting down the Bahama grass; nothing but the rustle of wavelets on the beach and the sun high and the day already hot.

He looked at his watch. It was eleven o'clock. He got up and searched.

There was no-one in the house, no crew on site, no-one at the jetty or on the boat. He might have been the last man left in the world.

He took the Pontiac and drove toward town.

Doing fifty round a corner he saw the road closed just ahead, a tree-trunk across oil drums and a dense crowd of natives.

He slammed on the brakes and threw over the wheel, feeling the rear break away and begin to slide, the wheels bump into the ditch and out again and the car bucking, lifting, about to go over as he whirled the power steering and the back lashed round ... and then he was right amongst them as they scattered and the thump as he hit someone and the clang going into an oil drum and the car shuddering to a stop with the motor still running.

They were all around him at once, with black furious faces and pink mouths yelling, and he saw the machetes and the drunk fury of them and the man lying by the side of the road where he had been thrown and he knew, whatever had happened, this was no place to be.

Even as they had their hands on the bodywork and were grasping for him he rammed the shift into gear and the wheels were shrieking and scattering stone as they spun for grip and the car fishtailing through the crowd and screaming everywhere and bodies falling away except for the two who had climbed onto the hood and now slid against the windscreen with the force of his acceleration to be held there with faces mashed against the glass with bloodied noses and mouths wrenched wide with terror.

His foot stamped down and he could see nothing at all but wrap-around flesh and features till he leaned out to look around so much black bulk and throw the car into the approaching bend and watched them slip, hands clawing at air, fall, bounce and slide ... in the mirror now only crumpled shapes slithering across the tarmac till they hit the ditch and dropped from sight.

Blood and brain racing from the sudden rush of adrenalin, he gunned the battered car back the way he had come.

His house was as he had left it, the site deserted, the bulldozer abandoned upon the beach.

In his office he picked up the telephone to hold it for a long moment in one hand with the other poised upon the dial. He set it down slowly. The line was dead.

He stood concentrated in thought, analysing the courses open to him. He had kept a gun in his bedroom. When he looked for it now it was gone.

He walked out to inspect the car. The front was pushed in and a rear wing had crumpled at one of the concussions to scrape upon the tyre. With a pickaxe he levered it away, ripping the metal till the wheel ran free.

Then he drove out of the development, taking the same road but this time going down it little more than a mile till he came to a narrow track which led into the trees. Though barely the width of the Pontiac he had seen it used by ancient trucks to collect the banana crop. He turned onto it, revving the motor in second gear, and rammed the car through the jungle, branches whacking against the sides and his vision never more than five yards ahead down the green tunnel, the wheels flinging up a dense cloud of dust behind his unruly passage.

After fifteen minutes he reached a tarmac road, turned onto it and drove more decorously. Two miles further and he came to another barrier built in the same fashion, this time manned by only three of them.

He came slowly to a halt. They approached the car.

'What's this?'

'Roadblock, man.'

'I'm going to town.'

'No movement without pass.'

It was spoken with pantomime authority as a child repeating an instruction learned by rote. The man was no child, however, but over fifty, a fat black in jeans and a T-shirt, wearing an armband. The others stood close behind him. They carried new Armalite rifles and all three of them were drunk.

'I have a meeting with Mr Le Roy in town.'

'No movement without pass.'

'What's this nonsense about?' he demanded.

'Internal security. No movement without pass.'

'But I need to go to town,' he insisted.

'Don't ya go to screaming and hollering. Without pass you don't get through here no how.'

'So how do I get a pass?'

The question confused the black.

'I get it in town, right. Look, be reasonable. One of you can come with me. You. You come!'

Almost he bluffed his way through. If the black had been alone he would have made it, but the man had his reputation to maintain before the others. He took refuge in anger and raised his rifle threateningly.

'Ya get outta here, man, ya hear me. Come back when ya got a pass.'

Just shrugged.

'You've got bad judgement,' he said. 'Who gives you this authority?'

The negro stepped to surer ground.

'Ruling Power, that's who, man. Government done gone changed, ya hear. Mr Maxwell he's the big man now. Ya go fuck yo-self, whitey.'

On the drive back this time not adrenalin but anger squirted through his veins, a seething mix of hatred for all blacks and fury at himself. If there had been a coup how could he have been so stupid as not to have known. How could he have grown so slack, he who had always planned for everything with such meticulous attention, rehearsing the scenarios, setting up the slip roads, the secondary options and fall back position. Marvin must have known it was coming. Had he become so dumb that he chose a man who would betray him. Yet Marvin had warned him about the plane. So how did that add up?

He switched on the car radio. Calypso from Trinadad with a competition for a free luxury funeral. Nothing but static on the waveband of the local station.

There was nobody on the roads. The jungle pressed closer along the verges, each bend concealing some unwelcome surprise.

When he topped the ridge and looked down over the development all appeared exactly as he had left it. The completed houses along the peninsula each on its landscaped site and each, unfortunately, empty. The club-house with his bungalow beside it against the picture postcard setting of the jungle, the mangroves, the palm trees and the beach, the sea, the jetty and his boat at its mooring.

The boat. His look jerked back. Something had changed. The boat floated low in the water, its deck awash, wallowing in the gentle waves, a creature already dead.

A spasm of fury shook him. His grip tightened so fiercely on the wheel that the metal frame twisted within its plastic skin. He looked down with astonishment at the buckled shape between his hands. He willed himself to breathe slowly. He blinked to clear the burning in his eyes. Suddenly he was calm again. In control. He drove back slowly to the house.

In the old days when he had fought his way through another jungle he had survived and won by means of certain strategy. Only a single tactic had application now.

Then the jungle had looked very different. To the casual eye it was invisible beyond the country club lawns, drawing rooms, swimming pools and tennis courts, those homelands of the rich that he had chosen for his manor. His devices then were many and intricate but one was constant: he always carried on him as much cash as possible. He knew that with a large sum of money in his pocket he smelled different. Even in that world where wealth was the norm it gave him an edge of advantage, minute but valuable: it made him feel better.

Now in the house he emptied the wall safe of 2,000 US dollars and a wad of local currency which he distributed between the various pockets of his lightweight suit. He searched again for the gun though he knew it was gone. Then he collected a jerrycan, cord, a flashlight and a plastic bag and tossed these into the car.

He drove down the dirt track which led to the point. He had reached a decision and when he got to the headland above the sea he did not hesitate for longer than the moment it took to throw out his things. He sat up on the back of the seat so his legs were clear. He reached down and shoved the gear selector into drive. As the car began to move he jumped clear, landing on his feet upon the dry cracked earth.

The car crawled ponderously up the slope. It reached the top and the front wheels dropped down and the steel chassis clanged on the rock. For a long second he thought it was stuck. Then it slid forward, scraping across the stone. It lurched over the edge and dropped sheer, somersaulting slowly as it fell.

The crystal water splintered white on the splash. Concentric waves surged outward from the sudden hole, slapping on the rocks. In less than a minute the surface was calm again and the sight of the car fifteen feet below water, belly up on the white sand, was perfectly sharp and clear from where he stood.

The sailboat was gone already. There was nothing he could do about the plane and the house with all that was in it, and five years of work wasted. But there was a bitter satisfaction in denying them the car. He glanced at his watch. Past three o'clock. Three and a half hours to sunset. He scrambled down the cliff to the tiny beach, undressed and stretched out on the sand, knowing that he could not be seen from above for he had come often to this secret place to sport with his little playmates.

There was nothing to do but wait. They would find the car in time of course. But the rest of this day and the night was all he needed.

When they came to the house and found the car gone they would think he had dodged the barricades and got away by road. They would reckon he was headed for the airfield. Even if he could make it undetected on foot through the jungle it would be pointless to try. The plane would be guarded and immobilised and they would be waiting for him there. That was no way to get off the island. No way at all. The only possibility was by sea. He needed a boat and he could not walk to it.

He hid out on the beach till evening. Once a plane came over and quite low but inland and hidden from sight by the cliff. Two engines – so maybe it was the coastguard Cessna and they were looking for him. But it was day one of the new regime and a revolutionary government must surely have a lot else on their minds as well.

When the sun burned down over the horizon and the light started to go red he prepared to depart. He folded his clothes into a plastic-wrapped fortune cookie around the money and lashed the bundle to the jerrycan. He knotted the other end of the rope around his waist and when the ball of the sun touched the sea's rim he waded into the water and started to swim. He moved at a slow, easy crawl. He reckoned the village was five miles down the coast and he was in no hurry. The cord tugged gently at his waist and the jerrycan floated behind him.

There was no twilight. Suddenly it was night.

When he was halfway out into the bay he paused, trod water, and looked back. The moon was up and the whole sweep of beach curved bone white across the distance. His house stood out against the dark line of the coconut palms and every window was ablaze with light. There were fifteen or twenty vehicles there with their headlamps on and a whole crowd of people swarming under the trees. There was a bonfire going and the sound of reggae music and laughter and victory wafted out to him across the water as his stolen liquor stoked their celebration.

Fury tightened his muscles. His fists clenched. He went stiff with anger. He wondered what they were burning. It had to be books. Those were the only things they would consider not worth looting.

He kicked out and resumed swimming. He slid through the water at a strong regular rhythm, turning his head every fourth stroke to snatch breath. The sea past his ears washed out all sound from the shore and after a while his rage cooled and his mind cleared. He did not stop again until he was beyond the headland and the cape shut out the view behind; then he paused only for a moment to take his bearings.

He calculated the time to be 7.30. He had wrapped his watch amongst his clothes for barracuda hunted at night and they were dumb enough to strike at the glint of metal.

He ploughed on, four strokes to a breath. An offshore wind had come up with evening. Waves cuffed him across the face as he rolled to take air.

One hour later he was floating opposite the village. In the moonlight he could see shanty houses clustered under the trees. Lamplight showed in their glassless windows and he heard the steelband music on the radios and the sound of voices from inside. There was no movement on the beach. As he came closer he distinguished the fishing boats pulled up on the sand. He aimed off, swimming for the shadow of the mangroves at the head of the creek.

When his feet touched bottom in the estuary he stood and tasted the water. Salt. He went in further till it was too shallow to swim and he was easing his way forward on his elbows. It was not people he was afraid of but the pack of dogs which infested every village.

As the channel narrowed he felt the river's current thrusting him back. He tasted again and shifted the water round his mouth like a man sampling wine while the waiter hovers, bottle in hand.

He spat. This was no Chateau Lafite. It was brackish and foul but it was drinkable – or would be tomorrow in the heat of the day when he was desperate. He filled the jerrycan until only a pocket of air remained to keep it afloat, then screwed back the cap. When he swam out of the creek the load attached to his waist slowed him like a sea anchor.

He approached the beach so slowly he caused no ripple. To anyone watching from the shore his head would have looked like a floating log.

He hung in the water and studied the boats. At the end of the line was one smaller than the others whose stern still rested in the sea. It was about twelve feet long and the sail was bunched unwrapped on the boom.

It was the only one he would be able to set afloat unaided and it was almost certainly not seaworthy. Its owner who had not pulled it out of reach of the mildest storm would not have troubled to keep it in condition. Ratpoor, they despised their possessions. So abject scarcely could they afford to buy food, yet they seldom fished. They disliked both the effort and the sea. He had never seen their boats further out than a half mile from shore.

He came on low in the water, fingerwalking across the bottom to hide in the shadow of the stern. He pulled himself up on the transom and looked into the boat. Splintered oars. A rusty tin. A litter of lines tangled on the thwart. The bottom a swill of filthy bilgewater gleaming in the moon. The overpowering stench of rotten fish.

He had come to this island on an executive jet, wearing a Brooks Brothers suit and with a line of credit for three million dollars. He was leaving it naked with what he could carry in the hand. He sighed and swung his jerrycan aboard.

First he tried to shift the boat from its seaward side, using its bulk to mask him from the shore. But he could not budge it. On hands and knees he crawled onto the beach. He set his shoulder to the bow and shoved.

Still he could not shift it. The water in the bottom weighed it immovable. He rested, gasping from the effort, his muscles trembling.

He bent, linked hands beneath the keel and lifted. The water sloshed into the stern. He strained up and heaved forward. The boat slid two inches on the sand.

He glanced behind him. The nearest hut was less than thirty yards away. He could plainly hear a man and woman arguing. He crouched and heaved again. The boat slithered down into the water and floated.

But at the last he had no luck. He had set one foot on board and with the other was pushing off when a dog rushed snarling down the beach. He thrust off hurriedly, grabbed up an oar and poled away. Within seconds two more dogs dashed out from the huts barking furiously.

He pushed around the bow, threw down the oar and hauled the sail up. The rusty hoops ran clanking up the mast.

There was a whole pack of dogs lined up on the shore baying their heads off.

He felt the wind on his cheek as he cleared into the estuary. The boom swung across with a jerk and the sail filled.

There were children on the beach now yelling and the dogs frantic in uproar. Adults were running from the huts and a whole hullabaloo was starting up behind him.

He laid dead before the wind, paid the sheet out and secured it. With one hand reached up to the tiller he crouched in the bilge and set to bailing.

Soon the racket on the shore grew fainter. No fishing boats were put out after him.

Sighting west by the stars he headed in the direction of Trinidad. That island was 70 miles away and if he missed it the next shore was South America. But if a ship did not pick him up he would be thirsty by then.

The moon was dipping down toward the horizon. The breeze was lessening. He had been going two hours.

He had just checked his watch and seen that it was after eleven when he heard the motor of a power boat behind him. He looked back in sudden fear. When he saw the bright beam of light and the speed it was coming up on him he knew that he was done for. He ran the sail down fast and packed its white canvas out of sight and lay on the thwarts so the boat's profile was minimal but these precautions served for nothing.

The coastguard launch came scudding over the surface with its searchlight scouring the sea and they were onto him right away.

He stood to face them. They rammed alongside the sailboat with such force that its planks splintered and he toppled into the bilge. Two men sprang down from the deck. He had no time to raise his hands far less speak, reason with or beguile. They picked him up bodily and flung him aboard the launch.

Then he was on the floor of the cockpit and the gorillas were all over him with cudgels and working on him with their boots.

For three days he lay in a cell without food. The temperature was 125° at noon and never less than 100° at night, yet he often shivered and longed for something more than the ripped silk shirt which was his only covering. There was no bed, no bucket, no furniture of any kind. Sweating and trembling, he lay in his own filth upon the concrete floor. He was in great pain.

They took him out at the same hour every night, somewhere

between two and four AM when the flame of life burns never closer to an ember.

They led him to another room with shutters closed, a sink in the corner and a naked bulb the only light, breathless and sweltering and the air foul with the sour reek of fear.

There were four of them there behind a trestle table. He had seen none of the men before but he would remember every detail of their appearance for ever. Mr Yes, Mr No, Mr Kiss-my-Arse, and the Doctor. It began in a quite civilised fashion. He was seated in a chair which faced them. The questions started.

What was his name? The name of his company? Where was it registered? When? With what capital? Who controlled it? How long had he worked on Belida? How many houses had he built? What price did they sell at?

Now he saw the direction of the interrogation. How many men did he employ? What was their contract? Their hours? Their pay?

He kept his composure and answered the questions calmly.

Mr No was the first to show anger.

'You are selling these houses at a quarter million dollars each. How much does it cost you then to build them?'

He explained why it was hard to calculate exactly. There was the value of the individual sites but also their share of the considerable cost of setting up the development. Their cost could not be assessed merely from the material and labour which had gone into their construction.

'What is your profit on the sale of these houses?' asked Kiss-my-Arse.

'We are not yet into profit. We are operating at present in a loss position.'

No's face was congested with fury.

'Loss! You are selling houses at a quarter million dollars and you are paying your men five US dollars per day. How do you justify that?'

'They are unskilled labour and I am paying above standard rate on the island. It is true that in the United States a construction worker earns more but he is a trained man handling sophisticated equipment and ten times more productive.'

'You are saying these men are stupid?'

'I'm saying they are untrained. In the States it takes three weeks to build a house. Here it takes eight months.'

'You are saying they are lazy?'

No had risen from the table and was pacing the floor invisible behind Just.

'I'm saying ...'

A ringing blow struck him across the side of the head.

The questions came harsher, faster, overlapping.

'So why you come here, man? Cheap labour?'

'My corporation decided ...'

'Dumb niggers? That what you're thinking? You rip off your *own* people like that?'

Just answered hotly, 'We've got five million dollars invested in the development of your island. We employ a local workforce and pay them above scale. We ...'

A blow knocked him to the floor.

They had worked themselves up to a rage by now and though they continued to shout at him they were no longer interested in his answers.

He was picked up and forced over the table. His face slammed against the wood. All four were yelling at him, generations of hate spewing from their mouths, years of resentment and enforced civility. They loathed him and this was their time. Time to even the score.

He ceased trying to answer and concentrated only on hanging on. An inch from his eye two flies copulated on the planks. It seemed the last normal happening left in the world.

He felt a grip on his belt, hands wrenched at his trousers, the material ripping and a burst of mocking laughter. His mind reeled. A fog of horror clouded his brain.

A figure entered his narrow band of vision. The Doctor, walking away, something writhing in his hand. A snake? He was doing something at the sink. A hose. A length of garden hose which he was screwing to the tap.

Another body blocked his view. His hair was gripped, his head flattened to the table.

His muscles convulsed in agony fierce and unbelievable. It was like a blade going into him. A scream broke from his mouth, instantly cut off as he clenched his teeth. A rod of fire was thrusting up him. Endless, the pain was endless, impossible to endure.

'You trying to make monkeys of us, man!'

And the Doctor turned on the tap. A harsh crow of laughter then silence while they watched.

It was as if boiling lead were filling his guts. He felt his intestines leap and twist. He threshed up, his spine snapping straight before his head was smashed down again, face into the table.

He was coming apart. His belly was distending, blowing up huge under the pressure. A terrifying inhuman noise roared in his ears, the sound of his own screams. The pressure was agonising, impossible. He would explode, split open, burst upon the floor, his entrails spattering up the walls.

How long did it go on? For ever. Endlessly. An eternity of pain.

Then they let him go and he shot upright, staggering, his hands clawing round behind him. His legs folded and he collapsed to the floor, his knees drawing up to his chin and blood and mucus dribbling down his face, moaning, and conscious only of the pain. The searing cramp of agony.

At that moment there was only the pain. The rest was afterwards. The ignominy, the horror and the hate, all that coming much later when he lay on the floor of his cell. Later. Along with the decision to kill.

It was like that for three days. On the fourth the pattern changed.

He was given melon to eat and a mug of sweet tea. He was

ordered to clean out his cell and they brought in a chair, a trestle table and a bed.

'You no go work today,' said the jailer.

Only long afterwards did he comprehend that this was Sunday.

On Monday Marvin Le Roy came to visit him.

'Thanks for coming so quickly,' Just said. 'Really good of you to make so much effort on my behalf.'

Marvin looked around the cell, his face wrinkling in distaste.

'Smells bad here.'

'Where the hell have you been?'

'You don't look so good,' said Marvin as he seated himself on the only chair.

'Get me out of here,' said Just from the bed.

The lawyer hitched the crease of his white trousers.

'I don't think you quite appreciate your position. They're not through with you yet.'

'I will see those niggers dead. Get me out of here.'

An expression of sadness appeared on Marvin's face.

'Yours is the contemptuous violence of the oppressor, Just. It is not the attitude to facilitate relationship. You won't learn. It is a historical mistake and a historical penalty which you are paying.'

He was beaten and bloodied and empty and thirsty and so weak he could hardly push himself up on his elbows or raise his voice.

'You're a lawyer. Get me out of here.'

'Not so easy,' said Marvin, 'And threats won't work. The British are not about to send a gunboat to rescue you and indeed there has been no mention of your name in the press at all. It's the new President you are up against. You debauched his daughter.'

Just sighed. 'I taught her,' he said. 'I taught her music and books and the art of conversation. I showed her what it is to be a civilised human being. I taught her clothes and style and grace and how life could be in a world not inhabited by brutal savages.'

Marvin giggled. 'You wormed your way into her schoolgirl drawers and had your lust on her.'

'That too,' Just agreed readily. 'I taught her lessons for which she will be forever grateful. Most important of all she learned she cannot stay on this stinking island.'

'You broke up the family. You came between father and daughter, man. You know how men are about their daughters. It's for that you're being punished.'

Exhausted, the man on the bed sank back upon the mattress.

'All right, Marvin. How much is it going to cost?'

'They want the key to your safe deposit in Port of Spain and a letter of authorisation to open it.'

Just sat up again abruptly.

'*They* do? How do *they* know about it?'

'That's what they want, man. I'm telling you.'

Just looked at him with loathing. At that moment to the list of four targets in his mind was added another name.

'Up yours with a meathook,' he said.

The lawyer rose and dusted down his trousers.

'As you will.'

He banged upon the door for it to be unlocked. He looked at the man on the bed, frowned and shook his head in the resigned gesture of one who deplores such wrong-headedness but cannot be bothered to remonstrate.

'Goodbye, Just.'

They took away the bed and the other furniture. He was given neither food nor water.

Lying upon the bare floor he tried to rest and prepare himself for the ordeal which he knew to lie ahead.

Flies buzzed around his unhealed wounds. He was tortured by the thought of water, of diving in cool green depths, of frosted glasses and ice-cold drinks.

Vengeance and water were the alternating obsessions which filled his mind but, as the day drew on, it was the second which became the more consuming. He was bruised everywhere. The rough concrete scalded his skin. He sought endlessly for a new position. His mouth was caked and parched, his tongue a wad of dust.

'I will kill them,' he thought, and hate nourished him and kept him from surrender.

At the same hour of the night he was led to the interrogation room with wrists bound and a hood over his head.

He blinked in the light as it was removed. The questions started immediately.

Where was he born? His mother's name? What was his father's job? How much did he earn?

They were the same four behind the table but this time there was also an empty place at its head. A chair with arms.

Where did he live as a child? What size was the house? How much was it worth? Where did he go to school? What were the fees?

Always that overriding interest in money and evidence of privilege. The questioning served for no purpose except to inflame their anger. Its outcome inevitable, he answered them defiantly, unshaved and filthy in his ragged shirt.

He concentrated intently upon his interrogators, noting every detail of their appearance, each facial expression and mannerism. Their voices, their accents were printed indelibly in his mind. No matter how many years later he would recognise these men again instantly.

How long did he remain at school? What did he do afterwards? His first job? How much was he paid?

The voices became harsher. Mr No sprang from his chair to walk the room.

Where did he live then? What did it cost?

No cuffed him about the head at each reply. Just's ears rang from the blows and there was a dismal emptiness inside him at the inevitability and stupidity of it all. His words were thick and broken in his parched mouth, his voice uneven. His stomach had tightened to a hard knot.

AIYB—C

A hand dragged him roughly from his seat. His ankles were trussed. He felt his legs raised. He was hauled up till he swung upside down, roped to a pulley in the ceiling.

His shirt had fallen around his face to blind him. He heard the slop and clang of a bucket slid in place beneath him. He felt himself lowered till his hair brushed the surface.

Then there was silence. The questions, the taunts, jeers and mocking laughter had stopped. In the eerie quiet he hung there, the stink of piss filling his nostrils and the blood draining to his head.

A door was opened. The mutter of voices. Footsteps on the wooden floor.

He spun slowly on the rope, his shirt front fallen open by half an inch, a gap in the curtain. Feet framed briefly in the narrow split of vision. A man's legs below the knees. Pressed khaki uniform trousers seamed in golden braid. The fifth man. The chair with arms. The gorgeous trousers stopped too short, showing bare black ankles, calloused feet in plastic sandals and filthy toenails. Through Just's pain he felt a twist of contempt. Monkeys!

A jerk on the rope. At a rush he went down into the pail. Unprepared, he had not taken air yet an eternity went by while he threshed and held his breath. His head banged desperately against the side of the bucket and the man who watched stepped backward so his splendid uniform would not be splashed.

Scalding acid in his mouth, eyes and ears, he breathed and drew in fire, threshed and struggled for endless seconds before oblivion came. He plunged through all the choking circles of hell into thickest stinking night. Then darkness. Nothing.

'What are you trying to prove by holding out? They have the time. They're working on instruction and they'll go for a week or a month if necessary. What are you trying to prove, Just? Now or then, the end will be the same.'

Marvin Le Roy straddled the only chair, well dressed and sure of himself.

Just raised himself inch by inch against the wall till he sat propped, his legs splayed.

'Cigarette,' he said weakly.

'You can't take it,' the black told him, ignoring his request. 'In the end you'll crack so tell me now, man. Save yourself the pain.'

Just stared back through red-rimmed eyes. His shirt hung in blood-soaked rags, his limbs ached. His skin was bruised and streaked in filth. A question formed in his parched mouth, the words slurring out in an unintelligible mutter. The lawyer leaned closer.

'What's that, man?'

'What happens to the development?'

'It's been nationalised. Under government control.'

'Who's going to live there – now?'

'The matter is under consideration. We may proceed with it as a multi-racial project.'

'*We?*' queried Just. '*We?*'

'They have asked me to prepare a report on its economic potential.'

Just said, 'Suck scum, nigger. Your mother fucked lepers.'

Marvin looked pained.

'Really! What do you hope to achieve by this attitude? I am your only friend. It's no skin off their arse if you fail to survive though I think I can persuade them it is inadvisable. They still have a lingering suspicion that whites possess mysterious powers. I can convince them your death would cause trouble. They don't know you are alone as you are, my friend. So very alone.'

He could not endure much more, he knew. He had lost count of time now and lay in an aching limbo shot with pain, his mind fragmented as a broken mirror reflecting scattered images of a reality which leaked with horror.

But he was not so finished that anger could not revive him.

'Give me a cigarette,' he demanded.

Marvin flicked open a pack and held it out. Just's hand wavered toward it and he watched in desolation as it was withdrawn. Marvin lit a cigarette, bent down and placed it between his lips.

'You're gonna die, man. What good's a safe deposit to you then?'

Just sucked hungrily on the cigarette, felt the harsh burn, the flash along his nerves. I'll kill them, he thought. Kill them, all of them.

'Look. It need not be so bad as that. When all this dies down I'll talk to them, about tourism. I'll convince them it's best to look legal and pay you compensation.'

Like hell you will, thought the man on the floor.

'They can't afford to scare people. They have to attract tourists. Bring in foreign currency.'

Starting with mine, Just thought. With two hundred thousand dollars in Trinidad. Five years of hard graft.

'Play ball and they'll let you go. Put you on a plane,' Marvin said.

Out, he thought. Away. Clear. To wake whenever in whatever straits, but free. It was like some impossible dream.

'Look, man. You've had some good years, yachts, girls, high living, the fat of the land. You're a gambler, you must have known it couldn't go on for ever.'

He had not, though. He had been having such a fine high time he had thought that it would never end.

'A guy like you, you'll manage. You'll come up again. You win, you lose, you win again. What you going to prove by getting dead. You're being 'ornery, that's all. Tell you what: hand over that safe deposit and choose where you want to go to. Then, if you don't make waves, in a year I'll guarantee you government compensation of ten thousand dollars. How's that for an offer?'

Not for a million, thought Just. Not for a million would he forgo the chance to kill them.

He stared back stonily then dropped his cigarette and let his eyes fall lest they should betray him.

'OK,' he said, 'do it like that. OK.'

It was over. The lawyer sat back. He looked not elated but exhausted, as if he too had staked all upon this outcome.

'Now get me something to drink,' ordered Just. 'With ice. Quickly.'

It was in this fashion that Just lost all he owned and came to be evicted from the garden of earthly delights. He was left with nothing. At the age of forty-six his life returned to Go.

Six

Next morning was the first time Just saw the boy at the pool.

He was in the bathroom where he had been examining his face at the mirror before shaving. There was no trace now of that pallid flesh around mouth and jaw where he had cut off his beard and no sign remained of the swollen bruises which had encircled his eyes. Only by stretching the skin over his cheekbones did he reveal the fine but livid scars which in time would fade to white and become invisible.

He was pleased with his face – he looked both different and younger.

He turned toward the basin to slot a fresh blade into his razor and glanced from the window over the sunlit river bank and the rockpool below.

A figure was standing on the boulders which formed the dam.

So hidden had seemed this place where they lived, so secluded and private to themselves, that instinctively he drew back from the light; whoever was down there had come with intent.

Just watched, razor in hand.

It was a boy seventeen or eighteen years old, dressed in sweater and jeans and carrying a walkie-talkie radio. He stood upon the rocks gazing into the dark water, now less turbulent and swift than when they had just come to the mill.

From the high window the man regarded him with hostility, continuing to resent this intrusion even after he saw it was no radio in the boy's hand but a telescopic fishing rod whose extended section resembled an antenna.

The boy jumped lightly to another rock and studied the still water behind it. Finding nothing there to interest him he moved on till he reached the wall of the ravine and scrambled up, using the branches of the figtrees as handholds in the climb. He emerged at the top of the waterfall and continued up the bed of the river until he was lost to view from the window.

Shaved and dressed, Just came downstairs a half-hour later and found the girl in the kitchen preparing breakfast. An untidy mess of eggs spattered and fumed on the ancient stove and the room was filled with the smell of coffee. She was naked but for a pair of pants. Her hair was tousled and her eyes still heavy with sleep.

He ran a finger down her spine and kissed the nape of her neck as his hand cupped her firm little buttocks.

'I have to buy you some clothes.'

'Tomorrow,' she answered lazily.

'Today.'

'No way. It's Sunday.'

Always she had repulsed his attempts to buy her clothes. The gymslip was the single thing he had persuaded her to wear. Persuaded was not the word, however, but bribed.

He drank only coffee but watched with pleasure as she wolfed down a major meal.

'So what do you want to do today?'

'Swim. Work on my tan.'

She ran a crust of bread around her plate to sop up the last of the grease.

'I have to buy the English papers,' he told her. 'Drive down with me to the airport.'

She shook her head.

'You go. I'll hang out at the pool.'

She could not be permitted to remain here alone. Not now, with the boy around. He offered another bribe.

'Come. You can drive.'

Her eyes flared.

'You mean it?'

'Only till we ...'

'Oh man!'

She sprang from her chair and ran excitedly from the kitchen to get dressed.

The motor raced alarmingly. When she released the clutch the Ferrari shot forward with a squeal of shredding rubber. Coming around the corner she stamped hard upon the brakes and the car slewed across the road, sliding broadside up the hill.

A parked car blocked the road. The old couple from above were in the act of getting into it through a door held open by a tall man with upright military bearing.

Both let out cries of alarm and skipped backward as the Ferrari skidded to a stop beside them. Even the field commander executed a rapid and surprisingly nimble retreat across the ditch.

'I say ...!'

'Really ...!'

'Too too terrifying ...'

'Mr Law, how *could* you?'

The general snorted with indignation, his jaws champing as if chewing on something intensely displeasing.

Henry wore a threadbare linen suit, Yvonne was in tweed. Going to church, they said, the English church in Nice, and this was Brigadier Markham in baggy tweeds who growled and grumbled unintelligibly, not liking the look of this flashy pair at all.

They set off again; bounding up the hill in a series of kangaroo leaps until the girl got the feel of the delicate accelerator. He asked,

'How did you learn to drive?'

'Me dad taught me.'

She spoke without looking at him, frowning in concentration.

Just settled back in the passenger seat and resigned himself to violent death.

From the top of the ridge the road wound perilously down the Var valley at the bottom of which the sea gleamed azure blue, decorated by three white-sailed yachts. In the limpid air the runway of the airport was clearly visible with a miniature aircraft far below them coming in to land.

A bevy of racing cyclists swept down the road ahead of the car, alternately pumping muscular legs and coasting wide on the hairpin bends.

The girl muttered furiously, blipping the accelerator, then with a blare on the horn roared past in a hair-raising burst of speed. Captivating pubescent, he had always sought them in this mould, adolescent and wanton with a taste for the older man. But this was the best by far. Toothsome morsel, last and finest of a delectable line.

He laid a hand on the rounded thigh, brown and silky under the coarse texture of the jeans. The car swerved violently.

'Lay off! You'll cause an accident.'

At the junction where the country road joined the coastal highway which led to the airport Just repossessed the car in the face of violent protest.

'Can I drive back then?'

'If you're good.'

'If I wear the gymslip tonight then?'

He looked at her sternly and she giggled, catching her lower lip between pearly teeth.

As the glass doors slid wide and he entered the airport concourse . . .

'How utterly bloody, First Class is full,' boomed a voice . . . and his step faltered. He hesitated for a second. Marianne scampered ahead in high good spirits and he followed. Ridiculous, he told himself, he was a different man. No one could possibly recognise him.

Here the English Abroad were gathered in force. At this time of day, when the direct flights from London arrived and departed, this was their club. House guests were being met or wished goodbye, bluff blustering men and badly dressed wives with vinegar voices; loud, embarrassingly loud, in their opinions. At the newsstand Just heard attitudes expressed for which – under a less benevolent regime – the speakers would have been dragged from their 'plane upon arrival at London Airport, propped against the nearest wall, and shot.

Today, Sunday, the English dominated the concourse. Most were not passengers, however, but local residents who, fled from their homeland, sought the company of their compatriots. The midday flight brought in the Sunday papers and the expatriate colony assembled to collect them as by rite. All that they read would move them to dismay or anger, yet all shared this perverse wish to learn the worst, to draw reassurance from reports that, each week, their country went further to the dogs.

Here, in community, they bitched and grumbled, formed clubs, played bridge and golf, listened to the Queen's speech on Christmas Day, despised, criticised, complained about, patronised and colonised the French.

Just stood behind Marianne who was poring through the magazine racks, *Playgirl*, *Seventeen*, *Yachts and Yachting* . . .

'I shan't be a moment,' he said and stepped across the hall to a shop displaying luggage, briefcases and radios.

'Something rather good,' he explained to the saleslady, 'that looks good and has FM and Shortwave.'

She smiled at him pleasantly and opened the showcases, leaving him to choose while she served another client. Just looked the best sort of customer, gentlemanly, mature, well dressed and obviously rich. Anyone could see he was not a thief.

He selected a Sony in black and stainless steel of fine design with a solid heavy feel in the hand. He paid and watched while it was wrapped.

At the newspaper counter he found Marianne standing with one arm around a fat bundle of every Sunday paper and the other gripped above the elbow by an elderly man with bloodshot florid face and russet moustache who, surprisingly, was clothed in an old camel-hair dressing-gown below which poked crumpled pyjama trousers, black socks and walking shoes.

To Just's annoyance, rather than wrench herself free from this apparition, the girl seemed perfectly content in his clasp and indeed was listening to him with every appearance of lively interest.

He bought cigarettes and cigars at the tobacco kiosk. By the time he had paid she was beside him.

They walked out to the parking.

'Who's your friend?' he asked, his tone light and amused.

'Wants me to meet his son. Come up to the house and play, what!'

She mimicked the plummy voice. 'How or-fully or-fully. Can't sit down to luncheon without the Sunday rag, I say what, what. Stuck up toffee-nosed creeps.'

He raised his fist.

'Up the revolution! Hang the creeps! Let Piccadilly run red with blood! But aren't I one of them?'

She wriggled into the passenger seat.

'Yes, but at least you're a crook.'

'Please! If I'm taking you to lunch we'll have a little respect shown around here.'

'And I can drive? Yes? Yes? Yes?'

She clambered on top of him and thrust her wet ardent tongue into his ear.

'I'm feeling ever so horny. You ever done it in a car?' she asked.

He pushed her off, promising to debauch her after lunch and in high good spirits turned the car onto the autoroute in the direction of Cannes. He gunned the motor and the acceleration pressed them back into the seats as the red needle climbed around the dial.

'Yeah, man, go! Hit it!' she cried. 'Where are we going?'

'Le Moulin de Mougins.'

'What's that when it's at home?'

'The best restaurant around these parts. Could you manage a little something?'

'Could I ever! Right on lover!'

For the first time in his new identity he felt secure enough to visit a public place of this order. In Paris, though he had stayed at the Crillon, he had lurked in his suite, nursing his black eyes and living from room service. He was recovered and well now. His morale was excellent. It was unlikely that anyone he knew would be on the coast at this season yet, if by chance they should encounter a familiar face, he was confident he could not be recognised. He was very different now from that bearded man in jeans who had run around London during the last two years hustling trade in a mid-Atlantic accent. He had loathed that personality. It was a fine relief to be back in his own skin and wearing decent clothes again, the Ferrari burning up the road at 200 kilometres an hour with, for passenger, this juvenile hoodlum inspiring him to lust.

He reached over and dropped the package in her lap.

'A present,' he announced.

'For me?'

'For my enchantment, the demure Miss Marianne Brent.'

She ripped off the wrapping.

'Wow!'

He glanced at her. She was ecstatic, gazing at the radio with lips parted and an expression of flagrant joy illuminating her face, childishly transported by delight. Enchanted – enchanting. His heart turned over.

Only three or four miles inland from the over-developed coast the autoroute swept through low hills of pine forests with no view of the sea but, to the north, the glittering peaks of the Alps. Then the Ferrari howled into the broad curve above Cannes with the gulf dramatically revealed below them in panorama.

He slowed and pointed out the distant beaches already speckled with ordered rows of umbrellas in front of wedding cake hotels, the fishing port, the yacht basin, the casino and, beside it, the new marina where the really big boats were moored.

'Who owns them?' she asked.

'The rich.'

'What nationality?'

'The rich are their own nationality,' he told her and took the Cannes exit, turning inland.

'Muggins?' she asked, reading the sign. 'That's where we're going?'

'Pronounced Mougins. But Muggins sounds much nicer.'

Trees and a tall hedge bordered the road. He turned into the gravel drive and gave the car to a uniformed attendant.

He escorted the girl through a discreet door along plush corridors to a panelled room, the bar. She asked, 'You're sure it's all right me wearing jeans?'

'The only thing that matters is that *I* should be well dressed. Then, with me, no one will stop you. My respectability is your passport.'

'Respectability! That's a laugh!'

'Now, now,' he cautioned.

She stuck out her tongue at him then glanced guiltily up the corridor.

As soon as they had sat down she grabbed the leather card to read through the list of drinks.

'Nevertheless,' he said, 'tomorrow we'll get you some clothes.'

'Can I have a daiquiri?'

'Of course, if you insist. Personally I'm going to drink a couple of glasses of old-time champagne.'

'Made from grapes like grandpa used to tread?'

'Older than you, anyway.'

He ordered a half bottle of Krug '45 which opened with a richly modest pop and flowed into the glass with the merest trace of bubbles, light and dry across the tongue, cool down the throat.

'Super wine,' she said. 'Jolly good bubbly, what! Why are all these English living here anyway?'

'Always have been. Cannes was started by an Englishman and the British replaced the Russians who invented this coast.'

'I can't see the Russians coming to a place like this,' she remarked.

'Not any more. They lost influence in 1917 through reasons beyond their control. But the English, then the Americans, have been installed here ever since except during the war.'

She asked, 'Whose side were the French on during the war?'

He accepted the proffered menu.

'A good question. Opinions differ. Now, what do you fancy instead of the Sunday roast in Willesden?'

'Salade de truffes de Vaucluse,' she read aloud. 'Lay off. What's wrong with Willesden?'

'You know better than I, surely. I've only been there to drop you home.'

'No *salade de truffes* there?' she asked. 'That what turns you off North London?'

'Amongst other things. Do you miss it?'

'*Miss* it? You must be joking, mate.'

'You don't miss modelling? Your friends?' he pressed but, by then, the waiter stood beside them and she did not answer. She was silent while he ordered and then she asked, 'Do only the rich live here then?'

'I used to think so before I met our old neighbours.'

'When you were here, were you rich?'

'Sometimes,' he said. 'I passed for it. It's not wealth that matters but the appurtenances of wealth.'

'The what? Were you on the fiddle then?'

He smiled.

'I wouldn't put it quite like that.'

'Tell me about it.'

'I wouldn't dream of it.'

'Please.'

'Certainly not.'

She pouted.

'Go on. Tell me.'

The carre d'agneau was served and proved faultless. Just ate with keen pleasure, drinking his way into that particular state of well-being induced by a superb meal. In response to her curiosity he continued to discourse on that world which he had known so intimately more than a decade before, though he did not describe his role within it.

He explained the rigid dates which govern the seasonal migrations from St Tropez after the fourteenth of July to Monaco for the galas and the gambling, the grandes soirées royally graced, which lasted until the tenth of August when suddenly the harbour would wake empty with the yachts dispersed at sea and headed for Sardinia, Corsica, Portofino or the Greek Islands and anyone still on the coast was a leper, socially dead.

'Who are they?' she asked. 'What sort of people?'

'It's not just the rich, though they're the focus. It's a whole milieu. Very mixed. Industrialists, tycoons, gilded youth, deposed royalty, Arab sheiks, arms dealers, hookers, gamblers, con-men, ponces and gigolos ... The cream of their various professions. Everyone selling something, even if it's only themselves ...'

The memory of those long nights returned clear and sharp as he talked, the fragrance of perfume and cigar smoke in the gaming rooms crowded at 2 AM. The hush and clicker of the chips, the fat cats seated at the tables and the restless drifting groups. The driving rhythms of vanity and envy, greed and lust tangible on the air. Everyone dealing, everyone out to score. Hustlers and marks preying on each other, hunters and hunted in interchanging roles.

'Is that what you wanted,' she asked, 'that kind of ego number? To be rich and part of them?

'Certainly not. It's a competitive and exhausting life. There is no rest and no shade. Invitations are bought at vast prices. There are parties at which not to be seen is the mark of Cain. The rich have their agonies as do the poor, just as sharp but of a different nature. Beneath all that jazz there's an edge of desperation. They are insecure.'

He had known a photographer who covered the season for *Vogue*, a man privately courted and publicly ignored or waved away, 'No Press! No Press!' He was an honest man who refused bribes of a thousand dollars to publish photographs for, though they affected to despise it, these brilliant creatures were greedy for publicity. They needed to see and read about themselves in the pages of glossy magazines to be really sure that they were living up there amongst the gods and really having such a fine high time. They needed confirmation and reassurance. To be convinced.

'Why? Does it tempt you?' he asked the girl.

She wrinkled her nose.

'Man, no. Heavy! It's not my scene at all.'

They had finished eating now and were having coffee, the girl smoking a cigarette and the man a cigar.

He said, 'The most pleasant condition is anonymity, but wealth is important for it enables you to live simply.'

'Simply?' she asked. '*Simply?*'

'Sure. Your laundry is taken care of. The driver parks the car.'

He dusted a fleck of ash from his sleeve.

'If you're really rich I suppose you can even afford to be badly dressed.'

Looking up, he caught the waiter's eye and nodded for the bill.

She said, 'There's only one thing I'd want money for.'

'What's that?'

'To buy the mill we're living in.'

'If you are that determined you'll get it. People always do. But you'd be bored to death living there.'

She denied it vehemently.

'No. I'd paint it up and decorate it. Do my own thing there. I'd really get into myself.'

He suppressed a smile and took a wad of money from his pocket as the bill was set before him.

'Wow!' she remarked, watching him lay the money upon the table. 'That's over a hundred quid. We only had two courses.'

Her voice was coloured by awe. Waiters set back their chairs as they rose to leave.

'Yes,' he said lightly, 'One can manage on very little, provided it's the best.'

Seven

'One can manage on very little,' he said.

Evicted from Belida, Robert Just had returned to London obliged to do exactly that. He was penniless.

Or almost. His total capital was £150 which he discovered remaining in his London bank account. With it, he looked in Soho for a familiar face from long ago and spent over half on an unregistered handgun. It was an extravagance; he did not need it yet, but one day he would fix them, Marvin and the others. He did not know how or when but that day would come and with a gun he was ready for it. It made him feel secure.

He dressed in sweater and jeans for he owned no other clothes. He grew a beard. He lived off baked beans and eggs which he cooked on the gas ring in his room where his only entertainment was watching television.

He worked as an office cleaner. Perhaps he could have found a job more agreeable and better paid if he had used the telephone to locate contacts he once had known. But he did not want to tap on previous acquaintance. Those people knew him as a winner and he would not allow them to see him beaten and down like this. He would not ask for favours.

Nevertheless, what he was doing was ridiculous. He came to see it. He survived, he ate, but he was merely supporting life. It was gruelling self-punishment and outright foolishness. He knew hard work was no method of becoming rich. His only problem was that he was skint and suffering from a grave loss of confidence. The niggers had had his cash. They would not have his balls.

For London and New York, Just held a number of moral IOUs. In both cities people owed him favours. Well, it was time to call one in. He had no illusion about their value; indebtedness caused strange resentments, but it was time.

The day following this decision he came to the Collingham in Belgrave Place at twelve noon exactly. It was a fine Sunday morning in June. He was the first customer in the pub.

A heavily-set man in his fifties with grizzled hair was bent behind the bar setting bottled lagers onto the cold shelf. Just called for a beer and Hamish had poured it and brought it over before he stared in wild recognition, let out a bellow and banged it down, not spilling a drop.

'Robbie laddie! I could nae recognise you behind the foliage. It makes my heart glad to see you and how're you keeping?'

Just laughed with pleasure.

'Fine. Great. In the pink. I'll buy you a beer, Hamish.'

'You will no so!'

The publican roared and looked at Just acutely.

'I'll start you a slate, Robbie. A gentleman should not have to be paying for his own drinks.'

Another customer entered, a young man in a denim shirt who ordered a campari tonic. While Hamish was serving it Just carried his drink to one of the wooden tables and sat down on a bench.

After a few moments of hearty mine host exchange with the new customer Hamish drew himself a pint, came over and settled his bulk on the bench beside Just. He nodded at the opposite wall.

'What do you think of the new light fittings then?'

'They're ghastly,' said Just.

'You ignorant peasant, you've been living with the nignogs. I'm telling you these are the latest thing and very sophisticated too.'

The oak panelling which Just remembered had been covered in striped wallpaper.

'What *have* you done to this place? You've ruined it.'

The landlord was not at all discomfited.

'You've no taste at all, at all. This scheme was executed by a professional decorating establishment. Buggers' Regency it's called.'

'You didn't invent that,' Just said sharply and Hamish boomed with laughter.

'No, laddie. That was said by a wee ponce that comes here who calls himself an advertising art director or something and's very good at repartee.'

He took an enormous pull from his beer and set the glass down half empty.

'Well then,' he continued in a quieter voice, 'so you've taken a fall have you?'

'It's as obvious as that?' Just asked.

'Aye, laddie. It stinks from every pore.'

Hamish rose to fetch more drinks.

'You'll be excusing me, Mr Lyle,' he called to the campari drinker, 'but I've a black sheep to minister to, long missing from the flock.'

He directed his voice to the ceiling and bellowed, 'Mary. Come ye down and attend to the bar.'

When he was back beside him on the bench Just said, 'You're right. I'm on my ass. Will you stake me, Hamish?'

The florid face clouded.

'Aye. Maybe so. But to what indeed?'

'I need a big one,' Just said, and the other answered immediately, 'Never met one who didn't,' then pulled at his nose and shot him a swift sidelong glance.

'Of what nature of tickle were you thinking then, exactly?'

'Well ... it's hardly dignified to go scrambling up drainpipes for a man of my age.'

The publican was still studying him closely.

'Only one job you start at the top – digging a hole, that's not your style either, is it, Robbie?'

Just yawned, pretending an indifference he did not feel.

'Don't fash yourself, Hamish. I'll find my own trouble.'

He turned his head away and looked over the room.

The bar was filling up. The campari drinker had been joined by a peer group in casual clothes accompanied by a couple of girls, one of whom held a Siamese kitten on a lead. A young woman with pink healthy face and quick smile was now at work serving them from the bar. Hamish nodded to her in the same proprietary gesture he had used to indicate his wallpaper.

'Fine lass that. Looks like butter wouldn't melt in her mouth but she'd kick your balls in for ninepence.'

He paused before continuing in exactly the same tone.

'Then maybe I could put you in with some people where you could do yourself some good.'

'What sort of people?'

'A young lot, but keen. Dead keen I'd say ... though maybe somewhat lacking in experience.'

'You scare me,' said Just.

'Well, I'm thinking maybe you'd be the ... the ... what's it called?'

'Compensating factor? Older Statesman? Voice of experience?'

'Aye, something like that.'

'You scare the hell out of me,' said Just.

'No cause to, laddie. The blag's a doddle but I have a mind they're setting about it the hard way.'

'I don't want to hear about it,' Just told him.

'Of course you don't. It's a provincial establishment, down on the seaside with a nice climate and in the holiday season betimes there's a fair sum of filthy lucre stashed away there of a week-end waiting for the banks to open on a Monday, if you follow me.'

'It's not my kind of thing at all,' Just said.

'Maybe not, but they're good boys withal and reliable.

Ex-members of Her Majesty's armed forces and trained by her in the noble art of blowing a peter.'

Just affected a shudder.

'You're showing your age, Hamish. It's computer fraud today, asset stripping, Aussie mine shares. That's where the action is now.'

Hamish's colour deepened.

'You're managing to misunderstand me, boyo. These are common wee villains I'm putting you in with and the staff of this establishment's largely female and I'm thinking that with that stuck-up accent and your highfaluting ways you could be spending the weekend inside in a quieter and more orderly fashion than the way they're intending.'

'It's not for me,' Just said. 'Thanks but no. I told you, it's a loan I'm after. Will you stake me, Hamish?'

The publican shoved aside his glass angrily. 'A bloody millionaire, is that what I look like? A rich old soak and a soft touch in my dotage? Is that it?' he demanded. 'Is that what I bloody look like?'

His complexion had thickened alarmingly to a deep purple where the black veins swelled like ropes. His finger was jabbing furiously at the room and Just searched for its target ...

'A mark? A sucker?' he asked. 'When that one, that ponce there tried to tap me for ten grand. Only yesterday, ten bloody grand.'

Just looked in the direction of the stabbing finger, searched and identified a face altogether unremarkable, astonishing to be the object of such hot fury.

Hamish raged, 'You lot don't know the meaning of bloody money ...'

Just interrupted to correct him sharply. 'I'm not a part of that lot, and you know it. So stop giving me such a hard time. Are you going to stake me, or not?'

The storm abated as suddenly as it had swept over Hamish. With a handkerchief he dabbed at the spittle which had gathered on his lips, at the same time darting another sly sideward glance at the questioner.

'Aye, Robbie, but you'll cheat me,' he answered softly.

Just was stung.

'Hamish, I . . .'

The publican brushed aside his protest. 'Don't give me that! Me who's knowing you since you was in short pants and hanging false paper all over this town. You a con man and it's in your blood. You'd cheat your mother of her milk. How much do you want?'

'A couple of grand.'

'Too bloody much. You'll waste it poncing around buying Savile Row suits and down payment on a fancy car. The style's changed since you was away and it's you that's out of touch, boy. It's no more fluffy bathtowels and monogrammed shirts, you know. Not now. No more posh accents. People don't exactly distrust a man in a collar and tie but they don't rate him worth much either. Old fashioned, they reckon, a slow horse. It's the rough touch that does it now, boy. I'll let you have five hundred.'

Just complained, 'I don't feel happy with less than a grand in my pocket.'

'Too ruddy bad,' Hamish said. 'Five hundred and credit at the bar. Do your drinking here. Familiarise yourself with my clientele.'

He nodded at them.

'Them there.'

The crowd surrounding Lyle, the original campari drinker, had grown considerably, divided and spread across the room into separate groups engaged in their own conversations. Periodically one or other of those who formed these clusters would call out some taunt or challenge to a familiar entering the pub and for a few minutes the bar would be loud with general badinage.

A few surrounded the girl with the kitten, others sprawled on benches reading the Sunday papers. Others, including the man who had tried to borrow ten thousand pounds from Hamish, were gathered around a couple playing backgammon. All were in their twenties or early thirties, casually even cheaply dressed, yet with touches of display or extravagance, Cartier watches, Gucci shoes. They occupied the bar not only in the sense of their physical presence but because, gang-handed, the pub was 'theirs', enjoying its success through virtue of their fashionable patronage. This was not entirely true. In furtive conversation at the far corner Just recognised two regulars from an older trade. The place had been the haunt of felons before this lot were born.

'Have you been to the toilet?' asked Hamish and he switched his attention with surprise.

'What?'

'Have you seen what someone's written on the wall of my toilet: "The people here get up your nose but the beer's good."'

'Who are they?' Just asked.

'Advertising people. The new elite, I'm telling you. Trendy ponces on a screw of fifteen grand a year with expense accounts and credit cards and all. They make the ads in the magazines and on the telly, the commercials. The firms that manufacture that stuff spend millions of pounds to make us buy their rubbish. Pay it to these jokers to do the work.'

It was the longest speech Just had heard him make. There was both contempt and admiration in his voice as he continued.

'See that ponce over there in the cut-off shorts – Dalby. Took a whole bunch of bum boys and model girls to Jamaica for two weeks, twenty people, to make an ad that didn't last but half a minute. There's more to be made with a daft idea and a fancy spiel than in honest villainy.'

Just said quietly, 'I've always known that.'

'Sure you have and where are you now? Fucking skint! Look at them with their campari tonics and their sports cars and their dolly birds, and learn something. Take it from me, there's loot in that racket.'

All the while he listened Just's eyes remained upon the crowd with a casual regard whose detachment disguised its unwavering focus: the pinched features, lank hair and city pallor of the man who needed ten thousand pounds.

'What did he want it for?' he asked and Hamish's face flushed hot on the question. His voice harsh, 'What does he take me for?' he demanded. 'A cunt? Is that what I look like?'

'Well, why does he want it?'

'Spun me a whole cock and bull yarn about business and stealing the cream, a golden opportunity. A whole lot of cobblers. What it comes down to in the end he wants the loot to settle debts. He didn't fool me for a second.'

Just asked, 'What sort of debts?'

'That's the daft part. Not even his own but to pay off the mortgages and loans of a bunch of nancies he works with. He must take me for a sucker, would you credit it! Some kind of Christian charity for bum boys.'

Just's attention was still fixed across the room. He said, 'Will you introduce me?'

Hamish stared at him as at a madman. After a moment he said, 'You daft cunt, whatever do you want that for?'

'Do it will you, Hamish. Get him. Fetch him over.'

'Why?'

'Fetch him, Hamish. Tell him you've got someone who might come up with the ten grand.'

Paul Black was thirty years old and spoke still in the fierce accent of his native Glasgow. A slum child he had been, grown up whey-faced and lanky, used to castoffs and cold discomfort and the reek of deprivation. He spent money on his clothes now but, hung from his bony shoulders, still they did not look quite right.

He worked for a large company in Mount Street which made advertising films. He was a producer, he explained, one of several who obtained and administered but did not actually direct the productions. The creative function was executed by film directors. He mentioned several of their names which sounded vaguely familiar.

For the first moments of this talk Hamish remained silent. Then he entered the conversation with a sneer and thereafter treated Paul with patronising contempt. Unsure of how these two older men stood together, Paul became increasingly uneasy in their company.

'Would you care to lunch with me?' Just asked him. 'If you happen to be free that is.'

They ate at a small restaurant in Elizabeth Street surrounded by family groups in sweaters and jeans and weekend clothes and couples who talked only desultorily and read the Sunday papers with their meal while the afternoon sun dappled the check tablecloths and the waiters were patient and there was no haste to leave.

There was nothing about Paul which was charming, attractive or funny, urbane, stylish, even prepossessing; but over that meal, where the guest drank beer and his host a carafe of house wine, Just identified his quality and confirmed that his instinct in the pub had been correct.

The man was dedicated. He was consumed by a fire which would not let him rest.

Paul was incredibly ambitious, hard working and single-minded. He had come south from Scotland eight years before, and his first job in London had been as a messenger for this same company where he worked now earning nine thousand pounds a year.

Just was charming and attentive, encouraging him to talk. He did not like Paul, but certainly this did not show. He had no admiration for obvious effort and Paul's drive was incomprehensible to him for it was for success alone; he had no taste for the sweets of life.

'So why do you need ten grand?' he asked at last and Paul answered:

'That's the half of it. I want twenty thousand to start a company and Hamish said you could get it for me.'

'It sounds a modest enough request. Why not go to a bank?'

'I have. They turned me down.'

It was a business in which the investors could receive no sort of guarantee or collateral for their money. There was no plant nor real estate, no substance beyond the intangible value of the relationship between a company and the film directors contracted to work for it. Paul explained this to Just as he had to the bank when he tried to borrow twenty thousand with the expressed intention of immediately spending half of it on bad debts.

'Hardly the sort of news really to attract a punter or make his juices flow,' Just observed. 'How do you reckon that?'

Paul told him. The Teller Mostern Company where he worked had been in existence since the start of commercial television in England and, though it consisted only of the Mount Street office it was one of the largest of its kind and mounted films all over the world.

'Peter Meade who made the Rolling Stones films works for us,' he explained, 'and Thornton Duke who is directing the new Robert Redford picture, and Clovis Shephard the fashion photographer is also under contract to us.'

Just expressed surprise that such big-time and international figures should also direct commercials.

'It suits them,' Paul said. 'If they have two months between pictures or are preparing a script we can provide work which pays them so many hundred pounds per day. They all have tax bills or alimony to meet and, working for us, their life is underwritten. They don't have to take the next picture they are offered.'

But it was not these men whom Paul intended to divert to found his own company. They were too rarely available to provide more than the glamour dressing to an operation. Another league of film directors worked at Mount Street, younger men from advertising or photography who had not yet made feature pictures but whose talents were in demand by the young admen clients who frequented the Collingham and other fashionable watering holes. It was four of these whom Paul intended to steal.

'How?' Just asked.

'At Mount Street they are second-class citizens compared to the feature directors, less glamorous and less exciting. Also they are dissatisfied with Teller Mostern. It's too big and staid and old-fashioned for their tastes. Too respectable and dull really. They'd like to be part of something smaller and more trendy. Their contracts come up for renewal in the next few months and I know they'd come with me to start something, but the problem is they've all borrowed money from Mostern and one of them has a mortgage through the company. To start an operation of my own I need ten thousand pounds to discharge and take over their debts. The bank and Hamish can't see it somehow but it's good business. If you own a man's house or have guaranteed his son's school fees you keep his loyalty.'

'Tell me more about Teller Mostern,' Just said. 'How big is it?'

'Big and unprofitable. It turns over more than a million pounds annually but last year showed a profit of only twenty-four thousand before tax.'

'How do you know?'

Paul smiled, showing capped teeth. 'The accountant has the office next to mine.'

'Who runs the company?'

'Mr Mostern.'

'Maybe he's diverting profit, salting it away,' Just suggested.

'No chance of it. He's the model of respectability; chairman of a working boys' club, very active politically, all of that. No, that's not the reason. The company's overstaffed and inefficient. There are six producers doing the same job as myself and five of them are stealing money. I don't mean putting it in their pockets but living it up off their expense accounts, driving around in hired limousines, dressing their wives on the wardrobe budget. That sort of thing.'

'Why doesn't Mostern fire them?'

'He's too gentlemanly and I don't think he really cares. He gets a good living out of it himself and though he's spent twenty years of his life building it up he's not really interested any more. Or rather he cares more about the company's reputation as biggest and best than its profitability. A couple of years ago he found a new hobby which appeals to him much more.'

Just had finished eating and sat listening carefully as he sipped the last of his wine. His mind was racing. He had fingered a runner and his blood quickened at a whiff of the old familiar scent.

'What's that?' he asked.

'Politics. He got the Socialist Party as an account and put our best directors onto making their TV spots for the General Election. Did you see the campaign?'

'I was abroad.'

'They were sensational. *The Sunday Times* said it was our ads that put the party in. But they cost an enormous amount to make and the company carried the loss. We still do political films and it's the main reason we don't make money.'

His listener fiddled with his glass.

'That million plus of turnover. Who provides it?'

'Advertising agencies here and abroad. The work is actually placed by the writers or art directors who devise the ads. The Collingham's customers amongst others.'

'Does Mostern own the company?'

'Seventy-six per cent. The rest's in his wife's name.'

Paul Black was smoking, having pushed away his steak after a couple of mouthfuls. Unlike his fellow producers, food did not play an important part in his life.

'How soon do you need the twenty grand?' Just asked, and Paul answered instantly:

'Absolutely as soon as possible. To get the directors before they re-sign with Mostern I need it within a month. Are you interested?'

'In principle, but I would want certain documents – the audited accounts of the company for the last three years and a note of Mostern's personal expenses. Also a photocopy of his diary since the first of this year until the last forward entry.'

Paul looked astonished.

'Whatever for?'

Just said easily, 'Time spent in preparation is seldom wasted. There are other dreary maxims that apply. Can you get them?'

'Of course.'

'And another thing. I'd like to meet again and learn all there is to know about the mechanics of your business.'

Just raised his head and waved for the waiter. His fingers wrote on the air, calling for the bill in transnational mime.

Paul did not budge.

'Will you put up the money?' he asked.

'Well,' Just said, 'there's only one thing that worries me about that.'

'What's that?'

'The amount.'

Paul frowned.

'I *must* have that. The debts have to be bought and I need enough to cover salaries and the first month's trading. After that it is self-financing. The absolute minimum would be eighteen thousand.'

Just pushed back his chair.

'You misunderstand me. I'd feel a lot happier about the whole proposition if you were asking for a hundred grand.'

He had settled the bill with a twenty-pound note and now picked up two pounds and stuffed them into his pocket, leaving the change.

'Listen,' he said to the waiter, 'I have a black labrador to go home to. Would you wrap up the rest of that steak so I may take it with me?'

When they left the restaurant a few minutes later Paul said, 'Do you want to share a taxi? I could drop you home or we could have a coffee or something.'

'No, I'll walk. It's a nice afternoon and I want to ponder. I'll call you tomorrow.'

He could not allow Paul to see where he lived.

He strolled to Sloane Square then along King's Road, where a cinema was about to open and couples stood informally in the line, sleepy after a heavy lunch, with the bundles of Sunday papers under their arms, a little crumpled now.

Just carried a foil-wrapped package containing the remains of Paul's steak. He had two pounds in his pocket. It was all the money he had left in the world.

Eight

At rest, in perfect contentment, Just lay in the narrow bed, her thighs wrapped around his head.

They had passed an ideal day. Lunch at the Moulin de Mougins had been a dress rehearsal into the world, a *sortie* in his new identity.

Impeccable. The trial run had proved successful. Michael Law was at one with his face, that new countenance gradually revealed as the scars had healed.

Curiously, that alteration in his appearance had been accompanied by a change of spirit. He was conscious of an internal climate more benign and tranquil than he had known before. He was happy and at ease; his blood was calm. Peace had come to him since living in this house.

A memory stole back, the recollection of a night crossing and a course set for Calvi, the sky clear black and moonless, the sea jet and mirror calm exactly reflecting every star so there was no sea, no sky, but the craft floated through an infinite sparkling void. By the small light of the cockpit he had been reading *A Sea-guide to the Tyrrhenian Sea*:

> Whales off Corsica. The waters north of Cap Corse are unusually deep, and a yacht proceeding towards this cape from approximately the French–Italian frontier should not be surprised to see a school of large sperm whales. They are said to be ageing bulls who bring a few cows in from the Atlantic and spend their declining years cruising in these waters. These

mammals, which are very large, are no longer hunted, and are often to be heard when they surface on a calm night.

It was he: an old whale, scarred and escaped from the hunters, come to the warm sea, retired and cruising. This was the still point, here and now. The radio played softly from the chair which held their clothes. An electric fire warmed the evening chill. The girl slept. She was at ease in his company, feeling no nervous or restive edge. Despite the thirty years between them and no tastes shared, her mood was in phase with his. She too was happy here. She wanted to stay, indeed to own this place, to live here.

'Get my head together and do my own thing ... experiment with alternative lifestyles ... really get my own gig together ...'

His lips moved, forming a smile. Enchanting half-wit. Why not though? Why not? He was home and dry. Why not bag it, stay, raise walls against the world? Behind them live in sport and revelry with his lissom teenage bride.

The future stretched ahead a warm and gentle ocean glowing in the sun.

He shifted his head minutely between her legs and brushed his lips across the hair to kiss the delicate damp curls of the sleeping child. Old whale cruising the summer night.

Nine

Just had telephoned the Teller Mostern company the day after meeting Paul Black.

'... No, a personal matter. Mr Redman suggested yesterday in New York that I call Mr Mostern and invite him to lunch.'

'Mr Redman of Coca Cola?'

'Mr Redman of the State Department. J. Walter Redman.'

'Mr Mostern is out of the office just at present,' she told him. 'All his lunches are gone for this week but he could give you Friday the thirteenth.'

'You don't think that's bad luck?'

'For him or for you, Mr Just? It's not the same thing. Shall I confirm it?'

'Please do,' he said, 'the Tiberio at one.'

He pictured the secretary as she put down the phone. Tall and blonde, he thought, crisp and foxy and young. From the sound of her voice she had to be good looking.

Now that he had a scheme to work on Just felt much better. Revenge no longer obsessed him or dominated his thoughts to the exclusion of all else. It was not forgotten but set aside, a meal to look forward to, best eaten cold. Meanwhile, there was hustling to do.

The bright summer weather continued, supporting his new

mood where before it had disturbed him. The low in spirit have need of shade. He had longed for the heavens to open and the sky to fall.

With Hamish's £500 in his pocket he had become a different man, secure and confident. Getting up in the morning was again a pleasure and not the dreary ordeal of the last few weeks.

He was on the hunt for major funds.

He met three times with Paul Black who gave him the documents he required in a plain brown envelope. He listened carefully to all he had to say and did not mention that he had made an appointment to lunch with Mostern. He examined the books and trade magazines which he was given. It had always amused Just that man must construct a mystique around his occupation and a bank trainee pass two years behind the teller's grille before deemed worthy to progress. With the possible exception of surgery Just believed that any job could be mastered in three days. In less than a week of attentive study he was familiar with the workings of the TV advertising business. Familiar enough to chat convincingly. Sufficiently familiar, that is, to punt something.

But he needed a mark.

Chance is a lover of crowded places, and the jostling throng. She frequents the market place but not the hermit's cave. With the money in his pocket, Just put himself about.

Chance found him in a rainstorm.

He had met Paul in the Collingham for a sandwich lunch and was walking from Hyde Park Corner toward Knightsbridge when the first heavy drops began to fall. He ran to a bus shelter and signalled an approaching cab. It had drawn to a stop and he had the door open and his foot raised to enter when a plump figure perspiring from its streak across the road burst through the opposite door.

'No,' said Just, stepping into the cab.

The portly young man wedged himself into the seat.

'I say, this taxi's mine.'

'It's not,' said Just.

Fleshy features crumpled into petulance, then recognition flared in the buried eyes.

'I say ... aren't you Robert Just?'

Just studied him. Twenty or twenty-one in an expensively baggy, blue striped suit.

'The name's Morar,' he said, 'stayed in Rex Motram's place in Belida. Don't you remember?'

Just recalled a fat schoolboy burned raw by the sun. Russell, Earl of Morar, had a strawberry-coloured face and a haughty strangled voice, member by right of the Lords of the Earth, raised on second helpings of over-rich food.

'Of course.'

'Perhaps one could share. Where are you headed?'

'Jack Barclay's,' Just lied.

'I'll drop you.'

The taxi turned into the Park at Bowater House and doubled back toward Piccadilly. Russell asked, 'Buying a car?'

'Picking one up,' Just lied again.

'Been a bit of trouble in Belida, hasn't there? Think I saw something in the papers.'

'You could put it like that,' Just said.

'Caused you aggro, did they?'

'Nationalised me.'

'I say! What rotten luck.'

'Happily we'd seen it coming.'

'Yes? Got it out, did you?'

'Well one couldn't exactly move the bay.'

'No. Suppose not.'

Russell's beady eyes were fixed on him with interest.

'You fly, don't you? Still got a plane?'

'I rent one.'

'And fly it yourself? Yes? How does that sort of thing work?'

Their taxi had negotiated the turn around the Hilton and was driving along Piccadilly much too fast. In less than four minutes they would be in Berkeley Square and Russell would take longer than that to reveal his point. But at Stratton Street the lights changed to red and held them.

Russell said, 'Bad luck, that revolution. Must have put you in a bit of a spot.'

'Yes. Fortunately I had another ball in the air.'

His lordship puffed himself up with importance.

'Look,' he began weightily, 'I don't know how you're placed of course but it just so happens I know of something which may be of interest to you.'

He preened his feathers, thrilled to be in a real man's world.

'Unlikely,' Just replied, 'I'm busy on my own scheme at the moment.'

'Yes . . . well . . . this wouldn't take very long actually. Not more than a couple of days in fact. Good money. Five thousand pounds.'

The taxi had stopped outside the Rolls-Royce showroom.

'It's a fair daily rate,' Just admitted as he got out and walked away. 'You must tell me about it some time.'

'I say . . . !' Russell called after him.

Just looked back at the damp face projecting from the window.

'It doesn't just depend on me you know, but I'm meeting my . . . er . . . my associate in the Ritz bar this evening. Why don't you join us . . . about seven?'

' 'Fraid not. Couldn't possibly make it before half-past. I'll see how I'm placed,' he said and nodded goodbye. Turning, he crossed the pavement into the showroom. Through the gleaming motor cars a salesman approached with manner aloof and eye fishlike on Just's attire.

'Can I help you, sir?'

'Yes,' he answered briskly, 'though you don't have what I want here. I'm looking for an S. 3 Continental bodied convertible. Not earlier than 1963. Can you find me one?'

'A superb car,' the salesman observed warmly. 'Perhaps the most elegant and beautiful model ever built.'

'It must be in mint condition and either white, black, or midnight blue.'

The car salesman was listening with attention, his dress and bearing suggesting some high-ranking member of the diplomatic service.

'I think I know where such a car might be available, but the price would not be less than fifteen thousand pounds.'

'The price is not so important. If you get it up to the showrooms I'll come in next week. Now, I'd like to use your telephone . . .'

He called Paul who had just returned to his office.

'. . . Is it called Spotlight?' he asked. 'That register that lists actors and performers?'

'Of course. I have a set here. Do you want to pick them up?'

'I'll be in the lobby of the Berkeley,' Just told him. 'Do you have a messenger?'

'I'll send them right away. Casting a part?'

'Sort of,' said Just, 'a role for an old trouper.'

Mr Thornton met Just in the Bristol Hotel at six o'clock that same evening. He entered the bar with diffidence, a man in late middle-age and shabby suit, older than his Spotlight portrait, unused to such places, an *Evening Standard* in his hand, lunchtime edition, picked out of a bin in Green Park.

'A gin and orange if I may,' he said.

Then Just questioned him about his work.

'Not much call, not now,' said Mr Thornton, 'what with family entertainment dying out. Tried it out for the telly, yes I have, but it's not the same. Doesn't do for the box, they tell me, no call, no demand for it.'

Just explained what was wanted and Mr Thornton looked flustered. He smoked a cigarette down to the last quarter inch, impervious fingertips stained to ochre brown.

'Don't know what to say, I'm sure,' Mr Thornton said at last, rather ill at ease.

'Then shall we say thirty pounds?' Just suggested. 'Plus a bonus for results.'

Mr Thornton coughed apologetically, 'As to expenses ...'

Just passed him a fiver.

'I'll have a go,' said Mr Thornton. 'Not guaranteeing anything mind you, but I'll do my best.'

He gathered up his evening paper and left.

Just waited at the Bristol. If he had owned a suit and shirt he would have taken a taxi back to his room to change. But he did not so, instead, he went downstairs and asked the cloakroom attendant to fetch him scissors and razor.

He removed his sweater, washed, then trimmed his beard. He was still lightly tanned by the West Indian sun, his body hard from tennis and swimming despite the weeks he had passed in London.

He tipped the attendant two pounds and returned to the bar where he drank Coca-Cola until Mr Thornton came back at 7.40, slightly tipsy and the worse for wear.

He listened carefully to what he had to tell, twice asking questions, once recalling him when his recital strayed.

'Anything else?' he asked.

'Not that I recollect. Couldn't take notes you understand, not in the circumstances, and my memory's not what it was. They were about fifteen feet from me and one was in profile. I lost a lot of him, I fear. Still, hope you've got what you want, that it's satisfactory.'

Just gave him forty pounds. He said, 'Even though it's no longer considered entertainment, Mr Thornton, I think we've found a modern application for your skills.'

At eight o'clock exactly he left the Bristol and crossed the road.

It was dusk in the street, dusk verging on night, the light which the French describe as 'between dog and wolf', that time when night predators stir and stretch, unsheathing their claws.

He walked swiftly across the street between the rush of traffic. Deep in his brain he heard the click. His head cleared to ice. The world fell exactly into place. He descended the stairs at a loose fast pace and entered the bar. Brass wall brackets with burgundy shades lit yellowing paintwork. The patterned carpet was rather worn, gilt chairs chipped, in poor repair. Grandeur past its prime. An atmosphere of luxury slightly run-to-seed which only the English and French recognise as being stylish. The marks were seated in an alcove at the far end of the room. Russell Morar and a still younger man with a plump resembling face. Both rose.

'My brother Edward,' introduced Russell, glancing pointedly at his watch.

'We'd given you up.'

'I got involved.'

They were drinking champagne.

'This all right?' Russell enquired, lifting the bottle from the ice-bucket as a waiter hurried up to serve.

An awkward beat of silence. They had been discussing him and he had interrupted them in mid-sentence.

Just sipped his wine and remarked lightly, 'I've scarcely been in England during the last few years but looking for signs of economic recession in Piccadilly one risks being crushed to death by a Rolls-Royce.'

Russell seized upon the topic with relief.

'Got your car, did you?'

'It's not ready yet. Next week.'

'Oh, what are you getting?' brother Edward asked.

He described the S. 3 Continental.

'Got a Jensen myself,' Edward said. 'Rusty's got a Ferrari but it's sick at the moment.'

'Ran out of road,' added Russell, 'wrapped it round a lamp-post.'

'Ah ... gilded youth!' sighed Just.

Both brothers uttered the same bark of token laughter. Then Russell said, 'Well ... glad you're here. Thing is ... well, not sure how to put this, but ... what we're going to talk about ... best it doesn't go any further.'

'Absolute discretion?' Just suggested. 'Could that be how you put it?'

'Yes ... well ...'

The wine was clean and sharp on his tongue. Lolling in his chair Just felt totally relaxed yet knew he could move twice as fast as anyone in this room.

Edward said, 'We wondered ... could you tell us a little how you fly your plane?'

'For that you need an instructor, but someone of your age accustomed to racy cars would probably need no more than ten to twelve hours to solo.'

'Ha-ha ... no I mean ... where you keep it and so on?

'My plane was nationalised. In England I rent.'

'And when you take it ... you charter for the day or whatever?'

'Whatever,' Just confirmed.

'And if you have it overnight you keep it at another airport?'

'Any field with more than 250 yards of level grass.'

'Oh yes?'

There was another pause.

'The thing is,' said Edward, 'we've got to trust you.'

'And the other thing,' said Just, 'is that I've got to trust you.'

The young man looked most surprised at the notion.

'But surely ...'

'Surely,' Just said, 'in a criminal undertaking trust is all.'

'Now wait a minute,' put in Russell, 'who said anything about this being criminal?'

'Oh come on,' Just remarked impatiently, 'you've got your hand on my knee so make the proposition.'

Brother Edward reached a decision. He said, 'A couple of years ago father died and we came into quite a bit of money. Then with death duties we had to sell the house and so on, and both of us are rather fed up with paying taxes actually. The things this government spends it on make me absolutely boil.'

Just said, 'Sterling's not too hot either. You'd do better converting some of it into another currency.'

Both brothers were taken aback. After a moment's silence Lord Morar said, 'Well, yes. That's what we were thinking. Actually we thought you might do the job for us.'

'An illegal mission?'

'Something of that kind.'

He sipped his wine and regarded their plump brightly-coloured faces above the rim of his glass.

'The trouble with that kind is that if it goes sour you can end in prison and that's very boring.'

'Well, I don't think ...'

Just continued. 'You see, you have to be so sure of who you are working with. Careless talk costs lives – that sort of thing.'

'But you can trust us,' put in Lord Morar with a show of irritation.

Just's eyes looked past them at a print on the wall. His tone was abstracted. He might have been discussing a theoretical point of ethics.

'Trust ... not only must it work both ways but backward as well as forward. The past as well as the future.'

Russell grew impatient.

'Yes, of course. Now what we want to do ...'

Just interrupted him, 'Don't tell me. I am not your man and the fewer people who know about your scheme the better. It should not be difficult to find the sort of pilot you seek. The job offers considerable opportunities to a dishonest man. He can either steal your money at once or complete the transaction and blackmail you for the rest of your lives. The decision is his. A classic choice; immediate capital versus steady income.'

'But ...'

Just continued, 'Your plan is imaginative, even ingenious, but it contains certain flaws. For a start, Lord Morar, when you disappear the TV networks and the press will seize upon your kidnapping with delight. Your brother will be overwhelmed by expert advisers. Every policeman in the British Isles will want to get his photo in the papers. The terms of ransom you will be unable to keep secret and in the full blaze of this notoriety you want me to transport a considerable sum of money to Switzerland and there make a dummy drop to your non-existent abductors and then secrete the money. Planes are not mice. They make a lot of noise and people tend to remember them. Then, redeemed, you must appear. Fit and well, healthy and poorer, no trace of your captors. Neither physical nor psychological scars and a tall tale which does not bear examination. Shortly after that all of us are sent to jail. "I'm sorry your Honour,"' Just concluded in a cockney accent, '"truly sorry, honest. We promise it won't happen again."'

Two mouths gaped. The expressions of the brothers had fallen, comically identical. The face of each resembled a smacked arse.

'How ever ...?'

'How did ...?'

Just savoured the long moment.

'Don't worry about that,' he told them at last.

'Just bear in mind that if you want to work with me you must be much, much more careful. Now ...'

He leaned forward in his chair and began to talk ...

At the Collingham, Hamish bellowed with laughter when Just told him, slapping the table with a meaty hand, 'They're all the same,' he said, 'all of them. Go to them in hurt or need and you don't get through the door. Kick 'em in the teeth and they buy you dinner, lick your boots, press lucre in your hand. Ponces!'

His exuberance overflowed in a hearty playful nudge.

'Lipreader indeed! You've kept your touch, Robbie boy, I'll grant you that. Lipreader ... the fucking cunts! I'll drink to that.'

* * *

Saturday afternoon Just took a walk through Mayfair. He strolled past the windows of Jack Barclay then cut the corner beneath the leafy trees of the square into Davies Street where a limousine passed him, delivering a tribe of Arabs to Claridges.

The shops were closed, the streets quiet and uncrowded. Parked cars were few. This was not a business area; solid Victorian façades decently concealed spacious apartments whose owners were spending the weekend at places in the country.

Outside the Connaught a uniformed doorman touched his cap to a couple entering a cab.

'The National Theatre,' Just heard him say. He turned into Mount Street and sauntered past Scotts Restaurant, its plate glass window incongruously meshed and sandbagged against terrorist attack.

Opposite number 44 his steps slowed and stopped.

Set back from the street by the width of a railed basement area it was a late Victorian house in red brick, large and imposing. Two columns supported a portico which formed the entrance, raised from the street. Ornamental metal grillework closed the sides of this portico and the same ironwork protected the balconies on every floor.

His casual gaze roamed the façade; a man, one would have said, with some interest in architecture, and half an hour to kill.

Heavy sash windows in white painted solid wood. The metal box of an alarm system was pinned to the wall at the second level. No exposed wiring even at this height. An expensive system.

Just moved on, nodding pleasantly to a passing policeman.

In Park Lane he turned north, the crowd thicker here, tourists and out-of-towners strolling tieless, chattering in English dialect and assorted tongues.

Beside the Cumberland Hotel a store window displayed a range of summer footwear.

He entered and sat down.

'Tennis shoes,' he said, and chose the most expensive in the shop, in white canvas with thick rubber soles, particular about their fit.

'*Black* polish?' the attendant questioned with surprise.

'Playing at night,' he explained, smiling, and wore them into the street, carrying his own shoes in their box.

He walked home through the Park, looking at the lovers feeding the ducks and the au pair girls and children and a straightbacked couple of uniformed nannies wheeling their charges through in prams.

He thought not much had really changed in the years he had been away. There were more black faces, he noticed, and fewer policemen. The streets were dirtier and the shops more tawdry. There was less style but the way the city functioned was the same; the same bland faces ruled it. Ten years ago this had been his territory. He was still comfortable here.

By the time he reached home the tennis shoes had softened to his feet. He passed half an hour colouring them black then switched on the television and rested until night.

At nine o'clock he bathed, combed his hair and beard and dressed in clean jeans and dark blue sweater. Under his clothes he tied around his waist the other loan he had got from Hamish.

At a quarter to ten he left the house and was walking the length of the dismal street toward the lighted thoroughfare of Earls Court Road.

A pub door banged open. A pair of drunken Australians, locked in mortal combat, spilled out into the gutter as he stepped around them.

He travelled by taxi as far as Hyde Park Corner. Paying it off at the Hilton Hotel he walked up Park Lane. The corner to Curzon Street was obstructed by limousines and a group of Arabs in excited debate outside the Playboy Club.

He strolled up South Audley Street and turned into Mount Street with the easy tread of one who belonged here. At number 44 he slipped his hand into his pocket in the gesture of a man reaching for his latchkey and mounted the four steps to the door.

From the shadow of the twin columns which flanked the portico he looked up and down the street.

A cluster of people were talking on the pavement outside Scotts. Two cars passed. He heard the doorman whistle for a taxi outside the Connaught, the slam of a car door, then an engine starting. A hundred yards away a cab swayed around Carlos Place and disappeared in the direction of Grosvenor Square.

The street was quiet. He swung a foot onto the railings and stepped up into the angle behind the column.

He felt the hit as he began to climb, a surge of the heart and thud in the gut as the rush got to him. A perfect mix of excitement and calm squirted through his veins. A stab of adrenalin and then his breathing steadied, deep and slow.

He reached one foot across to the windowsill and transferred his weight, then stretched and found a hand-hold on the lower of the overhangs which roofed the portico. Wedging his other foot higher in the angle he stepped up smoothly then shifted grip to the upper ledge. He glanced at the window fastening as he passed. Locked and wired; not that he would have tried this one anyway.

He moved his hand, fingered the base of the balcony railing, tested it for strength, and pulled himself up and over. He had planned the route that afternoon, considering its hazards, selecting every foot and handhold. There was no technical risk in the ascent. The sole danger lay in its exposure to the street and he went up fast; that first section of the climb had taken no more than fifteen seconds. Now, protected by the balcony, he examined the French windows.

Well built, small-paned. Wing nut fixtures and a nine-inch stop, securely plugged into the woodwork. Flex crawled down the inside frame in a shallow groove, putty filled and painted. A sophisticated system aesthetically installed, it must have cost them dear.

He could have taped and tapped out a window then cut the wires but he had no wish to advertise his visit. How security-conscious London had become. As he stood up to resume his climb he sighed; there had been no such problems when he was young and similarly engaged.

He was not in such good training now either. He realised it as he set both hands to the drainpipe and monkeyed up to the next floor level. As soon as he was organised he would take up exercise again. As soon as he had cash ... He climbed on.

Obscured by a tree, the streetlight dappled the house front with moving shadow. A car swept by thirty feet below him.

Two men had come out of the Connaught and were walking down the street in this direction, the voices quiet and clear.

'... The thing was a put-up job from start to finish. Ted as much as admitted it at dinner.'

A cigar glowed in the other's mouth.

Locking one foot between drainpipe and wall, he reached across with the other to place it on the windowsill, then shifted his weight to balance upon both. His free hand tested the window. Locked. But no wiring. A man who had climbed this far deserved to enter.

His hand moved to his waist and returned with a six-inch section of metal ruler tied on a cord.

Spreadeagled against the rough brickwork, he slid the blade into the crack between the wooden window frames. At the second try he felt the catch slip back. He pushed up the window and stepped down into the house.

The street lamp reflected from the white ceiling and bathed the room in a pale wash of light. Just saw four desks, each with a typewriter. In the corner stood an accounts' computer.

The door was open into a corridor. His feet moved soundlessly over wall to wall carpet.

He glanced into each office as he passed. Two desks apiece, executive and secretary's, a filing cabinet, framed prints on the wall. There was nothing to interest him here.

He passed the metal door of an elevator and arrived at a stairwell. He moved upward. What he sought had to be on top.

The staircase rose into another corridor, the carpet here deeper beneath his feet.

He opened the door of a high-ceilinged room with parquet floor, once a private library, now a conference room with refectory table laid for twelve with a dozen note-pads.

He stepped softly down the corridor, through an arch, into a small anteroom surveyed by a secretary's desk neatly bare but for a pair of telephones. In the wall a built-in ice-box and a cocktail cabinet. He was warm.

Two doors. One revealed a bathroom, comfortably appointed. A wardrobe contained a dinner jacket and two evening shirts on hangers. It would seem Mostern had the habit of working late and frequented people who dressed for dinner, Just reflected as he washed his hands of grime.

As he opened the other door which led from the anteroom his nose picked up the lingering fragrance of a good cigar.

The room was about twenty feet square with the domed glass ceiling of a conservatory. A suggestion was retained of that previous role in the shape of two rubber plants reaching the full height of the walls with twin cascades of sombre drooping leaves.

The far end of the room contained a large leather-topped desk, two telephones upon a table beside it. The corner opposite was furnished by a pair of sofas set at right angles around a square coffee table of stainless steel and glass upon which stood another telephone, a pad of paper, a cigarette box, two used glasses and an ashtray containing a single cigar butt.

Just sat down upon the sofa and let his glance play over the room. A bookcase held works of reference and a number of statuettes and awards. On the wall hung framed lithographs, a Picasso and two Matisses. If there were a safe it was going to make life that much more difficult. But he was not ready to go to work yet.

He leaned back comfortably in the sofa and emptied his mind to allow the atmosphere of the room to get to him, the personality to form of the man who worked here.

Mostern had been here during the weekend. The cleaners would have done the offices on Friday night. Just lifted one of the glasses and sniffed it. Brandy. He tested the dead cigar between his fingers and retrieved its discarded band from the ash-tray.

Unclipping a pencil flashlight he shone it for a second on the scrap of paper. Havana. Two men had come back here after lunch today.

There was no method of covering the glass roof. It would be too dangerous to use the electric light for the glow of the dome could be seen from the street.

He got up from the sofa and took down the first of the pictures. Using his flashlight he began a detailed examination of every foot of the room's wall space up to eye level.

Let there not be a safe, he thought.

Fifteen minutes of meticulous search failed to reveal one. There was no filing cabinet in the room. If there was anything of use to him it had to be in the desk. On each side of the kneehole was a set of three drawers, all of them locked.

Pulling up his sweater, he unstrapped a cord which had been tied around his waist. A loan from Hamish. Thirty or forty keys suspended from it, knotted at one-inch intervals along its length.

As he set it on the floor and crouched to the desk he heard a noise downstairs.

He froze, his nerves alert, straining at the silence. Somewhere in the building a door had banged shut. Standing up, he crept to the door ajar. He listened. Inside the house all was quiet.

He stepped into the passage and glided towards the stairwell. By his head came a clank which made his heart leap, a loud mechanical whirr. Someone was coming up in the elevator.

Swiftly he darted back the way he had come and into the bathroom to stand behind the door. His stomach cramped as he realised that the rope of keys still lay behind the desk. A desperate bird of panic flapped in his belly.

Ten feet away the elevator clanged open. A raucous laugh and steps going by in the direction of Mostern's office. Two voices, then silence.

The light had switched on in the passage. Viewed through the hinge crack the bathroom was fiercely bright. More voices. The sound of a drawer or cupboard opened. Suddenly – a shadow blocked his sight. He tensed. A man had entered the bathroom and was at the basin adding water to a glass. A broad blue back in policeman's uniform.

The man set down his glass and stepping to the lavatory unzipped his fly. Sharp noise of water. The man shifted on his feet, easing the weight.

Just was crouched, hands advanced and splayed, ready to spring. If the man moved further into the room they would be face to face.

The blue figure turned. A fleshy, pallid face with sore patches of cold beneath the nostrils. He picked up his glass.

'Needed that!' he called loudly as he went out.

Just relaxed, let out a long and silent breath. There had been something wrong about the uniform. Not police but security guards, on their rounds and stealing drink, he realised at the chink of glass from the anteroom. After five minutes they left. Steps past and the light going off. Rattle of the elevator door.

From the top of the stairwell his ear followed them down. Hum of the lift cable. Slam of the elevator at the bottom. Voices receding. Front door closing. Silence. From the window a car starting up.

His forehead and hands were wet and his nerves thrilled with fire. A tremor danced in his muscles and his neck had tightened to a knot of pain. He craved a cigarette. Suppressing the need he returned to Mostern's office and looked at the desk.

He picked up the rope of keys and weighed it in his hand but fear was still in him and the mood would not come. To calm himself he stepped to the bookcase and shone his flashlight on the shelves. *TV and Advertising Directory*, the *Advertisers' and Art Directors' Yearbook*, a crouched lion in bronze engraved

'Palme d'Or, Venice. Overall Best: Alka Seltzer 60 second commercial. Producer: Teller Mostern Company'. There were a dozen such awards.

Just sat for five minutes on the sofa, his head thrown back and eyes directed upward through the glass to the stars and high wrack of moonlit clouds. He emptied his mind and lost himself in the heavens.

Then he stood and with deliberation crossed to the desk. Picking up the length of keys he tried the first in the lock of the top drawer.

He worked swiftly, devoting less than five seconds to a key yet each essay told him something. A check, a turn, a further probe and the profile of the lock took shape as an identikit picture fills up on a screen.

One after another he tried the keys, selecting and fitting them to the hole with the aid of his flashlight then closing his eyes as he slipped them into place, would-be place, to feel the jar, the check, to discard and take up the next. He did not think. His mind was void and the sense entirely in his fingers. The seventh was it. He knew it was right even as it entered the lock, felt it with the sureness a piano tuner knows when the note is true. His fingers had perfect pitch.

He turned the key, pulled out the drawer and laid it on the leather top.

Working by the light of his torch, Just started to read through every piece of paper that was in the desk.

On Friday the thirteenth, Just was ten minutes early for his lunch date at the Tiberio. He wanted to give Mostern everything that came within his power, starting with the pleasure of a well-timed entrance.

Ordering a sherry at the bar he installed himself on a leather sofa which overlooked the stairs into the restaurant.

A quartet of businessmen descended talking in flat northern vowels.

Though he sat physically at ease the adrenalin coursed through his body in a sting of anticipation. His mind was needle sharp. Cards had been dealt; he had drawn and improved. He was ready, waiting only for his opponent to enter, pick up his hand and play.

A slim, well-dressed man came down the stairs at a run and with the same instinctive certainty with which he had sensed the key, Just knew that this was Mostern. A quick word at the bar then the man was coming toward him, flash of teeth and hand outstretched.

'My dear chap . . . do forgive me. Such a perfect day . . . thought I'd walk.'

Mostern was in his fifties, tall and handsome. Wings of grey hair swept back over his ears. An alert mobile expression, easy smile, open reactions. An actor's manner. A public face.

'Shall we go in?' Just suggested. 'Have a drink while we order?'

There was no fumbling for a gambit as they sat down.

'Used to eat here a lot,' Mostern remarked, 'but then the chef went rogue or took to drink or something. The food became very unpredictable.'

A waiter hovered.

'What'll you have?'

'A large whisky. Just ice,' Mostern ordered directly then his look came back to Just and he smiled almost shyly.

'Frankly I need it in the worst way. The most ghastly thing's just happened to me.'

'Then have a drink and confide in a stranger. That's sure therapy.'

'Yes? I hope so. Fridays are always bad but this was an especially full morning. Meetings one after another since breakfast. A list of appointments written into my book on every half hour. Twelve-thirty was the last one, to interview a new chauffeur; my own's going to Australia . . .'

His whisky was served. Mostern picked it up and swallowed a thirsty mouthful.

'Go on,' Just prompted.

'Well ... so the man came in. Middle-aged, sensibly dressed, short hair ... you know, suitable looking. So I told him to sit down and asked how long he had been in his present job and he said twelve years. Then I asked was he married, and the usual questions; did he think he'd like this sort of work ...'

Just was already laughing.

'Yes, well you've guessed of course and I admit I thought he was looking rather peculiar but we went on for a long time before he exploded.'

'So who was he?'

'The chairman of Unilever.'

Mostern shuddered elaborately

'No doubt after lunch I shall rationalise myself into believing I didn't want his account anyway but, really, I think I'm losing my touch, getting too old for this job. Do you know you are the only person over thirty I have lunched with this week. It's a great pleasure.'

This was an outright lie and, having studied his appointments book, Just knew it. But there was a quality about Mostern, at the same time self-deprecating and stylish, which was disarming. Just knew he was up against a man who deployed charm as deftly as himself.

Mostern glanced up from the menu.

'But how *does* one end?' he demanded. 'The only man who did it with elegance was St Exupery. Flew south into the eye of the sun and disappeared.'

Just asked, 'Do you know about Glen Miller?'

'Wasn't he lost in an air crash?'

'He was searching for St Exupery.'

Mostern looked amazed.

'No? What a fascinating theory.'

They ordered. Both men chose roast beef and Just selected a burgundy, opened the game and led.

'Now, Mr Mostern, I know in England the convention is that business is not discussed until coffee....'

'If at all,' interrupted his opponent, scoring a point which Just conceded with a smile.

'... but in the States where I have been working we have the habit of starting on the subject with the first martini.'

Mostern rearranged his chair at a slight angle to the table, hitched his trouser crease and set one leg across the other.

'You are my host,' he said.

So as the meal was served, Just started to play his hand. And Mostern picked up the spirit of the game immediately and responded. As a player he proved adept and swift, perceptive and intelligent.

He spotted quickly what Just was after, increased the ante, yielded points and gained some. He bluffed occasionally and well but he went always by the rules. He was a gentleman; he had no way of knowing his opponent was a cardsharp.

Throughout the course of lunch Mostern played with conviction and skill and finished still holding unrevealed his secret joker. He ended and went out certain that he had won – as in a sense he had for he got what he wanted. But he was unaware that every card in his hand had been examined.

Every one, including the joker.

Flushed by success, lightheaded and lighthearted, after lunch Just was tempted to have his beard shaved and his hair cut and order a half-dozen suits. The curse had been lifted. The beggar had been transformed back into a handsome prince whose first act would be to call for room service and order up; the royal finger poised above the bell ...

He stilled the impulse. Fate had dealt him a wardrobe and a

persona. Both were working. He would do well to stay inside them.

So he sublimated, went to Jack Barclay, signed for the Bentley Continental and ordered four hundred pounds' worth of stereophonic tape equipment. He telephoned a real-estate agent and made an appointment to view furnished apartments from £250 per week, centrally located.

Then he called Paul Black, saying, 'I think we ought to meet.'

Paul joined him for tea at the Ritz.

Just told him about the Morar brothers, their new partners, and Paul slopped his cup in excitement. His dour face kindled.

'You mean it? We've got the money?'

Just confirmed it.

'Fantastic man. You're really fantastic. I mean it. So when do we start the company?'

Just shifted his chair and picked up a sandwich.

'Well ... in fact we don't.'

The light went off in Paul's face. His joy collapsed. He looked so sad and woebegone that Just felt wretched.

'I don't know quite how to break this to you. There is, as they say, both good news and bad.'

'OK. That's the bad,' Paul said in a dull voice. 'So what can be good?'

'We're buying the Teller Mostern Company,' Just explained. 'You and I are going to run it. I think we can make a great deal of money.'

Ten

Sun blazed upon the plate glass window. Inside the office of the Notary Public in Lezat the air was lifeless, baked and dry, stifling.

Though the place was in a modern block everything in it, including the Notary himself was of the nineteenth century.

Perched beyond an enormous carved wooden desk, he was a tiny bald man with a complexion the same colour as the yellowed pages of the legal tomes which lined the walls behind him.

Just and Marianne, Henry and Yvonne, sat upon upright chairs in a semi-circle facing the desk. The old couple had been in a high state of excitement since early morning and had dressed carefully for the occasion. In the taxi which had brought all four of them here neither had stopped talking for an instant.

The Notary spoke good English with a heavy accent. Before him on the desk was the ribboned dun cover to the Act of Sale recording the purchase of the mills by Yvonne's parents more than fifty years before. Confirming that the property could not be divided and that both mills must be sold together, he explained to Just the conditions of an 'en viager' sale, then asked the old couple what price had been agreed.

Both answered together, £15,000 down, they said, plus £2,000 a year until their deaths.

The money must come from outside France, for he was a non-resident foreigner, and must be transferred into the Notary's client account. To prepare the new act he would need Just's passport and birth certificate. Now, in order to sign the *compromise*, which was the engagement of both parties to the transaction, what sum was intended as deposit?

Just answered with a show of embarrassment. The sale price had been agreed. He had proposed £2,000 as immediate deposit and written to his accountant in Switzerland instructing him to transfer these funds. Yesterday the payment had not arrived and it was only by telephoning today that he had learned that his accountant was on holiday ...

Henry and Yvonne were clearly disconcerted by this news. They reacted badly. Of course they realised it was not Just's fault but it was not what had been agreed. It was tiresome ... it was inconvenient ...

'A matter of days,' Just reassured them. Shortly he would have not only the deposit but the entire £15,000 in his account here. Next week, say, they could have the full amount. The transaction could be completed right away.

'Well yes, but ...'

'Now ...' Just continued, turning to the Notary, there would be no further delay. That, he guaranteed. If the Act of Sale could be prepared he would be ready to sign and hand over a cheque in ten days' time, as soon as possible ... if that would suit *monsieur le notaire*, of course ...

No problem. It seemed it could. The old couple appeared reassured. The *compromise* was signed.

So, it was done. The deal was settled. It was a major event, goodness yes, the most important happening in Henry's and Yvonne's lives for fifteen years. A celebration was called for.

The four of them moved to the cafe on the square where Just ordered champagne.

He watched both waiter and Marianne as the wine was served. Not a sign was exchanged between them, not a flicker of recognition. He would have preferred that there should have been for he sensed a tacit conspiracy operating to his disadvantage.

Yvonne cried out as the bottle was opened and raised a tremulous hand to her heart, the gesture theatrically overplayed. Just was conscious of amused and curious glances from the other tables.

'Jolly nice to have you here,' she carolled but Henry said nothing.

Both old people drank fast, their eyes on the bottle. It was years since they had tasted champagne. Henry's clawlike hand fiddled with the sugar bowl, setting out the wrapped cubes in dominoes upon the table.

'Simply super we'll be neighbours,' Yvonne continued gaily. 'Too awful you're going to want us dead.'

Just refilled her glass and attempted to set her mind at rest. Really, one house was enough, he told her.

Under cover of reaching for his wine, Henry's sleeve swept the sugar cubes off the table and into the paper napkin on his lap. Just, who caught the movement, smiled with tolerant understanding; he too had known the harsh voice of need.

'Of course we never for a second think about *you* dying,' Yvonne announced abruptly.

Her husband threw her a straight look and she was overcome with confusion.

'Oh dear! I didn't mean that. How frightful all this talk of death. And this should be a joyful occasion.'

Flustered, her hands picked at her frock in agitation. Just assured her that it was so. Marianne had not bothered to enter the conversation. With the rest of her generation, the rituals and civilities by which adults conducted their lives only excited her contempt.

By the end of the bottle Yvonne was definitely intoxicated. Her face was flushed and her voice shrill. When they stood to leave she stumbled and Just had to take her arm to prevent her falling.

They shared a taxi back to the mills. When finally they had delivered the old people to their house and returned to their own Marianne let out a whistle of relief.

Just agreed. 'That was embarrassing. We must take care not to become too friendly.'

'Wheee! Yvonne's worse than my gran. And ten times as noisy.'

She unbuttoned her shirt and threw it carelessly to the floor.

'I'm going to swim.'

'Have you got a birth certificate?' Just asked.

'Yeah, I got one for my passport. Why?'

'I haven't,' he said thoughtfully, 'and as my passport is in the name of Michael Law I don't see that I'm about to get one. We're going to have to buy this place in your name.'

'Yes?'

She kicked off her jeans and pants and, naked, made for the door. That she would be sole owner of two houses in the south of France seemed a fact of no interest to her.

'Coming to swim then?' she asked.

'No. I have to make a call.'

He took the Ferrari and drove back to Lezat.

The woman behind the grille glanced pointedly at her watch when he asked for a call to Zurich. It was close to five o'clock and the post office was about to close.

'Hallo. Dr Liebel's office.'

'I'd like to talk to him please.'

'Who is this please?'

'Mr Law. Don't you recognise my voice?'

'I am sorry, Mr Law, he is not returned yet. He is in South Africa.'

Was she lying? Face to face, he could have detected it; he had a keen instinct for these things. Over the telephone it was harder to be sure.

'Have you telexed my transfer yet?' he asked.

'I told you, Mr Law, we shall be transferring this as soon as our account is credited with your funds from Curaçao.'

'They have been there for four weeks,' Just objected. 'Dr Liebel told me they were being transferred nearly a month ago.'

'Yes, this is normal. It is not efficient in Curaçao.'

There was no warmth in her flat voice. She sounded impatient to be doing something more important. Just persisted, 'In that case you must advance me money from your client account. I need funds immediately.'

'No. This I cannot do without authorisation from Dr Liebel.'

'Well get it then. Call him. Hello. Hello.'

The line had gone dead. After a moment he heard her again beneath the crackle of electricity, '... shall be talking to him on the telephone in Cape Town tomorrow. How much do you need?'

'25,000 Swiss francs immediately and 100,000 of my own money within two weeks. I need this urgently, you understand.'

'I will tell him.'

A faint trace of humanity entered her voice in sympathy with his predicament.

'I am sorry, Mr Law. These transfers take time.'

'Perhaps, but I hope you will find a way to do it swiftly. I would take it very badly if anything snarled this up.'

'Snarled? Mr Law, I am not understanding.'

'Try,' he answered coldly and hung up.

On the way home Just stopped in at the Tabac for the English papers.

He had paid over the money and turned to go, his eyes glancing across the headlines, when the blonde woman behind the counter called him back.

'Monsieur, you have found your friend?'

'My friend?'

'The young gentleman who was looking for you.'

'For me?' he asked, puzzled.

'*Eh bien*, *monsieur*, I think so. He described the girl who is often with you and the white car which goes vroom-vroom.'

'An Englishman?'

'I think. Perhaps German.'

'What was he like?'

Her Latin gesture described more eloquently than words the permed and bouffant hairstyle of the unknown enquirer.

'Young. *Un peu ... farouche*.'

'No,' Just said, 'that is not for me. What did you say?'

'I say perhaps yes, but I am not knowing where you live. He was here only a little time. He is gone now, I think.'

'I see,' said Just, 'but it is another man he wants.'

It had to be a mistake. No one could be looking for him.

The sun had gone from the valley by the time he got back though the peak which soared behind the house was still aflame. He stopped the car as it came into sight. With the coming of evening a mist rose off the river and in this soft light the old stone of the two mills showed muted grey among the trees, as one with the landscape, the colour of age.

He stilled his racing thoughts. There was nothing wrong. The enquiry at the Tabac was not for him; in Switzerland these delays and aggravation were all too normal. One of the rules of life was that no money ever arrived when promised.

Marianne was not in the house when he let himself in.

He shivered, for the fire was unlit, and went upstairs to fetch a sweater from the bathroom.

From the window he saw her still at the pool. Naked, she was crouched upon a rock staring up at the house.

Unseen at the unlighted window he watched her fondly, impure elf, pale in the twilight. Her look was fixed. At this distance he could not read her expression but the set of her body was intent, pointed at the mill, squatted upon her haunches in the posture of a gargoyle. A deadly imp.

What was she thinking, he wondered. He could ask her later but she would lie. Despite the shallowness of her mind and the banality of her thoughts – which worried him not at all – there were areas of this girl which he could not penetrate, a sly and secret quality which excited him intensely.

Something white drew his eye, a movement on the further bank. He directed his look into the trees above the ravine.

At first he saw nothing. And then he became aware that he was not the only figure who from the shadows looked down upon the crouching girl.

A young man stood among the trees. As Just's eyes penetrated the gloom he recognised him in jeans and sweater and carrying a collapsible fishing rod in his hand. The same.

Just drew back from the window into the concealment of the darkening room. His area of vision shrank to a narrow view, centre the pool, bottom the girl and top the boy who watched the naked prey.

Narrow-hipped she squatted on the rocks, thighs splayed, face and juvenile breasts tilted up toward him. As he observed the scene the thought of all his other worries left him. His breath came short and a queer languor stole into his limbs, a voluptuous weakness flowed through him and made him reach out his hand for support as he swayed and would have sunk to the floor. Tightness gripped his heart and boiling fire percolated in his loins.

So endless, so drawn out it was, he could not have said how long the moment lasted while such stinging juice dribbled in his veins . . . but then the girl moved. She stood up. Her regard travelled the bounds of her property. She turned around and Just saw the shadowed curve of her slender back and the jut of her little buttocks as she faced the further bank and the shadows which concealed her other watcher.

Both flagrant and chaste she turned back and sprang lightly across the rocks to the steps which led up to the mill.

In the upper mill Henry had made his wife a cup of tea while she rested on her bed.

'Feeling better, dear?' he asked.

'I'm *fine*,' Yvonne said. 'It was just the wine on top of all that excitement.' She sat up straight. 'It *is* exciting, isn't it?' she appealed to him.

'Exciting?' He seemed to be considering. 'No, Yvonne, I don't think that's exactly the word I'd choose.'

'But the money ...'

'*What* money? It was said so harshly it startled her.

'But ...'

'We haven't seen any money yet, remember?'

After a moment she asked in a small quick voice, 'You don't think ...'

'He's too glib by half,' said Henry.

'Surely you don't think ...'

'There are all sorts of dubious characters roaming the world nowadays,' Henry continued. 'Well dressed, well spoken smoothies who can charm the birds off the trees. Spivs and wide boys. To someone like that ... well, we'd probably look simple.'

Yvonne said, 'I wonder how he made his money?'

'*What* money?' Henry demanded fiercely. 'Oh yes, he flashes it around. Loaded with it – he looks. You're a foolish woman to be impressed. He couldn't make the deposit. When it came down to it our Mr Law couldn't even come up with £2,000.'

Yvonne had turned white. Her voice was tiny.

'You don't think he's ... a trickster?'

Henry did not reply at once. He had stepped to the window and was looking down to where, through the darkness, a light showed in the window of the lower mill.

'I don't know,' he admitted at last. 'But he believes he's very clever, does Mr Law. All I can say is that if he thinks he's going to pull the wool over my eyes then he's got another thought coming. You mark my words.'

Marianne stood before the mirror brushing her shining hair while Just lay nude upon the bed and watched her.

'Put on the gym slip,' he said.

The long firm strokes continued across that burnished helmet.

She ignored him. This one would be his downfall, he thought in a flash of prophetic vision. Uncaring, incorrigible, this little number would do him in.

But there was no pulling back now; the blood makes its peculiar selection, the flesh its own demand. His heart pounded, a drum in the chest.

'Here,' he commanded, a sharpness in his tone so she looked, brush poised in air, and caught him reflected in the glass. Her lips twitched in amusement as she saw his stiffening and the power she held over him.

'But you *told* me to do my hair.'

'Put it on,' he said.

She moved so slowly to obey, still wearing that sly and crooked smile, age-old in her whorish knowledge, schoolgirl slut finally consenting to place one foot up upon the bed.

'Tell me what you want,' she said, the angled knee, taut curve of thigh and glimpse of coral in the silky shadow.

'On the bed. Stand over me.'

He was rigid now and his senses reeled, tormented by that lazy impure grace as she stepped upon the bed, shifted weight and placed one leg astride his face.

'Like this? This what you want then?'

'Yes,' he breathed, 'Oh yes, yes ...' with fire and ice burning in his groin.

'Like this?'

'Yes. Squat!' he said, but she disobeyed, remained standing, rocked back and looked down at his lust; brazen, all awareness of Man's secret dark desires in that knowing smile.

'Do you want it?' she asked, flexing. 'Do you want to look at it?'

Then slowly she sank toward him, pink lips parting with damp and tiny click, lowering voluptuously upon him ... and poised there just beyond reach of his flickering tongue, squatted in lascivious triumph and display as his body writhed.

'You're a dirty old man,' she said. 'I know what turns you on.'

Obscenely splayed she squatted, the rosy petals of her parted sex wet with her own excitement.

'Dirty perverted old man,' she mocked as his hands clutched at the tense thighs then she, at the precise extremity of his need, the exact spasm of his coiling nerves, drove down upon his mouth with greedy savage thrust . . . the flooding salt sea taste and oyster squirming on the tongue as in the same instant his body shuddered and he too came and she laughed as it spattered on his belly.

She slept, but he could not. Sex had emptied him and into the void the demons rushed crowding in.

At midnight he was still restlessly awake. Thick and haunted, the darkness pressed at the windows of the silent house. He got up then, went downstairs, poured a drink and lit a cigarette.

He paced the flagstones with bare feet, oblivious to the cold.

At the paper shop, it had to be a mistake. No one could be looking for him.

Could they?

Eleven

One hundred thousand pounds was the price which Just paid for control of the Teller Mostern Company, plus the promise of a retainer of ten thousand sterling a year to Mostern for his services as 'consultant'. Also, as Just explained to Paul, Mostern could continue to use the company's directors to make political films.

'I don't understand it,' Paul said. 'He's spent twenty years building up this company to give himself income, prestige and a big business life-style. So far as I know he's never even *talked* of getting rid of it. Yet he agrees to sell to you over lunch. The first time you meet. Why?'

'Read the papers on Friday,' was all Just answered.

The hundred thousand was paid up by the Morar brothers. Their motive was straightforward: greed and a quasi-legal method of taking money out of England, for Just guaranteed them an untaxed twenty thousand a year in Dutch guilders. Meanwhile, in London, they ran cars upon the company and charged most of their lives as directors' expenses; the equivalent of another ten thousand a year plus fringe benefits of wayward delight.

As a result of the autocratic manner with which he handled the noble pair neither of them asked a single question on how Just proposed to run the company whose shares they owned.

Under the arrangement Just, who took no shares, was appointed managing director. It was agreed that he would draw a salary of twenty thousand pounds a year plus expenses which no one would question. Paul Black was to get twenty thousand

and the title of Deputy Managing Director controlling production. He took both titles and job seriously.

On that Monday when Just first went in to Mount Street, he found subtle pleasure in being shown around and introduced by Paul through those rooms which he remembered from six weeks previously when first he had entered them as a thief in the night.

There were four floors to the Mount Street building. On the first were reception and production offices; the second, cutting rooms and viewing theatre; the third, production and accounts. At the top was the conference room and Mostern's executive suite. Thirty-three people worked there on payroll, servicing seventeen film directors paid by contract.

Just gave Paul the executive suite, installed himself comfortably in the conference room, which came to resemble the library it once had been, and there did nothing for a month. Paul ran the daily operations of the company while Just roamed the building as a feared but unexpectedly charming *eminence grise*.

At first the Morar brothers came in almost daily, accepted drinks and patronised their new toy. Just would talk to them and take them off to lunch where they ate copiously and brayed approval. Then Edward went to Ireland for a holiday, Russell to California. Soon the company assumed its reasonable place amongst their other possessions, their Country Place, Social Set, their horses and their girlfriends. A profitable diversion, its activities engaged their interest but did not command it.

At the end of one month in Mount Street, Just fired thirteen people and increased the salaries of those who remained. Like shooting an admiral, the action served to encourage and stimulate the survivors. Overnight, from being a moderately successful and gentlemanly establishment, the company became ruthlessly hardnosed.

That Friday on which Just had told Paul to read them, the morning papers were headlined CABINET RESHUFFLE.

In the third paragraph of the story which followed, the new

Minister of Communications was named as Frederick P. Mostern (57), Winchester and New College.

The appointment was the reason why he had wanted to be bought out, the secret joker whose identity had been known at luncheon only to Mostern ... and to the cardsharp who was his host.

Following the Night of the Long Knives when he dismissed more than one third of the staff, Just's next executive action was to open a company in Amsterdam.

He explained his reasons to the Morar brothers.

'I want to build up the work we do for continental agencies and I aim to direct half our sales force into Europe to achieve this. All jobs they get will be contracted and invoiced from Holland. Holland will then subcontract to Teller Mostern, London, at a lesser price, skim off the cream, and keep the margin there.'

'Why not Switzerland?' Russell asked.

'To the civil servants at Exchange Control and Inland Revenue, Switzerland is a dirty word whilst Holland smells not of roses but tulips, most upright of all flowers. "Going Dutch" is a decent and drab idea. Holland's a flat dull country with a hard currency, fully convertible. Holland shall be our piggy bank and our slop fund.'

'Slop fund?' asked Edward.

'Our feature directors earn sometimes as much as a half-million dollars in a year. If we pay their fees illegally in tax free guilders, we will keep them loyal to us in the face of all competition. They are artistic and talented people, popular and much sought after. But, if we have them by the balls,' said Just, 'then their hearts and minds shall surely follow.'

He went on to discuss his plans to expand in Europe.

'The market is wide open for us. The young men in Agencies who hold these jobs within their grasp have as little to talk about in the evenings as anyone else. If they can let drop at dinner parties that they are working with the director who is shooting the new Robert Redford picture, and if doing so involves them in no danger or personal risk, how can they resist it?'

'How risk?' questioned Russell.

'Our rivals are small, fashionable film companies, more modish and trendy than we are, but less reputable. Some have been known to go bankrupt in the middle of a job. But at Teller Mostern we pay our bills and our taxes on the nail. No breath of scandal has ever clouded our name. Pretending to be a client, I took a Dun and Bradstreet on our credit rating. We are as solid and respectable as the Bank of England, and just as dull. It's a fine time for us to pitch for overseas work. Every day our prices become more competitive as the pound sinks in value. Last year, European agencies spent 500 million pounds on producing TV spots, and I reckon that, without difficulty, we could get a couple of million of it. Unfortunately, we must restrict ourselves to only a quarter of this amount.'

The brothers had been listening to Just with keen attention. The noughts were working magic on their minds, and they took his last statement with disappointment.

'Why?'

'We can't afford to become too successful because we can't finance the work. Look at it this way: if today one of our producers comes back with a promise of three, half-minute commercials, the price we'll bill these at is, say, thirty thousand pounds. But our client won't pay us until a month or more after we have completed and delivered the films. Yet we need about a third of that money right away for location expenses, technicians' wages, fees to the actors, etc. The next third is easier: laboratory and equipment hire, travel expenses, rent and overhead on this building ... bills that can wait a little.'

'And the last third?'

'Is profit,' said Just.

In two plump faces little eyes gleamed.

'So it's only a margin which needs to be covered,' said Russell.

'Three months or so until the agencies pay?'

'Nearer six.'

'Couldn't we borrow the money?'

'We can raise an overdraft. No problem about that. I've discussed it with our bank manager. But he has a technical requirement set by head office. We need a quarter of a million pounds, and overdrafts above fifty thousand require the personal guarantees of the company directors.'

Russell looked puzzled.

'Well . . . ?'

Just spread his hands expressively.

'Well . . . due to being nationalised by a pack of rabid niggers, I am not personally in a position to guarantee those kinds of funds.'

'Even so . . .'

'But if it is only a margin . . . ,' said Edward.

'If the money's due on contract . . . ,' said Russell.

'If it's only for six months . . .'

'If it's turning over $33\frac{1}{3}$% profit . . .'

Split the deck. Shuffle and cut. Shuffle and cut. Now draw a card . . . any card. Don't tell me. Right?

Glancing at his brother, Russell leaned forward to respond.

'Under the circumstances, Edward and I *might* be prepared . . .'

In the office and out of it, Just worked assiduously upon his role. His personal appearance did not betray the attention which he lavished upon it. His hair and beard grew longer. He cultivated an uncouth appearance, a mid-Atlantic accent, and the manners of a slob. He wore a T-shirt and jeans and rode in a chauffeur-driven Bentley.

Through diligent study, he knew more about the business than most of the people who worked for him yet he made no pretence to an insider's manner. Swinging a squash racket, he roamed the offices inspiring awe and terrorising by his casual passage.

He worked long hours and late. His private life was inextricably bound up in business. He travelled much, at first on scheduled flights, then by Cessna 310 which, on instalment, was added to Teller Mostern's assets and which he piloted himself.

Paul operated the shooting schedules and administered the work. Just took charge of sales and promotion, and set out to double the turnover.

'Do it better,' he explained. 'Or, if you can't do it better, do it bigger. People usually can't tell the difference.'

Twice a month he staged a flying carnival. He loaded up the plane with two directors, a pair of producers plus sometimes the Morar brothers, engaged airline seats for the additional cast, and went into Europe. On separate visits he covered Paris, Frankfurt, Hamburg, Berlin, Zurich, Geneva, Stockholm, Copenhagen, Milan, in each city taking a suite in the best hotel and there mounting a spectacular with champagne and music, girls and closed-circuit TV projection. Every art director, copywriter and group head in every major advertising agency found himself invited. Ignoring top management, Just concentrated upon the men and women who actually placed the work and who would only have felt restrained by the presence of their employers.

Under Just's direction the parties were excessive. Dom Perignon was served. On closed-circuit system, sequences of his directors' feature films were transmitted, intercut with the best of their commercials. The best food decorated the buffet. Models and actresses graced the guest list, along with the best from Chez Claude. Mummers and jugglers were provided, tumblers and jesters, but the film directors were the stars, the producers were their panders, and Just was ringmaster of the whole travelling circus.

Their orgies were bad for the health and hard on the liver, exhausting and demanding of the spirit, but contracts came in as friends were made and bought, their texts chattering back over the telex to be caught by Paul in London. Interpreted into breakdowns and budgets, construction and shooting days, studio and director requirement, they were then telexed out again, translated now into confirmations and acceptances, quotations bid and instructions on invoice, rattling back over the wire to Madrid and Milan, Frankfurt and Munich, the markets through which the carousel had passed – translated into money.

At the end of the first year of Just's control, the annual turnover of the Teller Mostern company had risen to the equivalent in various currencies of two and a half million pounds.

Twelve

'I am sorry, Mr Law, but Dr Liebel is not returned.'

Just replaced the receiver carefully, then picked up the five franc pieces piled ready to slip into the coin slot and put them back in his pocket. It was serious now.

That morning, before shaving or washing, he had gone downstairs and taken a knife from the kitchen. Kneeling before the fireplace in the huge main room, he had cleared out the soap and dust with which he had refilled the cracks then, with the aid of another blade and a knife sharpener which he used as lever, he prised up one of the flagstones which formed the floor.

He took out the slim bundle of money which remained in the hiding hole and counted it.

'Running out?'

Marianne stood on the spiral staircase, a towel around her waist.

'Purely temporary,' he said and, bending to put his weight behind the stone, he slid it back into place.

She called from the kitchen.

'Hope we've enough for food. There's not a thing left in the house.'

'There's nothing to worry about,' he told her. 'Expectations are good.'

But now his face was grave as he walked from the post office to meet her. The day and the tree-lined main street were bright. The pavements were crowded; the well-stocked shops contained a cheerful bustle of activity and were doing good business. The sight did not please him as it had before, impressing him now as familiar and banal, no longer foreign. He had come here to escape, yet responsibility and care had found him out already. He had a property to buy, a payment to meet and funds in the pocket barely adequate to live. Worst of all, a cloud no bigger than a man's hand had now swollen monstrously to fill the sky. Was Liebel avoiding his calls? The implication was horrendous.

At first he thought Marianne was not there, at the café in the square where he had told her to wait, and then he caught sight of her, partly obscured by the waiter's back. The young man was leaning forward to talk to her, his knuckles on the tabletop. The girl's hands rested beside his upon the table, loosely grasping a pack of cigarettes.

The waiter straightened up hurriedly as Just dragged back a chair.

'Monsieur?'

'A brandy with ice.'

He flicked his napkin over his wrist and moved away.

'I thought he couldn't speak English,' Just said.

'Oh yes. He worked last summer in Ramsgate.'

'Ramsgate!'

'He's a student in Nice. He's only doing this until he goes back to college.'

'A very good-looking young man,' Just observed.

'He's neat. He's a very together sort of person.'

Her manner was unaffected, her enthusiasm without guile.

'Maybe you should do something about it,' he suggested spitefully. Her face fell. She looked at him oddly. She seemed about to say something, then checked and held silence.

He stood up abruptly.

'Right. Let's get the shopping done,' he said.

He strode through the cobbled streets of the Old Town and she followed at his heel. The narrow passage was lined upon both sides by food shops, their displays of vegetables and fruit, fish and meat, set out on boxes into the busy lane.

Always before he had found it charming. The unhurried manner in which the locals did their marketing, the ceaseless gossiping exchange, lack of urgency and assumption that no one could be pressed for time. Now it irritated him. He picked up a pack of coffee and thrust it into her basket.

'This is silly.'

She had taken out the package and was examining it.

'What?'

'This is 8F50. In the supermarket it costs 7F25. I know you don't care what you pay for things, but if we're short of money it's just stupid.'

He shrugged.

'As you like.'

He pushed his way through the throng, past a tiny square and fountain where children played and splashed, under an arch and out into less crowded streets.

She caught him up.

'Look. This is a drag for you. Why don't you give me a hundred francs then get the car and wait outside the supermarket.'

'A hundred francs won't be enough.'

'Yes it will.'

He gave her the money and watched her as she walked off, basket in hand, tight little body in worn jeans and faded sweater. As soon as the money came in he would burn all she had and force her into new clothes.

He fetched the Ferrari and sat reading a paper in the parking lot until he saw her come out pushing a trolley containing three bulging paper bags. He helped her stack them behind the seats.

The way out of town led past the post office. On impulse he stopped just beyond it, then reversed back into a parking space.

'I won't be a minute.'

He went in and did what he had to do. Then he rejoined her in the car and they drove back to the mill.

In the kitchen he helped unpack the supermarket bags, taking out the things she had bought and laying them on the table for her to put away. So involved was he in his anxious thoughts, so concentrated upon the situation and the limited choice of moves now open to him, that he was for a while quite unaware of the objects he was handling, until a familiar label caught his attention.

'Caviare?'

He looked at the tin in his other hand.

'*Paté de foie gras?*'

The tin was marked 3F. The caviare bore a sticker reading 7F80.

'What's this?'

'Special offer.'

'I don't believe it. You didn't buy all this for a hundred francs.'

'Sixty three actually,' she said, then grinned widely, 'I switched the labels.'

They dined well that night. They had caviare and champagne and foie gras and cold pheasant with Château Lafite at 2F70 the bottle and, though she would have preferred Coca-Cola, she joined him in the wine. She said,

'I was thinking . . .'

'Yes?'

'That *viager* thing. It's a pretty weird arrangement.'

'It only exists in France.'

'I mean . . . it's like forcing people to live together who want each other dead.'

'So's marriage,' he observed.

'I mean, it would be so convenient if something happened to them.'

He asked, amused, 'You're thinking of doing them in?'

She was frowning. 'Well, accidents do happen, as they say.'

Then, as her eyes moved, she let out a cry of terror and started back, gaze fixed in horror, her face stricken. He turned quickly.

A pulsing spot of light had entered the open window and was drifting toward them. The size of a pea, it floated at the girl emitting incandescent stabs of green-tinged light.

'Cor. What is it?'

'A firefly.'

It settled upon the table and, fascinated, she bent her face down to it, jumping nervously as it crawled toward her.

'Pick it up.'

She stretched her hand out uncertainly. Without wavering in its track, the insect clambered up onto her fingers. She set her chin on the edge of the table and brought her hand to eye-level. Rapt, she studied the throbbing ball of light and the tiny fragile creature that was its core. Her hair had fallen across her face. She seemed twelve years old and his heart turned over as he looked at her.

The firefly climbed to her wrist, then suddenly took off and flew in a purposeful curve to the window. Mouth open, she watched it flicker away into the darkness of the overgrown garden.

'Thank you for a superb dinner,' he said. She blinked and brought her attention back to him.

'Stolen apples nothing,' he said. 'All of it tastes sweeter.'

'I thought you needed something to cheer you up,' she said. 'After the telephone call, I mean.'

He had been feeling fine. But on that reminder he sagged. Suddenly he was horribly sober.

'I did. But I hope I'm wrong.'

'Why?'

'Don't ask,' he said.

Next morning he called again.

'Hello, this is Dr Liebel's office,' the secretary answered. Just spoke in an American accent.

'Hi, this is Mr Capsis here, calling from Rome. One of Dr Liebel's clients recommended I call him about a problem I have here, can I speak with him, please?'

The girl replied without hesitation, 'He is on the telephone just now, Mr Capsis. If you give me your number in Rome I will ask him to call you back.'

Just's mouth went dry. His heart lurched in consternation and dismay. He felt his palms go cold, his stomach clench.

'No thank you,' he said. 'I'll deal with this myself.'

Thirteen

Robert Just had set out to embezzle half a million pounds and had given himself two years to do it.

That was his new task.

It had taken him hard graft and a chapter of his life to acquire what he had had on Belida. The revolution there had ruined him. His happiness, his peace of mind, his wealth had been snatched away by black and brutal hands.

He had been humiliated and robbed. The men who had done it to him he hated with a cold deadly passion. When his plan in London was complete, when he had done what he intended and was free again and rich, he knew that his just indulgence would be to even up the score. He had patience and it could wait, but he was wed to those men who had misused him. He was linked to them by the intimacy of the torturer's domain, that white-tiled place where learned professors hopped like frogs and faithful wives screamed and laughed and pleaded to betray their husbands. Between Just and them existed a carnal bond. He knew them with that insight into the other's darkest nature shared by torturer and victim, partners in the same foetid congress of unholy pain.

Almost they had broken his spirit and finished him off. Because of them his life had returned to 'Go'. Now, at the unsuitable age of forty-six, he had started again on the long road around the board.

Just's brief hours of private life were spartan. He rested. He exercised. He swam regularly and visited a gymnasium. He kept himself in shape, to counteract the amount he had to drink and the meals which he was obliged to attend.

Despite the flagrant excess, greed and conspicuous consumption of the world which surrounded him, he remained aloof, living in a felon's isolation, his eye cold, his smile faked.

Food, wine and the pleasures of good living, which once had meant so much, counted now for nothing and love itself was dead for him. He lived without emotion. When, late at night, he could not sleep and his nerves were drawn tight as wires and the drink and the cigars were an ache behind the eyes and his mouth tasted of dust, he would go out and prowl for something young enough to ignite and purge his blood.

Once he found himself in a rip-off club in Bond Street, sleazily opulent and criminally run in cooperation with the local law. There was nothing for him at the bar; a workforce of hookers, pallid of body and mind, slack-fleshed in adulthood. Then, while he drank, a sly voice took him at the elbow and he looked down on a black girl with plump rouged cheeks, thick lips and tombstone teeth showing in a fleshy grin. A greedy schoolgirl with a crude and stupid face, not seventeen he knew.

He bought her a drink and took her home and paid her four times what she asked. He had her undress and pose for him. She obeyed his instructions with sullen lethargy, folding her lurid underclothes on a chair, and showing off a heavy, blue-black, almost purple body which in five years would be fat and prematurely middle-aged.

A sour smell came off her which recalled those hovel villages he drove through, scattering chickens, on his way to the capital in Belida. He ordered her to wash, following to the bathroom to observe as she crouched and soaped herself. Then he took her to bed and with clinical and abstracted lust practised lewdly upon her body.

In the morning, after he had thrown her out, he discovered she had stolen a table lighter.

* * *

From the production budgets of overseas jobs, Just was siphoning off fifteen to twenty thousand pounds each month into the account of the company in Amsterdam. He kept the Morar brothers fully informed on the state of this account, two-thirds of the money was theirs under the arrangement. When, from time to time, they asked for cash he paid it to them, not from this fund, but out of the London company on a director's loan account. They were well satisfied with these arrangements, mindful of the nest-egg of real money illicitly accumulating in Holland.

Although the brothers were born to wealth, their childhood had been passed between a home in the country, large but not luxurious, and an expensive yet spartan public school. They had controlled disposable funds for a couple of years before Just had picked them up, but their experience of the lush life was restricted and local, and they were unused to the cornucopia of fleshly delights which he spread before their eyes.

They were more than happy with their directorships and the tacit understanding that they should play no part in the running of the company's business.

Sometimes, in the afternoons, they attended the screening of daily rushes with girlfriends and cigars, their feet resting upon the chair in front. Then they would show off the building with expansive after-luncheon pride, walking their friends through the cutting rooms and discoursing upon techniques of editing before bringing them upstairs to take brandy with Just, seemingly unaware of the resentment and ridicule wafting in their wake.

Though Just was busy, he never grudged them time, devoting a couple of lunches and two or more evenings per week to their entertainment. Stroking the marks was the essential ritual which underpinned the whole operation. They gave him few problems, for they were greedy, but not ambitious.

The only trouble they did cause was when they insisted on coming to Sweden. A spot of aggravation had surfaced a couple of days before that, in another part of the pond. The fact that so much money was being diverted to Holland, combined with the increased turnover from Just's promotional forays abroad, resulted in a constant strain upon the company's liquidity in London. Though it was owed more than a quarter of a million pounds on the books in invoices outstanding, Teller Mostern was perilously short of ready cash.

The bank loan guaranteed by the Morar brothers bridged this for several months and would have sufficed to maintain the position for much longer, had not the success of Just's efforts produced a flow of new films requiring finance.

On Friday, 28 April, Mr Moss, accountant and company secretary, came to Just with the announcement that the payroll cheques could not be covered.

'What do you mean they can't be covered?' Just demanded.

Moss was a sandy-coloured man in middle age with a taste for vintage wine, a younger second wife and a facial twitch. He had little in common with the other members of the company and took no part in the evening drinking, darts, record playing and entertaining, which prolonged office hours until eight or nine PM. Mr Moss went home punctually at six o'clock.

'Well ... I mean to say, we haven't got it. We're right at the limit of our overdraft facility.'

Just noticed with irritation that the man's tie was stained with food.

'It's irrelevant. You know perfectly well what's due to us. Issue the cheques.'

He turned back dismissively to the papers on his desk. Mr Moss did not go, though he shifted awkwardly.

'I'm not sure I can do that.'

Just waited, saying nothing.

'Frankly, I'm preparing the figures for the auditors,' said Mr Moss, 'and to tell you the truth, I'm not happy about the state of the accounts.'

'Oh, you're not,' said Just, his voice wooden.

'As I say, we're doing good business, I know, but whether or not we're solvent ...'

Just's hand slammed the desk top.

'Listen! Listen carefully because I'll explain it once. This company's more successful than it ever has been. We're hot and our numbers are running. The bank and our creditors are staked right in there with us, riding our luck. Do you seriously think they're going to pull the plug on us now, when we're winning?'

Moss looked startled by the vehemence of Just's outburst.

'But ...'

'There is no place on this ship for a faint-hearted man. Life is not endless and caution kills. We are pirates on a hostile sea, Mr Moss, and like it or not, you are of the crew ...'

Just's words danced on. When he chose to, he could dazzle and mesmerise, weave castles in the air, enthuse, seduce, beguile. Yet the accountant proved stubbornly resistant to his skills. It was because the man had a drab and prudent spirit, Just decided next day, thinking back to the encounter when he was in the plane. He epitomised an attitude particularly British, a pride and satisfaction in proving something cannot be done. The best solution would be to fire him, of course, but Just needed his signature to the accounts. Perhaps he could be compromised ...

Just did his best thinking in the plane during those times when he flew alone. He found a lucid clarity of detachment up there above it all. But the plane was not invented that did not have to land.

He flew into Stockholm in the late evening, coming in low over the swamp and black water of the tundra in the flat dull light and lost, it seemed, on the bleak edge of the world till the ground below solidified into forest and the lights of the runway slid up from the gloom.

He was there to attend a shoot for a New York agency. The job had come out of nowhere, a request to engage a Czech director named Kadek and to film three commercials in the north of Sweden. On contract, it was worth 150,000 dollars – a not especially large amount for an agency which, Just ascertained, spent more than a hundred million dollars a year on television.

The job was being produced by Paul Black, who had already been there a week. Just was dropping in only to meet the client and to get his fingers on a larger slice of that multi-million dollar cake.

He took a taxi into the city and checked into the Hotel Angleterre, where the gang was staying. There was one message for him at the desk: Lord Morar had called to say he would be in Stockholm on Friday and wanted to meet. Just called him back immediately from Paul's room, where he was catching up on the job over a drink, but there was no answer from the London number.

When he put down the telephone Paul continued with his briefing, 'Tab and Clive are from the Agency and a bit neurotic, but professional at least. The trouble is they've got their client along, Peppard, and he's a monster.'

'In what way?'

'In every way,' said Paul, with feeling.

The trip had started badly for Peppard, it seemed, when all his luggage was lost on the flight from Kennedy, a catastrophe compounded by insult when he was denied entry to the hotel dining room through not wearing a tie.

Just's first sight of him was fifteen minutes later when Paul took him along the corridor to be introduced.

Crowned by a fur hat, a moon-faced man stood upon the coffee table. His large body was banded like a hornet in vivid stripes of black and yellow ski attire. At his feet knelt his agency executive, struggling to fasten his boots.

'You brought news about my laundry then?' were the first words he said to Just.

Next day, the party flew to Norrbotten in the very north of Sweden, where cars waited to drive them yet further north, beyond the snowline, where crew and director were set up and waiting.

'We've got this old man in the sauna, a real grizzled oldster – and Swedes live longer than anyone on earth,' Clive, the agency man, explained to Just. 'A fact, a statistical fact, and why we're here in Sweden. Hemingway see, and he's in this sauna nude and like sweat pouring off him and then he gets up, goes over and opens the door and steps out and ... wham! Imagine, he steps out onto a *snowfield*. Miles and miles of vast, frozen, wraparound, arctic ZILCH, and colder than get out. Well ... he runs over to the hole he's cut down to the freezing water below. Splash! In he goes. Wow! *What* a way to start the day! *What* an after-shave!'

Peppard regarded the desolate site with a shudder.

'Land of the midnight sun,' he observed. 'Man, you could lose your marbles in a place like this. Not a shop for miles.'

Dressed in thick protective clothing, the crew were set up upon the ice.

'I've got on thermal underwear and two pairs of 'lectro-insulated socks,' said Peppard. 'Me, I don't give a shit.'

He had no need to, for the trailer which accommodated the clients was luxurious and well heated, equipped with coffee and soup dispensing machines, and an observation window from which to watch the action.

The camera crew, electricians, grips and various other members of the unit numbered twenty-five. Just was aware that it was not essential to employ so many people. But in a job at this price it was necessary not only that the work should be done but that it should be seen to be done.

'Watch how you shoot him; no hair, no tits, no crack in the arse. That's network regulations,' the agency man warned the director.

Kadek, the young Czech, had never made a commercial before, though his feature picture was currently receiving critical acclaim at New York art houses and the Curzon in London. The agency's choice of such a man as director was due partly to his talent but more because, this week, success came in his flavour.

Kadek had adapted quickly to life in the West. His first encounter with Paul when his fee was decided, later meetings with the clients to discuss script, cast, location, all had taken place over meals. He noted that in this world food was free, and the fact made a powerful impression upon him. Now, at every occasion throughout the day, he called constantly for refreshment. Choosing camera angles on the ice-field, positioning lights, dodging in and out of the log hut which housed the sauna and the old man broiling inside, Kadek was never without a sandwich or cake in the hand.

'Take a photo, will ya,' demanded Peppard, pressing a camera into Just's hands. 'The two of us, me shaking hands with the director. That guy's a very famous commie. Everyone's heard of him.'

The next day all returned to Stockholm. Peppard went ahead in a helicopter, attended by one of the agency men who had ordered it for him so that he might return via a mink ranch to pick up some pelts, then spend a few hours on the town before returning to New York the following day.

'My wife's just ape about Swedish crystal,' he explained.

He distributed fur hats to everybody as parting gifts. The agency men were terrified of him. Sales director of a five-million dollar account, tyrant for a season, he swung in the catbird seat of power, dispensing favour, banishment or death by whim, not unaware of the fragility of the cords which held him up. He was a man who achieved peace only in the act of purchase, perhaps also in lechery for he intended that night to be taken on a tour of the city's notorious sex clubs.

'S and M, bondage, topless shoeshine, you name it, what I'm after is a real shameful experience. Lead on,' he ordered, 'Lead me to the pig of my dreams.'

The Morar brothers were waiting for Just in Stockholm. He had intended to stop them coming.

'But why are you here?' he asked.

Russell looked sheepish.

'We wanted a meeting with you.'

'Couldn't it wait?'

He was tired and unshaved after a night on the train, wearing the clothes he had slept in.

'Well, actually we wanted to go back with you through Amsterdam, so that we could get our share of the money.'

'Idiots,' said Just, 'if I was going to embezzle it, don't you think I could have had it off you by now?'

Russell went scarlet.

'Not that,' he protested, 'not that. Mustn't think that. But we've been talking with a tax accountant chap we met. One can get 15% investing it in real estate in Liechtenstein.'

'You're a fool,' Just said shortly. 'Don't you realise what we're doing is illegal? I told you not to talk.'

'But we ...'

Fury rose in his throat. He said, 'I can't afford partners like you. You may send yourselves to prison but I object to you doing it to me. Your money is on seven-day call on the Eurodollar market, earning 6%, but I need two weeks to replace you as financial partners. You may have it then and I never want to see you again.'

'Of course we ...'

'It is not that you are fat, useless and idle which I object to,' Just added with cutting emphasis, 'But you are stupid – and *that* is unforgivable.'

Five days later in London, the brothers called him up and invited him to dinner. They were on their best behaviour, striving to converse and entertain like adult sophisticates. Towards the end of the meal they became flushed with port and embarrassment, huffing and blowing and making business with their cigars as they asked him to reconsider them as associates.

He treated them to a show of anger, before which they cringed like naughty schoolboys, becoming hysterically affable when, later, he was seen to relax and they basked again in his good graces.

The money stayed where it was, in an account with the Algemene Bank Nederland in Amsterdam controlled by Just's signature.

He would not be hustled by the Morars or by anyone else. He would steal it only when it reached half a million pounds and he was good and ready, and not before. That had always been his plan.

Fourteen

Without waking Marianne, Just rose early, bathed, shaved and dressed with more than usual care.

He put on a blue shirt, grey flannel trousers, black shoes with buckles and a double-breasted blue blazer ornamented by heavy brass buttons.

He glanced into the overheated room where the girl still slept, window closed and electric fire burning through the night. She had thrust back the bedclothes and lay upon her front, face turned sideways and swollen with sleep beneath the tousled mass of hair.

He bent and kissed the downy hollow in the small of her back, that warm valley from which the buttocks swelled so sweetly and firmly. He left her sleeping.

He did not make coffee at the house but drove to take breakfast at the airport in good time before his plane.

Locking the Ferrari, he tipped the attendant well as he left the car park so his first human contact was a smile.

In the restaurant overlooking the runway he ate a light, well served meal in an atmosphere of calm, *Time* magazine propped against the wicker basket of croissants, his mind clear and passions cool. He was happy not to have brought his gun. He had considered it, but the possibilities of detection were so high that the idea was nerve-racking. This way he could enjoy his breakfast, a well-dressed Englishman of a certain age who would read out impeccably on the metal detector.

When the Zurich flight was called he paid his bill, finished his coffee, then strolled down to the departure gate carrying his leather grip.

Boarding a plane never failed to give him pleasure, even if he was not to fly it himself. In quitting the earth was a special sense of liberation, an excitement quite separate and distinct from the anticipation of arrival.

It was a bright and cloudless day. The plane flew over the Alps; miniature below, each peak and ridge sharp as a white knife.

At Geneva he changed planes, walking through an antiseptic corridor past a checkpoint and into that section of the airport which lay in Switzerland. After a twenty-minute wait he caught the plane to Zurich.

The airport bus ran directly to the railway station which was his destination, yet he chose to travel there by taxi for the same reason as he had in the past shaved and changed his shirt before every confrontation. The least sense of additional well-being represented an edge of advantage over an adversary. Even if it went unrecognised, it was enough that Just should feel it.

It was 12.30 in the morning; a sunny day in Zurich.

Bahnhofstrasse, the main shopping street, runs directly from the station to the lake. Just walked its length, carrying his leather grip. He stopped three times, first at a delicatessen and butcher's shop where he bought two kilos of raw venison, the second only briefly when he paused by the solid edifice of Credit Suisse and looked across Paradeplatz at the first floor windows of Dr Radman's office.

His last halt was a gunshop where he bought a weighty and expensive toy: the perfect replica of a Colt .45 automatic pistol.

Containing such boutiques as Cartier, Gucci, and Grieder, Bahnhofstrasse is one of the most prosperous two kilometres in the world. Yet, unlike Bond Street or Madison Avenue, few Rolls or big Mercedes were visible here and the dress of men and women on the busy pavements was more or less uniform, decent and unostentatious.

A prudent nation, thrifty and discreet, not given to show, reflected Just, not for the first time, then entered the Hotel Bauer au Lac and felt wrap around him the cocoon and hush of luxury, that subdued and velvet murmur which perfumes the lobbies of only the very best hotels.

He gave his bag to the hall porter. In the restaurant he was shown directly to his table by a window overlooking the lake, which he had booked by telephone from Geneva airport.

He had nothing to drink to start and only a half bottle of Montrachet accompanying a light meal of caviare and *truite au bleu*.

Having finished *Time* magazine, with lunch he read the *Herald-Tribune* and *Financial Times* or, rather, seemed to read. To any observer Just's attention remained upon the page, the only occasion he even glanced up was that nod to the waiter to take away his plate. Yet, old habits die hard and his trained ear had picked up early the conversation between two Englishmen and an American at the next table. Like himself, they were preparing for an afternoon meeting. Their table was three yards from his and they spoke mostly in low tones, yet not low enough for, by the time coffee was served, he reckoned he could have sent two of them to jail. Not that he would wish that on anyone – and gone were the days when he would put the knock on them himself.

After lunch Just permitted himself a single brandy. He lit a cigar and, for the first time that day, rehearsed what he was about to do. There were two places where it could go foul and, in his mind, he travelled a little way down the branch roads which led from them. Two places he could see. But the unknown could gape open at your feet wide and startling as a chasm.

He always felt so amazingly well at times like this when he was about to start the play, never more intensely alive and aware than now.

It was 2.30 PM.

Summoning the waiter he paid his bill. He recovered his grip from the hall porter, stepped out of the hotel and took a cab to Paradeplatz.

Paying it off he entered the building, ran lightly up the flight of stairs, pushed open a door and walked into Dr Liebel's outer office.

The face of the secretary reflected no emotion whatsoever. A phlegmatic nation the Swiss, but also she did not recognise his face. Not until he spoke. Then something happened – no change of expression but a flicker behind the eyes.

'Is he alone?' asked Just.

She shook her head. 'He has a client with him.'

'I'll wait,' he said.

Throwing his bag down he sat and picked up a magazine.

After a moment the girl took up the internal telephone and reached her finger toward the button.

'No,' Just said.

He said it very quietly yet distinctly, with his eyes upon her. The girl hesitated, and what he did not go on to say got through to her. She felt the place where they sat become cold and she knew something very frightening was about to happen. She put down the telephone and withdrew her hands behind the typewriter. Her fingers blundered on the keyboard and an electric staccato of three letters rapped upon the paper. Then Dr Liebel's door opened.

'*Ja? Unser Freund Schroder wohnt auch dort ...*'

The accountant was speaking to his client who came out first, and had stepped three paces into the outer office and level with Just before Liebel appeared in the doorway.

The first man turned at the door, setting his hat upon his head, said goodbye and departed. Dr Liebel directed an expression of polite query at his unrecognised visitor.

'Please, have we an appointment?'

'Yes and overdue,' said Just.

Only if you had been watching for it would you have seen it, that instinctive animal tensing of the body under the clothes. Only for a second, then the accountant was back in full possession of the blue striped suit.

'Please forgive me, Mr Law. You look ... different.'

'I am,' said Just.

'Shall we go inside?'

Liebel glanced at his secretary.

'Fräulein Stahel, when is my next appointment?'

The girl's eyes dropped to her desk.

'Three-thirty, Doctor.'

'Then we have time. Please come in, Mr Law.'

Just entered. He placed the grip by his feet and sat on one of the two chairs which faced the desk.

Liebel was already in speech as he settled himself into his accustomed position of control.

'I do not wish to criticise your private life Mr Law, but it is hard for me to work for you effectively if I cannot reach you. It is not convenient to have no telephone number. I have wished urgently to speak with you since ten days.'

Just smiled pleasantly.

'You are having problems then?' he asked.

'Problem is too strong a word. Fortunately until now I have avoided problems. But action must be taken. There have been certain changes of management in the company which I use in Curaçao.'

Just crossed his legs.

'Of what nature?' he enquired.

Liebel appeared to hesitate, then reached a decision for candour.

'Well, to speak frankly, the local lawyer who runs that corporation has been sent to jail.'

'I'm sorry to hear that,' said Just. 'That must be an unpleasant experience for anyone.'

'Yes, I think so.' Liebel looked at Just levelly. 'For any man.'

Just said, 'Tell me more about these things which aren't problems.'

The accountant minutely adjusted the position of the leather pen and pencil set on his desk.

'Under these circumstances I did not think it wise to proceed with the transaction. Fortunately your funds are intact.'

'That is good news,' said Just.

'With patience I have no doubt they can be recovered and rerouted.'

Just said in a pleasant conversational tone, 'I think I'd rather have them now.'

Liebel's manicured hands made a further fine adjustment to the pen and pencil set.

'Procedures must be followed. Do not press me, Mr Law.'

In one swift and even movement Just crouched and swept the gun from out the grip. It was the action of a tennis player coming in low to return and, momentarily, Liebel recognised it as such until the sight of the gun purged all other thought from his mind. With an athlete's grace the crouch became a spring as Just launched himself across the desk, his hand with the heat reached out before him.

Liebel's face shocked white as he thrust away. His chair shot back and his shoulders slammed into the wall. Propelled by his own momentum his body half-rose to stand.

The outstretched barrel of the Colt took him full in the mouth with Just's weight behind it. The steel smashed through his teeth and rammed down his throat.

Just had not intended to take him thus. Liebel's involuntary recoil had yielded up this target.

His scream of pain was choked. From the man's grossly distended mouth a gargle of blood bubbled out around the barrel of the gun. For seconds he was held there, spiked against the wall. Then Just withdrew his hand and Liebel's slid down behind his desk.

Just walked away then and opened the door to the outer office.

'Miss Stahel, please lock the front door.'

The girl stared at the gun, unable to move. Just held out his other hand.

'The key, please.'

After a second her arm slid with weird languor to the desk, pulled back the drawer and, still in the same sluggish and underwater motion, reached in and handed Just the key.

He locked the office door, slipping the key into his pocket.

'Join us, please.'

She rose to her feet languid as a sleepwalker and drifted into the room where her employer still was slumped hidden behind the desk. Just directed her to a chair.

'Get up, Doctor Liebel,' he ordered.

There was a horrid choking, gagging sound from the other side of the desk.

Just repeated his order. The coughing stopped and now could be heard a shuffling and grunt and cumbrous shifting as of some beast in its sty. The head of Doctor Liebel rose above the desk, eyes wild and mouth a bloody cavern, front teeth dangling loose.

Not a sound from the secretary at first. Numbed by horror she stared at the apparition. Then her jaw sprang open and a wild shriek of laughter tore from her mouth. A gasp of breath ... then screech upon screech as she whirled over the precipice and dashed down upon the rocks.

Just stepped forward and slapped her across the cheek with his open hand. Her laughter ceased as abruptly as it had begun. Hunched forward, eyes rolled to show their white, she peered up at him in mortal terror.

Just turned to the desk.

'Now I'll have the key to your safe.'

It was not unwillingness which delayed Liebel's response but physical incapacity. One hand securing his mouth, with the other he felt for his pocket. He gave over the key, mutely pointing to a picture on the wall.

Just lifted it down to reveal the safe. He set in the key, turned it and swung open the metal door. First he took out the money, dollars and German marks. He tossed the wads of notes upon the ground.

'How much is here?'

Liebel tried to answer but only a plopping came from his ruined mouth, a wet groan.

'Write it,' Just instructed.

Turning back to the safe he started to go through the papers.

There was a real hazard attached to living in too civilised a country, he realised, a place with no poverty and little crime, its citizens well ordered, government sound and police effective: a man felt himself inviolable. In any other country all of these documents would be kept guarded in a bank vault.

He flicked through the neat folders, glancing into each before he dropped it on the floor. Meanwhile, he spoke – his audience came to believe they were hostage to a madman as they listened to his words.

'On the whole one tries not to be too concerned with these matters,' he began, 'but recently I have not been able to avoid noticing how dramatically the cost of living has increased. Food, clothes, airline tickets, everything becomes more expensive from day to day ...'

Liebel held poised in his hand the pen from that desk set which his fingers had been arranging so fastidiously at the moment lightning had split the world. When the gun went through his teeth that crescendo of agony had obliterated all else; now terror came flooding back. There was no knowing what this violent criminal would do next. Through the wrack of his pain he struggled to comprehend Just's measured discourse.

'Up and up the prices go. But, recently, I have been struck by one exception to this rule, a service which has not merely remained stable through these years of galloping inflation but actually gone down in price.'

Just paused to lend weight to his words, and then continued,

'I am referring to the cost of murder. Nowadays, the provision of commissioned death is at a discount.'

Liebel had finished writing. Elbows on the desk, both hands supported the lower half of his face. Bright blood seeped between his fingers and dripped down his cuffs, startling in the rich glitter of its crimson.

Just said, 'In this buyers' market the price of your deaths in one case is 10,000 dollars. In the other – for everything is cheaper in London and the Irish quote in sterling – it is costing me 4,000 pounds. Or, rather, costing you Dr Liebel, for I see no reason why *I* should pay for the inconvenience which you have caused me.'

Thrown down by Just, the files were on the floor now. All that remained in the safe were a few small jewel boxes and three cheque books.

He opened the boxes and tipped out a thin necklace, diamonds in platinum, matching earrings, two clips and a ruby ring. A groan came from behind the bloody hands of the man at the desk. Just said without pity,

'Quite. Your wife's.'

He turned his attention to the cheque books, crossing his fingers before he looked.

Two were in the name of companies, the first cheque of one already counter-signed by the necessary partner. The third was clearly Liebel's personal account.

Back turned to the room, he permitted himself a sigh of vast relief: all three accounts were held at Credit Suisse.

He brought them to the desk and looked at what Liebel had written.

In a wavering hand was marked, ABOUT 11,000 DOLLARS.

'Now, let's say the jewellery is worth 150,000 francs,' Just calculated aloud and ignored Liebel's squawk of protest.

'So you owe me then rather more than 1,320,000 francs plus my fee for today with expenses, plus of course the necessary cost of your deaths; if we round the figure off ...'

He looked at the secretary.

'Fräulein Stahel ...'

She started unpleasantly at the sound of her name.

'Please telephone the bank and tell them you will be there in ten minutes to collect 1.4 million francs in large denomination bills.'

Her pale face had tensed, mouth drawn back in a tight grimace and teeth clamped upon her lower lip. She trembled violently.

'Compose yourself, Fräulein Stahel,' he said.

Just gathered up the cheque books. He boxed them into shape then dealt them on the desk in front of Liebel, their covers identical, three cards face down.

'Now Doctor, from some combination of these accounts I want cheques made out for that amount.'

The accountant snatched for the books but Just slowed him with a warning.

'How you do this is your choice but all over the world penalties for overdrawing on inadequate funds have become stringent. I must tell you that in this case they are particularly severe: you will be shot. So I urge you to consider well.'

After a second Liebel grabbed the first book towards him. He opened it in a movement oddly abrupt.

'Please ...'

Fräulein Stahel's voice was thin.

'Yes?'

'Can I drink a glass of water?'

He allowed her to leave the room to fetch it, following her to the open door. Filling it, her glass rattled against the tap. Just said, 'Don't be afraid. My only complaint is that your manner on the telephone is rude, but that alone does not merit the extreme penalty. Up to now I have had no reason to kill you.'

Back in the office he stood looking from the window to avoid making her nervous while she placed the call. It was unlikely that her employer normally had need of such a large amount in cash.

Yet, in this country, bank secrecy was an article of religious faith. He counted upon Fräulein Stahel to inspire no doubts.

He took up the two cheques which Liebel had written and studied them. They were dated correctly, with signatures legible and resembling. One was for a half million Swiss francs, the other made out for the sum of 380,000 dollars. On it was a brilliant dot of blood. Just blotted it carefully.

'I said Swiss francs.'

Leibel removed a hand from his dripping mouth and gulped like a goldfish.

'Is dollar account.'

Just gave them to the secretary.

'Now, I should tell you more about your deaths. The first fifty per cent has been paid and both are contracted. Yet a telephone call from me tomorrow can stop them ...'

He looked hard at Fräulein Stahel.

'I do not think you will want to prevent my making that call ...'

And then at Liebel.

'... even though it does mean wasting the first fifty per cent of your money, Doctor.'

The accountant made the grotesque imitation of a laugh, toadying to the avenger.

'Fräulein Stahel, do you feel able to fetch the money?'

'Yes, Mr Law, I will get it.'

He gave her Liebel's attaché case, first tipping it empty upon the floor. He told her, 'If there is any problem, telephone me here. Let it ring twice then hang up as though it were busy. Call again immediately.'

'I understand.'

'Do not hurry. But do not linger. You will make me very nervous if you are too long in that bank.'

'I understand. I will be quick, Mr Law.'

He accompanied her to the outer office and saw her off, locking the door again after her departure.

Watching from the window he saw her cross the street. He started the stopwatch when she went through the doors of the bank.

'Now get undressed,' he told Liebel.

When the accountant hesitated he said impatiently, 'Come on, man! Do as I say and you'll come to no harm.'

Slowly Liebel's hands moved to loosen his tie.

First removing the raw meat and the few other things in his grip, Just then arranged on the floor beside it a selection of files from the safe.

'These shall be hostage to your continuing good behaviour. You will receive them back gradually ...'

He glanced at his watch. Two minutes fifteen seconds gone.

'When I leave from here I shall disappear. Do not attempt a hunt or to set men after me. In the event of harm befalling me I have taken further precautions which I have not told you about. I frequent low company and have discreditable connections. Be assured that so long as thugs accept money for performing violence you will never be safe.'

He moved to the window and looked across Paradeplatz to the solid frontage of Credit Suisse. Three minutes fifty seconds.

Liebel was standing shirtless, bemused and bloody behind his desk.

'The trousers,' Just snapped.

He had them off and was in the act of laying them upon the chair when the telephone rang. Both men froze staring at it. Once. Twice. They waited. It had stopped.

Just took a deep breath. Gun in hand now, and pointed at the Doctor, he stepped back to the desk.

It rang again. He picked it up.

'Yes?'

'They do not hold here this amount of dollars.'

The secretary's voice was impersonal, without emotion.

'You mean they won't honour the cheque?'

'No. Cheque is good. But this is written dollars. They do not have this dollars cash. They must get.'

'Draw it in Swiss francs at today's rate. Do not linger. I am restless, Fräulein Stahel.'

Liebel stood in his underpants. He had a powerful body in good shape. His mouth was still bleeding, dripping down his chin to speckle his chest hair with glistening scarlet. But he was no longer in shock now; physically he was in condition to try something.

Just kept the gun on him.

'The briefs,' he ordered.

Five minutes thirty-two seconds. From the window Just looked down. Two men came out of Credit Suisse together, rapidly down the steps, disappearing almost at a run into Bahnhofstrasse.

His stomach cramped.

A sudden sound spun him around, gun raised and aimed. But there was no cause for alarm. As a bull who, entering the arena, will establish his citadel, that spot to which, hard pressed, he will return always and where, in the end, he will choose to die, so Liebel, naked and slowly, was resuming his position in the executive chair behind his desk.

Six minutes fifteen seconds.

Those two running men were late. They had been in a hurry to catch their train. They had headed toward the station. But, building with the seconds, he felt the wince of paranoia.

Six minutes twenty-eight seconds.

Why were they not trying for a taxi?

Six minutes thirty-three seconds.

Because their car was double parked.

Six minutes thirty-eight seconds. *No one* double parks in Zurich. Six minutes forty-two seconds.

The Swiss are too law-abiding for that. They have the best police force in the world.

Seven minutes two seconds.

Fräulein Stahel came out of the bank.

She walked briskly, the attaché case heavy and her arm straight, crossing obliquely down the wide flight of steps. Headed here.

His eye remained on the door. A woman. Two women. Then an Arab with attendant. Then suddenly three men coming together and moving fast.

His heart lurched.

Two up, the third a pace behind. In step. Dark overcoats. Hats. All under forty. This was trouble.

Fräulein Stahel was half-way across the square. Suddenly the third man veered and stepped in her direction, moving to intercept her before the door. Just's fingers clenched on the useless toy in his hand. But then, after only two steps, the man turned and called out to his companions, raising his hat. The others halted. The man pointed and said something and one of the others was laughing.

Blood flowed back to his knuckle as his hand released the toy.

Fräulein Stahel disappeared from sight directly below the window where he stood.

He unlocked the door.

When the secretary came into Liebel's office, case in hand, her boss's naked torso projected above the desk as he sat stiffly upright, mashed mouth lurid and a gun pressed to the side of his head.

'Lock the door!'

He snapped open the attaché case. It was crammed to the brim with sealed bundles of blue and white money.

'You did well, Fräulein.'

'Thank you, Mr Law.'

Her face was frozen with nerves but she was in control.

He tipped it all out into his grip. On top he laid the files and then the venison. He threw the attaché case to the secretary.

'Pack Dr Liebel's stuff in there.'

He straightened up.

'We are leaving you now, Doctor, but Fräulein Stahel will bring back your clothes later.'

He took up the telephone wire and tore it out. He tossed the safe key onto the desk.

'You may tidy up while you wait. A dentist can fix those teeth and you are alive. Stay grateful. Don't get ideas. Remember, there's no revenge so sweet that your death won't sour it. Come, Fräulein Stahel.'

On his way through the outer office he ripped the telephone from the wall.

It took them ten minutes to the station. Walking together at a brisk pace, each carrying a case, they resembled businessman and secretary. They did not speak.

At the station, on the big board he saw the next train left in seven minutes, its destination Basle. He bought her a first-class ticket and said, 'There is time for a drink, if you like.'

'No, Mr Law. I am too frightened.'

He escorted her to the train, settled her into a seat and stowed the attaché case containing Liebel's clothes upon the rack.

'I am sorry this has been so bad a day for you. But it's over now.'

He put his hand into his pocket of jewellery and drew out the ring. It was the first thing his fingers encountered.

'I hope you will accept this in apology.'

She shrank away, drawing her breath in sharply.

'Mr Law, I cannot.'

'It is mine now. Allow me to give it to you.'

Her eyes were riveted upon it.

'Never. I cannot wear this.'

'Then as a memento.'

He made to give it to her. Her hands were clenched. From a height of six inches he dropped it into her lap.

'Goodbye, Fräulein Stahel.'

She looked up sharply.

'Good afternoon, Mr Law.'

He left. Coming back down the platform toward the exit he glanced through the window into her compartment. She sat rigid-backed, hands pressed to her sides, eyes down. Diffused through the station roof, the evening sunlight illuminated that side where she sat with a dusty haze in which the ruby on her skirt glowed richer than Liebel's blood.

He dumped the toy Colt into a station trash bin before taking a taxi to the airport. There was nearly a two-hour wait before he could board the plane to Nice. During that time he allowed himself just a single drink.

Only when he was in the aircraft and the wheels actually left the ground did the rush of success hit him. For a moment it made his head swim with joy.

He had an urge to talk to his neighbour in the seat beside him. He tried to pay for his drink and the man protested, startled by such effusive friendliness. Just checked himself in the assumption that everyone shared his exhilaration. This was the mountaineer's and burglar's euphoria in which men betray themselves after the event. Holding silent, he looked down over the twinkling night-world, his heart soaring with triumph.

Off the plane at Nice airport he waited his turn dutifully, bag in hand.

'I have something to declare,' he said, opening it up.

The Customs man peered inside. 'But what is it, monsieur?'

'Venison.'

'But no. This is not possible,' the man protested. 'No, not at this season.'

'Frozen,' Just explained.

The man's mouth dropped. His shoulders raised.

'But how will you cook this?'

'I thought to roast it.'

'I think not. The flavour is gone now. Perhaps as a civet, slowly with a bouquet garni.'

'Yes?'

'As long and slowly as is possible. And even then it will be better eaten on the second day. But only the Swiss would freeze venison.'

'Also their hotels are poor now and they are no longer so clean or so efficient,' agreed Just, zipping his bag. 'Look at the way this package is wrapped. It has come undone already and is bleeding everywhere.'

Arriving at the mill an hour later, there was no light showing at the windows.

He let himself in. The big room was in darkness though the remains of a fire smouldered in the grate. He sniffed. Below the smell of woodsmoke was the acrid trace of marijuana.

He set down his bag and switched on an infirm table lamp. The ashtray which lay revealed in the pool of light contained some twenty butts. They were of three kinds, the brown Rothman tips which Marianne smoked, four or five handrolled roaches, and one other brand. He picked one up and examined it. Filtered Gauloises. Who? A fierce knife churned in his belly. Who had been with her?

He set the cigarette stub down. After a moment he glided toward the spiral staircase. He moved fast and softly up, fingertips running on the wall.

Her door was ajar. The twin bars of the electric fire cast a ruddy glow through her overheated room. The sheet kicked away, naked, she slept upon her back, flushed face turned to the side. Her hair flung forward on the pillow exposed the neck and its delicate shadowed nape. The hot air reeked of marijuana and the sweet sour musk of her body.

He saw with a lurch of the heart the bruise upon her narrow thigh.

She slept upon her back, one leg drawn up and its instep resting upon the other's knee. The neat triangle which hid her mound was a blonde band between her legs fringeing the dewy glister of her pouted lips.

He took her without undressing. He spread her legs and went into her while she was still asleep and she woke with a cry. He took her brutally with no regard or interest for how she felt, the fire of jealousy fuelled by the curdled adrenalin of the day's events. She reared up with a scream. She was still stoned and the shock of waking flashed into excitement. He came within seconds. She dug her nails fiercely into his shoulders and cried out again as he scalded into her ...

Fifteen

'*Pardevant Maître Jules Guizol, notaire à Lezat, soussigne ont comparu* ...'

Perched behind his vast carved desk, the Notary continued to read out the Act of Sale. His audience was the same as at the previous meeting, sitting upon the same hard chairs, in a semicircle facing the desk.

'... between Madame Yvonne Joan Wilkinson, residing at Lezat, born in Brighton, England, 23 June 1911, holder of *carte de séjour* number ...'

She was wearing a calf-length frock which gave off a pungent smell of mothballs. Her expression was vivid with interest as she listened, a bright smile pinned upon her face. It was better than any party. This was the most important day in their lives for fifteen years.

The attitude of both as they listened was as if they were concentrating on a fascinating lecture delivered by a dear, loved friend, upon a subject which enthralled them. At the end of every paragraph, when the Notary drew breath to continue, two heads dipped forward in acknowledgement as to a point well made. A gracious bob of approbation.

'... and Mademoiselle Marianne Gladys Brent, student, resident of London, born at Willesden ...'

The girl sat slouched in her chair, gazing out of the window and taking no interest in the proceedings. Socially free, she sensed no obligation to demonstrate enthusiasm which she did not feel.

'... *l'aquereuse ici presente l'immeuble ci-après designe* ...'

The telephone rang. The Notary paused in his reading and answered it without apology. Just distinguished a conversation about probate of a will in the archaic forms of Napoleonic Law, where ties of blood and rights of family precede the intentions of the deceased. The Notary hung up. His eye returned to the page without glancing at his audience.

'... *l'aquereuse sera proprietaire à compter de ce jour de l'immeuble presentement vendu* ...'

Henry's hands lay folded in his lap like claws at rest, mottled in brown blotches on skin as shiny and white as wax. The old couple seldom went out of doors. Just recalled that he had never seen them sitting in the sun. Why did they come here, he wondered. Why did they live in this foreign land, where they clung so fiercely to being English; when the papers and the treats, the gossip and the chums all came from home.

Yet, what would they be back there, he reflected. Objects of ridicule? Aged caricatures in reduced circumstances, disliked for their accents and manner? Here, at least, they were eccentrics, neither fully understood nor 'placed' and, therefore, not representing the same detested class. Here they received polite attention, and the smiles afterward were tolerant, even kindly.

Also, they had a particular standing and merited a certain respect in the district through being owners of a large and important property. Ex-owners. Now they would be rich – in their terms, if not in his – or at least comfortably off for the rest of their lives. He wondered what difference the money would make to them.

'*Moyennant une somme de cent quarante milles francs que Mademoiselle Brent a payée et moyennant une rente annuelle* ...'

When he had levered up the flagstone and buried the money beneath the floor of the living room, Just had kept out twenty thousand Swiss francs for living expenses, and a hundred thousand which he had used to start an account in Marianne's name at the Banque de Paris et des Pays Bas. A cheque signed by her lay on the Notary's desk, together with her passport and birth certificate.

'... *en outre le notaire soussigné affirme qu'à sa connaissance le present acte n'est modifié ... Fait et passe en l'étude du notaire soussigné.*'

The tiny man turned the last page and laid it upon the others. He reversed the pile face upward and passed the sheaf of papers to Henry, eldest of those present. Every page had to be initialled by all parties to the act.

The Notary pinned Marianne's cheque to the cover of his file, returning her passport and birth certificate. Bored, she signed with a listless hand. The property was hers. The fact meant nothing to her, it seemed. Just marvelled at her indifference.

Sixteen

A flock of sheep blocked the road into St Paul de Vence. An old shepherd with a dog beside him walked unhurriedly behind, indifferent to the line of motor cars which had built up at his back to crawl at the same timeless pace. Just slid the Ferrari into position behind a Lincoln Continental with the white and azure plates of the Principality of Monaco.

St Paul de Vence was the prettiest and most famous of all the perched villages of the Coast. Its high walls and battlements crowned a bluff at the side of a valley and dominated a view of green and wooded country rolling to the sea.

The Lincoln, a Bentley, a Citroen Maserati further up the queue of cars were certainly headed for the same destination as the white Ferrari. Just had reserved a table for dinner at the Colombe d'Or to celebrate the purchase of the mill.

But, for the moment, the way to this delightful and chic establishment was obstructed by sheep and traffic was immovable. Just slipped the gear lever into neutral and resigned himself to patience.

His glance strayed. He started most unpleasantly and clutched at Marianne's knee.

'Look!'

A car had drawn up on the other side of the road and from its window the driver was in the act of photographing them through a telephoto lens. Just raised his hand to mask his face.

'Look there!'

He was a young man in his middle twenties with keen hard features beneath a bouffant mop of hair. It was exactly the man described enquiring after him at the newspaper shop.

Marianne asked, 'What are you going on about?'

'Can't you see him?' Just hissed. 'Over there!'

'What about him, then?'

'He's photographing me.'

'You?' She laughed. 'Don't be stupid.'

Just glanced surreptitiously across the road. The man sat waiting for a clear shot, the long barrel of the lens aimed directly at his face like a gun.

'It's *him*,' Just said.

Marianne's eyes rolled heavenwards in exasperation. Her finger jabbed at the horizon.

'Look there.'

He did. The valley was filled with purple shadow; in the distance the ragged line of mountains glittered in the sunset. It was an impressive and picturesque sight. Anyone might want to photograph it.

The line of cars eased forward. Just shifted into gear and drove into the village. The man in the Fiat remained as he was, intent on focusing his view.

'You're right,' Just said. 'I'm sorry.'

'Honestly. The way you go on. Whew!'

In Just's opinion, the Colombe d'Or was the best hotel in the world. It had only twelve rooms which were neither the most expensive nor the most comfortable he had known, nor indeed was the food of undue distinction. But it was staggeringly beautiful. A flagged courtyard was contained on two sides by stone walls thick with climbing flowers. The third side was formed by the house, the fourth a void, an open view across the valley to the Alps, whose snow-capped peaks blazed in the last of the sun as Just and Marianne entered the massive wooden door from the street.

The terrace was set for dinner. Some fifteen tables were ranged beneath the orange trees, each illuminated by a lantern which cast a warm yellow light upward into the greenery.

All but a few of these tables were occupied by guests. As Just and the girl were shown to a place in their midst, he became aware of a peculiar concentration of attention on the part of these diners. Few were eating or drinking and the gaze of every one of them appeared to be directed fixedly at the view.

'Is terrible,' said the head waiter.

He nodded across the valley and now both man and girl distinguished the object of this common interest as a red glow which enveloped the further side of the valley, more sullen in colour than the brilliant spires of the distant peaks, but more menacing. A forest fire was burning up the hillside, growing in size as they watched and flaming more fiercely in the gathering dusk.

'Will you have a drink before dinner, sir?' the waiter asked.

Half a mile away a miasma of smoke hung above the trees. Perched upon the battlements and separated from the conflagration by the deep plunge of the valley, the restaurant where they sat was in no danger. Fanned by a breeze, the fire crept away from them up the slope toward the main road to the coast. It was here that the fire-fighting crews were attempting to halt the blaze. Arcs of water drenched the hill from a dozen red fire trucks which lined the road, each transmitting from its cab a whirling beacon of crimson light.

Just shifted his interest to the menu and ordered for both of them. He glanced across at Marianne and warmed with possessive pride. That day, immediately after leaving the Notary's office, he had insisted on buying her clothes. Without enthusiasm she had accompanied him into the shop, and lagged behind as he discussed her with the saleslady. An expression of bored suffering written on her face, she had allowed herself to be measured and appraised, reluctantly tried on the clothes selected for her, and showed no pleasure in their purchase.

He was delighted by the result of his insistence. The white shirt and blue, pleated skirt were childlike and demure, veiling without hiding her nubile form. For once her hair was brushed and combed, tumbling in soft curls around her elfin face which was turned in profile, mouth slightly open as she gazed with enthralled fascination at the progress of the fire.

When Just set back his chair and stood, the movement did not divert her concentration.

'I'll be a moment,' he murmured, and went into the hotel. Two decades had passed since he had been here, yet he recalled perfectly the layout of the building. On his way back upstairs from the Men's Room, he turned off, opened a door and let himself into the dining room, empty today as usual during spring and summer when the outdoor terrace was used for meals.

The walls of the sombre room were entirely covered with paintings. At the turn of the century the auberge had been a Bar Tabac, the haunt of artists, notoriously indigent, who settled their bills with a painting in lieu of cash. The collection had begun thus involuntarily with the Impressionists. Waxing rich, the family had added to it over the years. Five of the canvasses Just recognised: a Braque, two Picassos, a Leger, a Matisse. Several million dollars' worth of original paintings were hung here.

On impulse he closed his eyes. Blind, he walked a precise and accurate course between the closely-set tables, detoured the fireplace, halted, raised his hand, touched the window which gave upon the road and set his fingers on the latch. Opening his eyes, he smiled. Twenty years ago he had stayed here for a week and planned exactly how he would steal those five canvases. Afterwards he had abandoned the project. It would have been churlish to rob a place where he had enjoyed so fine a time. Not everyone had such scruples. In the interval someone else had done them over and now a burglar alarm wired the window. Well, they had learned something. He returned to the terrace.

The girl was no longer at the table.

A stab of alarm pierced his heart, astonishing him by its intensity. It disconcerted him to be suddenly so vulnerable.

'Mike! Mike!'

She waved excitedly from another table where she was seated amongst four strangers, enjoying the fire.

'Over here, Mike!'

The two men in the party did not stand as Just approached.

'I say, better view from here. Front row of the stalls, what? Do join us,' one said.

He framed what was to be a refusal and glanced at Marianne. No longer looking his way, she had been heavily engaged in conversation by the stouter of the two women in the group.

'Grab a pew!'

The affable fool pushed back a chair, picked up the wine bottle and filled to the brim another glass. Reluctantly Just sat.

'Saw you at the airport. Sunday paper round.'

Just remembered. Old russet moustache in dressing-gown and pyjamas.

'Here on holiday are you?'

'For a few days,' said Just. 'Travelling.'

He was seated at the end of the table opposite a withered monkey-like creature with a ravaged but once pretty face. Now the florid host introduced her.

'Lady Amstel,' Just heard him say.

'Nadine Glenda Grant, and that's my boy,' he added, waving vaguely to the far side of the table where a twenty-year-old leaned forward to enter the conversation with Marianne.

'I say, see over there.'

Across the valley the largest congregation of pompiers were now assembled by a house standing directly in the path of the approaching blaze. In the floodlights from the road and the eerie glow of the flames, its owners could be clearly distinguished as tiny figures in summer dress among the black protective clothing of the firefighters spraying high arcs of water on and around their house.

'Do you feel *safe* here?' Lady Amstel enquired earnestly of Just.

'It seems to be moving away from us. I don't think we shall burn tonight.'

'No, I don't mean that. *Here*. Here in France.'

Just stole a glance up the table. Marianne was saying something now to Madame Grant.

'... really icy cold. Just an amazing physical experience,' he overheard.

'Safe? Why yes,' he answered. 'Don't you?'

'Oh no! We have a villa here you see. Certainly *not* safe. I feel safe in Switzerland,' she volunteered.

Just smiled inwardly. 'I don't particularly,' he said.

'If one has a villa here it's ghastly. We're on the Cap, you see, and we fence the property, but they keep tearing it down to get along the sea shore. They land in small boats and picnic, leaving broken glass and mess everywhere. Deliberate, of course. One puts tar on the rocks but the fishermen still come and sit on the ladder and won't move, so one has to step over them to get into the speedboat. I talk to them but, of course, they know I'm English. They hate us. Of course we have a *gardien*, but he hates us too and his dog won't go for them.'

'Yes, rather. Must come out in the boat,' the red-faced man called across to Marianne. He turned to Just.

'*Must* come out! Go out to the islands. Care for water-skiing do you?'

'I don't like the sea,' Just said.

'No matter. Come over and we'll lunch at the house. Let the children play. Rodney's pretty good: acrobatic skis, jumping, he's into all of that.'

'Into it', thought Just with contempt and loathing for this loud and so-sure-of-himself condescending ass-hole.

The food which he had ordered came served to the table where they sat. Now he saw no way of leaving, except by an act of calculated rudeness – thereby raising exactly the sort of curiosity and comment which he did not seek. He did not enjoy being here at all. Lady Amstel, that hearty merchant banker, stockbroker, Lloyd's underwriter or whatever he was, they were a tribe he did not wish to know. In England certainly they formed part of that same milieu as the Morar brothers. This was dangerous ground.

'Pity you're not staying,' Nadine Grant called across the table. 'Giving a party Friday. We *love* to entertain here, but it's difficult to find the *guests*.'

Red-faced's son was busy on the table demonstrating with knives and forks and a spoon ramped against the glass some refinement of his sporting skill. Eating heartily, Marianne was paying close attention to his tale.

'Yeah, that's keen,' she said, with her mouth full.

She looked enchanting tonight. The tanned column of her neck rose from the wide-collared shirt, the jut of her little breasts showing firm beneath the loose drape of the material.

'We'll go on the boat, Mike?' she called.

He nodded, forcing a smile, saw her turn back impetuously to the boy. Redface was saying, '. . . a Jew of course, but the best sort of Jew.'

What was he talking about?

This was a celebration tonight. The loot was here. The house was bought. The man with a camera in the Fiat signified nothing. All was well. So why should he feel this wrap of doom closing round him like a shroud? '. . . bought this place near Grasse. Far too big for us. Rodney and I just rattle around inside it, and the girl when she's here. Don't know why, grounds, gardeners, price way over the odds. Must have been drunk when I bought it. Still, can't stay in England, what?'

'You're here often?' Just managed.

But who had been in the mill while he was in Zurich? Whose were the cigarette butts in the ashtray? What brand was son Rodney smoking? Did Marianne know him already?

'Simply not tolerable any more. Backs to the wall, tighten the belt another notch, nose to the grindstone . . . pay up, pay up, till they squeeze you dry . . .'

He looked over toward the fire, stole a surreptitious glance at Marianne. The pompiers had halted the blaze, saving the house, he saw. Where the flames had reached the drenched verge of the road, a dense curtain of smoke poured into the sky. By now, however, little attention was being paid to the event from the terrace of the Colombe d'Or. The fire was seen to be in control. The initial bout of interest which it provoked had subsided and the guests were concentrating upon their dinner.

'... Twenty of them broke down the fence and came in all drunk and tore up the shrubs. We called the *gendarmes* but they refused to come, said we must deal with it ourselves. They're so rude, the French. They hate us, Mr Law, don't you find. Or is it Lord Law?'

He shook his head numbly, dragging back his attention to Lady Amstel from the sight of Marianne's pert attentive face. The young man was writing something on a scrap of paper. He passed it to the girl. He had laid down his cigarette to do so – filtered Gauloise. The same brand as those butts he had found the night he returned from Zurich.

The fire had thrilled Marianne. When it was subdued he had seen the disappointment on her face. Now that glow was back. He looked at her flushed cheeks and dancing eyes and his blood churned with jealousy.

Although it was long past their usual bedtime, Henry and Yvonne had only just finished dinner.

'Coffee, dear?' he asked.

'Decaff?'

'Of course.'

'You know I think I'll have another glass of that delicious port first.'

She poured the ruby wine for both of them. They had bought it that day, after the Notary, when it became clear they were not included in the invitation to dinner. That had been a disappointment but the wine was delicious, rich and comforting.

She swallowed a mouthful and remarked, not without satisfaction, 'Well Henry, you were wrong.'

He was sniffing at his glass, his eyes hooded.

'Wrong?' he queried, though he knew perfectly well to what she was referring. He had been waiting for it.

'The money. The £15,000. He paid it.'

'In *her* name,' said Henry.

'Well ... it's his money.'

'I heard her call him Bob,' said Henry, his tone deliberately vague.

'Bob?'

'I heard her. His name's Michael, so why should she call him Bob? He could have asked us to dinner. *Not* very polite of him.'

'Rather rude,' Yvonne agreed. 'No, he's not quite a gentleman I'm afraid, but we did get the money.'

'In *her* name,' Henry repeated thoughtfully. 'Now that's scarcely the action of an honest man, I'd say. "Bob", and dressed up like a bandbox in new clothes and driving around in that flashy car with a girl young enough to be his daughter ... just who is he, our Mr Law, that's what I'd like to know.'

Yvonne took another sip of wine and smiled secretly. Henry could never admit he had been wrong.

'Still, we got the money,' she said again.

'You're naïve, dear.' Henry's voice was sharp. 'He's paid us £15,000, that's all.'

The wine had made Yvonne quite daring. Normally she was too frightened to argue with him. She said, 'And the *viager* rent, dear. The £2,000 a year. He has to pay us that or the place comes back to us. That's the law.'

She knew she had scored for Henry did not reply for ages, yet, when he did, his tone was not at all peevish but quiet, almost dreamy.

'Yes,' he said at last, 'I suppose a man like that would consider us the perfect target.'

Yvonne did not understand.

'Target?' she repeated blankly.

'He's paid us £15,000. The only thing we know for certain is that if we die tomorrow he owns a property worth five times that.'

The blood drained from Yvonne's cheeks. For a second she thought she was about to faint.

'Oh no! You don't think ...'

Henry set down his glass and looked her in the eye.

'I'm not saying so – yet. What I am saying is that I do not like what I have seen of our Mr Law ...'

As she listened, Yvonne's world seemed to be turning black at the edges and narrowing. Only Henry remained stable and real and he was very cross indeed as he continued:

'No, not one little bit. He is a pervert, brazen and immoral. What I am saying, though, is that if he turns out also to be a crook he is not going to get away with it. No!'

Just came back from the kitchen, where he had poured a last drink, and found her setting a match to the logs in the open fireplace.

'Is it worth it?'

She did not seem to hear him.

'If we're going to bed soon. You had a good evening?' he asked.

She wheeled angrily.

'It's all such a big deal to you, such a heavy scene. I was talking, talking that's all. He's a guy. Just a guy. Someone my own age.'

Folding a spill of paper, he lit it at the fire and held it to his cigar, warming the end in the flame.

'He asked you out?'

She shouted: 'They asked both of us. You heard. His Dad did.'

'And after dinner?'

'He was showing me the art. The Picassos. You told me about the art yourself. Please, Bob.'

He shook off the hand which she had placed upon his sleeve. Her face hardened.

'Fuck you, then, you dirty old man! You pervert! Know what I was really doing then? You want to know? All right then, you asked me. We had it off in the loo, if you *must* know.'

His hand lashed out and struck her on the cheek. His cigar shot spinning through her hair. She jumped away with a scream. He went after her immediately. Cornering her flight he got a hold on her shirt. As she wrenched away it tore off in his hand. He kicked aside the chair as she dodged behind it and jumped for her neck, gripping with both hands digging into the soft angle at the shoulders.

She shrieked as she stumbled to her knees. One hand bearing her down, he reached the other to the waistband of her skirt. The zip burst as he wrenched it down.

'Pig!' she screeched.

Twisting her head, she sank her teeth into his wrist. He tore his hand away, grunting with pain, then whacked it back across her head, gripped her hair and forced her down, ripping her pants to her knees.

The breath hissed out between his teeth. All his weight bearing upon the hand which flattened her face to the floor, he pulled open his fly. Her body convulsed forward as she felt him, an aborted leap which had her flat upon the ground, outstretched, locking her legs together and yelling in fear and fury.

Rigid with hate, he hauled her up, dragged her to the chair and forced her across it while she threshed in his grip, struggling to escape. He pushed her face into the chair. Forcing her thighs open with his knees, he drove into her. She shrieked and her whole body clenched in pain. He pulled back, then forced into her again in a fast savage thrust. A vengeful dagger, he stabbed her again, feeling her wetter now with fear or excitement he did not care, and again. Compelling her down with his hands and open with his legs, brutally he plunged into her again and again, her spasms inflaming him, scalding jealousy whipping him on, and a rancid pressure boiling and building in his groin till finally it burst and spurted in raw anger, hot gouts of fury, the poison draining from him. Avenged.

Her struggles had expired. When he pulled away, she slid from the chair. She collapsed whimpering to the floor and lay there upon the flagstones with all defiance gone. Her thin limbs looked crooked and her shoulder blades stuck up from her back like scrawny chickens' wings.

Her shoulders heaved. Her desolate body shook uncontrollably, racked by sobs. Frail limbs so strangely skewed, she huddled on the floor. Torn and dirty, her new clothes were rags now. She looked like a broken, beaten child.

The taste of victory curdled in his mouth. They lay apart. The fire died down and it grew cold.

Seventeen

At the beginning it had been pure joy with her. Moonlight on snow. The impossible midnight spring of a heart gone cold. The start of a time when all might be hoped for.

It had been New Year's Eve, ten o'clock at night and Just was alone in his flat in Farm Street. Television was on without sound and Vivaldi played over the quadrophonic system. Elsewhere, the Morar brothers were throwing a party.

'Ha-ha, no good asking you to wear a black tie, I suppose,' Russell had said. 'Doesn't matter of course, everyone's dressing down these days.'

He was invited there and to several others. He would look in, he decided. Slipping on a sheepskin coat, he let himself out into the quiet street.

The night was dense and cold. He felt in his pocket for keys to the Bentley, then paused. Later the streets would be lethal with errant automobiles as glassy-eyed inebriates struggled to pilot them back to suburbia. He was in the mood himself to drink tonight, though he did not think anything would shift the chill clarity of him now. He shrugged deeper into his coat and walked.

The door of the Church of the Jesuit Fathers in Farm Street was open. An arc of yellow light and gust of warmth and organ music came from within. Beyond, the gates into the gardens were open, unusual at this hour. He turned into them, taking the short cut to Mount Street. The trees stood back from the path, in the ghostly lamplight their outlines blurred, tops lost in the mist.

The gardens were empty. A window opened high up somewhere and a phrase of music filtered down through the fog, a girl's voice clear, invisible.

'Aubrey, it's going to snow.'

Which it did at that moment. A few flakes came drifting down and his own steps sounded muffled as he came out into Carlos Place. Across the road the illuminated portal and windows of the Connaught were visible only as soft rectangles of festive light.

Passing the Teller Mostern building, he stopped and looked up at the façade rearing up into the fog, effaced at the level of the first-floor windows.

A notion took him. Too simple of course; no risk attached in *that* direction for he would be able to explain the whole thing away with ease, this night of all nights, the constables in for a brandy, hats beneath the arm. And a Happy New Year to you too, officer! No, that side of it was nothing. No danger there.

Still! He took off his bulky coat and, rolling it into a ball, dropped it behind the railings into the basement area where he would recover it later.

Glancing into the opaque whiteness of the street he set his foot to the balustrade and began to climb.

When before he had made that climb the night was clear and dry and the only danger was the risk of being spotted from the street. Conditions were very different now. From the height of the first floor the pavement was invisible below. The brickwork of the façade was slick and treacherous, the ledges slippery with snow.

He surmounted the overhang of the balcony and, choosing now a route different from the one he knew, traversed to the adjoining sill then set his legs horizontal to the ground and chimneyed up between the buttress and the masonry supporting the window.

Wilfully he had reduced the margin of safety to its most slender edge. Here were no balconies with ornamental ironwork providing easy handhold. To come out of the chimney he had to reach up blind and feel for grip then stand on the wooden frame of the window and swing his body out over the drop, up and around the overhang. It was strangely exhilarating to be climbing in the poor light on such a difficult pitch.

Fascinated by the danger he continued the ascent. His hands were numb, but he was climbing now in a distinct rhythm, his steady pace carrying him on and up. By the time he reached the window of his own office he could have continued for another five hundred feet.

He let himself down into the room and sank to a kneeling position at rest against the wall, set back upon his heels. A muscle was jumping in the calf of his leg and his hands had a faint and rapid tremor when, filthy with mud, he stretched them out and examined them.

In less than five minutes he had recovered. He washed, poured himself a brandy with ice and, glass in hand, wandered down through the unlit building, the way memorised and certain, surefooted as a burglar in the dark. That faculty was as keen as ever it had been, he thought, but, to test it, he turned into the internal passage of the second floor. Seven steps in the inky black ... a hand out ... touch the door frame ... down to waist height and the handle ... he turned it and slipped into the room.

Filtered by the falling snow, the lamplight cast up beyond the window. The cutting room was illuminated by a pale haze in whose soft light he distinguished the scaffold shape of editing racks draped with lengths of film above their bins, stacked cans upon the floor beside an editing moviola the crude shape of a factory machine, a strip of film laced ready in its gate.

He snapped down the switch which lit the lamp. Set on automatic the machine clattered into life, film jerking through the window.

Dressed in a gymslip, the unknown Marianne leaped at him from the frame. Leaped and reached for him with the stretched out slenderness of her downy arms. Leapt in nubile shaft of tender frame into the barren ice-fields of his arctic heart . . . which missed a beat. Tripped and slithered, recovered at a faster pace.

The strip of film rattled through the gate. Marianne leapt toward him, landed, laughed . . . and the shot ended.

To resume again. A clapperboard, Take Seven, the slate clearing from the frame and the girl revealed, knelt in the middle distance of an all white-set, tensed upon her marks as a runner waiting for the gun, in gymslip, white socks, black shoes, honey coloured hair demurely hidden in a black beret, tiny grandma glasses perched upon her adorable nose and face all childishly intent waiting for her cue.

Which, when it came, sent her flying forward, racing up the ramp to hit the edge and leap, soar . . . arms wide, hat going, skirts raising up the unformed thighs, a tingling glimpse of stretched white knickers . . . to land with all that freed blonde hair cascading round her grinning face, and a throb like fire answering between his legs.

The strip of film quit the machine and curled around his feet. He breathed deep and blinked, coming to the surface.

After a moment he bent, picked up the film and threaded it through the gate.

He ran both takes again.

Poised upon her start, she had the fragile delicacy of a wild animal, some timid forest creature encaptured in the sudden light, bolting toward the camera, to hit, to fly . . . and in that soaring bound mysteriously to change, to become impure within the very process of the leap, a child with innocence belied, sly and aware, flaunting white thighs and brimstone loins.

The screen went blank. The film coiled to the floor. He strode to the door and switched on the light. An ache of desire stiffened his moves as he took down the first of forty or fifty lengths of film which hung from nails over the editing bin. He examined it on the moviola. A bottle, a household drink, in silhouette. A hand turning it into light ablaze. He snapped open the machine and ripped it out, tearing the film in his haste. Replaced it with another.

Three girls stood in line abreast. Dressed in the same fashion and of the age which moved him, normally he would have studied them with interest and the eye of a connoisseur. Now they held nothing for him. He discarded them.

The flash had been immediate, the illumination total and havoc roiling in his groin.

He set another section in the gate – another bottle. He wrenched it out and dropped it to the floor. He laced one more into the machine and his held breath left him in a sigh. His loved one stood there in the light.

This time she stood beside a table, a fragile white affair set with glasses and a single frosted bottle. With girlish grace she took up the bottle to pour, to fill one glass and, pouring still, to fill another ... and another ... and another ... all from this single foaming magic source; an event which, seemingly, she had not expected, for a droll expression of the utmost surprise overtook her face. Her eyes grew huge and she clapped a hand to her astonished open mouth, whilst its mate still clasped around the bottle with its splashing errant jet ... Then the film clattered from the moviola.

He took up the next strip. His body hurt with the pain of wanting. He took down three takes, looked and dropped them to the floor before he found another and watched entranced the cartwheel turning of her nimble limbs, calves kicking free and arcing rosy knees ... skirt falling back on immature narrow thighs and white pants chastely clasped around precocious loins.

In this fashion, taking down strip after strip of film to run them through the machine, Just passed well over an hour. He himself had no sense of time and no awareness of his surroundings. Stone cold sober, with racing exalted blood, he bent over the illuminated window on a tiny world where she flickered and danced before his enchanted gaze. The stealth, the cunning and the gun forgotten, feet rooted, limbs turned to feather, mesmerised and weak at the mercy of his prey. Lost, gone, helpless in the ache of longing, breathless and submerged.

So, when finally he turned from the machine and drifted to the window as a swimmer in need of air surfacing from the deep, he found a real world become unrecognisable, for, while he had been there, it had snowed, then cleared, and now the whole of London stretched away white and magic and beautiful beneath an icy mantle, its thousand roofs angled in planes of whiteness to the moon and glittering stars and brilliant sky. And bells were ringing everywhere in tintinnabulation and sweet cacophony of midnight sound with, under it, the strain of distant music and far cries of revelry and joy.

Transfixed by so much beauty and the brimming measure of his heart, Just stood smiling hugely at the night. It was the first true smile which had softened his face for nearly two years. His associates, seeing him at this moment, could not have recognised his look; indeed, afterwards from that night on, it was noticed there was something changed about him, some set of expression, element of bearing, *something* was different. It was enough to draw comment and cause discussion, though hard to pin down exactly what it was that was discussed.

But at that moment there was no doubt or question what it was, as the bells rang out and the moon glistened on the unmarked snow. No doubt at all, for all, all had changed. It was a New Year and he was in love.

Eighteen

'Why the fuck can't you wear jeans like everyone else?' Marianne demanded.

It was 11AM in the mill and Just was not yet dressed. He studied the dozen silk ties which hung on a rough cord across the bedroom door and answered easily.

'I could not afford to, any more than I could be seen with an ugly girl. You wear the clothes you're most comfortable in.'

She shrugged impatiently.

'Oh yeah? You're always on at me to dress up.'

In foul humour she flounced away, downstairs and out.

An old woman, all in black, was stooped outside the front door. A sack lay upon the ground which she was closing as Marianne came out of the mill and halted abruptly to avoid treading on her hand.

Rosy peasant cheeks, eyes bright as buttons of jet, the old woman smiled as she straightened up.

'*Bonjour*, mademoiselle.'

'*Bonjour*,' said Marianne.

'You are English?'

'Yes. What are you doing?' she asked.

'I speak a little English. American English. From the war.'

'I didn't know the Americans came here then.'

'But yes,' the woman told her. 'The Americans are landing in the Esterel. They attack Cannes and take many prisoners for the Germans. They are not fighting too much I think.'

'What have you got in that bag?'

The peasant shook the sack. The contents made a loose rustle like shingle.

'Here are *escargots.*'

'*Escargots?*'

'You say snails.'

Plunging in her hand, she drew one out and held it toward Marianne.

The girl examined it curiously.

'You eat that?'

'But yes. Is delicacy.'

Marianne's pert nose wrinkled.

'I must say it doesn't look very delicious.'

'Oh yes. In restaurants this is a plate which cost nine, ten francs at least.'

She took it gingerly in her fingers.

'How do you cook them?'

'You fry in butter. I shall give you some but first I keep ten days in sack so they evacuate.'

'Evacuate?'

'Do their business. You eat now and ... clack!'

The woman sliced fingers across her throat in a fast expressive cut.

'Dead?'

'Ah yes. Is poison.'

'What are you going to do with these?'

'We eat. I sell. To restaurants, to the English.'

She nodded up the hill.

'Really. They eat snails?' Marianne asked surprised.

'But yes. I go there now.'

She made a little dipping bob of her head and plodded away up the overgrown steps.

Marianne walked to the Ferarri, her thoughts busy. She sat in the car and saw the keys still hanging in the dash. She reached across and sounded an impatient pip pip on the horn to hurry Just.

It struck her as absurd that he took so long to get ready. She was always downstairs within five minutes of waking, dressed and ready to go. To go? That was a laugh. There never was anywhere to go to. Today was an exception; in response to her nagging he had agreed to drive her to Antibes.

She made another beep on the horn, longer and more insistent. When, a little later, he had still not come, she slid across into the driver's seat and started the motor. She touched the accelerator and the highly-tuned engine roared. She waited for a moment then slipped it into gear. Tongue bit between her teeth she eased the Ferrari onto the road.

In the bedroom, Just heard the note of the engine and stepped to the window. He saw the white car crawl out of the parking lot, jump as she fluffed the shift into second gear, then disappear slowly round the corner.

He frowned and hurried to finish dressing. He was not worried about the car but Marianne's dissatisfaction distressed him. She was not as happy and contented here as she had been. Not only was she growing bored but something had gone wrong between them.

No, he was not worried about the Ferrari. To drive off like that was a gesture only. She would go only so far as the place halfway up the hill where it was possible to turn around and would be back in a moment. Fifteen minutes later when there was no sign of her, he began to wonder if he were wrong.

Just had become definitely nervous and was standing outside the house looking up the road and debating what he should do when, finally, Marianne reappeared. She was on foot.

'What the hell's happened?' he called out, alarmed.

He saw that she was close to tears.

'I'm sorry, Bob.'

'Michael,' he said. 'I've told you that a hundred times. What happened? Are you all right?'

'I'm O.K. The car ... it's not damaged.'

'What happened?'

'I was only doing ten miles an hour but it just … went off. The steering …' She was crying.

'Where is it?'

She waved behind her.

'Up the hill. In the ditch. I never hit anything. It's not harmed.'

'Don't worry,' he told her. 'Don't worry.'

He walked with her to the place. She was right. The bodywork was undented but the car lay at an angle, both left wheels deep in the ditch. She was contrite over the accident.

'I don't know what happened,' she said again. 'It just wouldn't steer.'

'Couldn't matter less,' he reassured her, privately delighted at this opportunity to pardon and show benevolence. 'The garage can tow it out. I'll order a taxi.'

He telephoned from the upper mill. The old couple were quite a-twitter at their visit and Yvonne served cups of weak Nescafé while they waited for the cab to arrive from Lezat.

When it did, and when finally he had managed to extricate them from the insistent hospitality, Just told the driver to take them first to the garage in town.

There, he pressed a hundred-franc note into the mechanic's hand.

'If you would tow it out and bring it here, I'll pick it up this afternoon and settle the bill. I'm sure nothing's wrong but if you'd just check it over …'

After a show of protest the man agreed, rather ungraciously. Just got back into the taxi and rejoined Marianne.

They came to Antibes to score dope. The phrase was Marianne's, as was the plan.

When she had flown to join him in Paris, she had carried a stash with her in defiance of his absolute prohibition. He was furious when he had found out. Its discovery and her arrest

'Sunshine Minister in London – Snow and ice were forgotten this afternoon at Heathrow Airport ... steel band in flowered shirts beat out calypso welcome ... West Indian Ministers ... Cumberland Hotel ... conference to promote ... tourism ... Mr Marvin Le Roy ...' Marvin Le Roy ... Marvin Le Roy ...

Just stared in stupefaction. So intent had he been on the strategy of his wooing, so delightedly concentrated upon the phased seduction of this pubescent wanton eating beans on toast, then for a moment he failed to assimilate what he read. And then with a click deep in the brain and a shift to icy clarity its meaning became clear.

Marvin Le Roy had come to London. The man he most wanted to kill had delivered himself into his hands.

Just was at the Cumberland hall porter's desk at 7 o'clock that same evening.

'This envelope,' he said, handing it over, 'I want to be sure it reaches the Minister.'

The uniformed porter glanced at the name.

'To Mr Le Roy, of course, sir.'

'Without fail,' Just added and passed across money.

'Of course, the minute he comes in, you can count on it.'

He watched the envelope, which contained only a guide to London, slipped into a pigeon hole whose key hung in place. The addressee was not in his room. It mattered not the least; Just had no intention of visiting until the morning.

The room number was 508.

He knocked upon the door at 8.30 AM.

There was no response. After a few seconds he rapped again and more insistently.

'Wha ... what is it?'

The voice was blurred by sleep. Just knocked again.

'Mr Le Roy, sir!'

He heard a shuffling from within, steps across the carpet and the handle turning. A petulant black face was blinking in the light.

Just kicked open the door and burst into the room.

'Wha ... what ya doing, man ... ?'

It had not occurred to him that, bearded and without a tan, he might not be recognised. He jerked the gun from his pocket and rammed it into Marvin's face.

'Down, nigger!'

It was a rude awakening. Dressed in lemon-striped pyjamas Marvin tottered back, tripped over his suitcase and sprawled upon the floor.

Just advanced to straddle him. The black man made to rise.

'Bob! I've been trying to find you, man.'

'Stay down!'

Marvin paused, raised upon an elbow.

'What luck,' said Just, 'you've found me.'

'And I sure am glad, man. I've got good news.'

Just aimed the gun at his nose. 'Marvin, you foolish jigaboo, how could you have been so dumb as to let me go?'

'Good news, man! I got you money.'

'Oh, nigger,' Just said with contempt, 'don't you know there's no price to this.'

'All right if I ...' and Marvin thrust himself up to sit.

Just's foot lashed out and kicked him back.

'Down, I say!'

Marvin's hands flew to his wounded chin.

'Listen, Bob ...'

Just would not let him speak.

'Fool, I'm going to thrash you all. But you've made it easy so you're the first.'

He thrust the gun against his face.

'I've thought of this for every second since you let me go.'

Marvin said distinctly: 'You bin wasting your time.'

'What's that?' His voice was harsh.

The black man choked in parody of a laugh, gums twitched back on yellow monkey teeth.

'Wasting, man, wasting it,' he repeated in fake hilarity. 'Oh, brother, you're just too late to hack it, man. Too fucking late.'

Just snapped.

'What are you saying, nigger?'

'The three at your interview, remember?'

'*Interview?*' Just echoed. 'You call it *that?*'

'Don't make no difference what you call it now. All three are rotting in the grave. Maxwell done it, pulped them dead. And as for himself, the good Lord done it for you.'

Doubt struck into Just as a cold sharp arrow finding the heart. He said, 'You're lying, Marvin.'

'He's dying, man, shot full of dope and crazed and dying. You don't know what it's like there, Bob. No work, no food, every place all locked up ... gangs roaming in the streets with clubs ... shooting and beatings every day and the niggers scared shitless hidden in the forest. President's a wild man with the cancer eating out his brain, boozed and murderous and howling like a dog ...'

'Shut up!' Just yelled, his mind a turmoil, furious. He had been cheated, short-changed, betrayed. He knew Marvin was telling the truth; this was the same black irony that had haunted all his life. It was idiot, futile, the time he had schemed and plotted. Unnecessary instrument, the Fates had ignored him and gone about their business. His victims had been snatched from him; how terribly the end he planned for them had been fulfilled.

'You were lucky,' Marvin continued, calmer now, 'real lucky. Man be glad you're out of it. Like me, broke and on the beach but here and now never going back. The Doctor ... you remember the Doctor?'

'Oh, do I ever,' Just said.

'Dead too. Maxwell slit his belly and tied him to the hind legs of a mule.'

For the space of a heartbeat it gave Just pause and then he spoke: 'But that leaves you, Marvin. You'll have to do for all of them. On your feet!'

His victim made no move. Just bent, gripped the scruff of his silk pyjamas and wrenched him up, drove him over to the window and smashed his face into the glass. With the hand which held the gun he slipped it open, flung it wide and thrust Marvin over the sill. He pulled back the metal window till it bit across his neck.

The noise of Oxford Street flowed up to them, five storeys high. Far below the traffic surged and stopped, held at the lights.

Just pulled tight the window frame as Marvin struggled to be free, desperately twisting his head so Just saw the eyeballs rolling in pools of white. He said, 'You don't have to pay me compensation, Marvin. This is it.'

He dropped the gun then, put his freed hand to grab the threshing leg and heaved him up.

The bile of terror retched in Marvin's throat. With a choking cry he vomited. The contents of his stomach bubbled from his mouth and sailed splashing down toward the street.

On the other side of the road the minute hand of the great clock clicked up to touch the hour of nine. The bells pealed out.

And suddenly Just could not do it.

His victim was balanced in his grasp. From the torture and ignominy which he had suffered in that white-tiled room nearly two years ago a straight line joined to here. The glittering rails of his obsession with revenge ran directly from that point to now. And now, at the end of it, there was nothing here. That which had possessed him, forming the very core and centre of his being, suddenly was gone. Not pity stayed his hand; his will betrayed him.

He strove for the anger which would make him do it but vengeance was a dish gone cold.

Now, with his enemy hung in his hands, suddenly he was powerless. Except for the girl perhaps he could have done it. Now it was too late.

He was hollow cold inside and all at once it was absurd, this frantic nigger spewing down the wall as he shoved him out of the window. The tableau was a farce. He released his grip, stepped back in disgust and picked up the gun. Pinioned at the neck, Marvin's legs still kicked and jived.

Except for the girl, he thought, except for her. Between the midnight ending of the year and today he had not considered them at all, those men he aimed to kill. Not for a moment had he thought of them, he realised. His mind had been entirely filled with her. In that week his world insidiously had shifted and rearranged. His obsession had been displaced.

He took one last look at the yellow-wrapped figure humped over the windowsill then let himself from the room, slipping the gun into his pocket as he walked away down the corridor.

He was disgusted at his incapacity to complete the act, at this weakness and abject failure of the will.

He pressed the button for the elevator.

On Belida he had resolved to punish them for the torment they had caused him. He had prepared and planned for it as a man might a long and arduous journey. Its thought had lain under all he did, like a murmur.

Well, he had made that journey. He had reached his destination – so often imagined – and now he looked about him in disappointment and dismay for this was not the place he had thought. Yet it was not the place, he realised, but the traveller who had changed. Himself, his world, had altered. The way had not ended; it still lay ahead.

The doors slid open. He entered the lift and hit the button to descend.

The demon which had possessed him for so long was exorcised.

He was an empty house. And to that barren vacuum space life itself came rushing and flooding in. Marianne.

From the hotel lobby he telephoned her and asked her to meet him right away.

Twenty

Just had set out to steal half a million pounds and had given himself two years to do it. He did not achieve his goal, either in sum or time, but at the date that he absconded he had embezzled £387,000 and spent one year and six months in doing so.

The irony was that he could have made himself that much and more entirely legally if he had remained and continued to run the company properly for, under his management, Teller Mostern was a runaway success. But he could not bear to wait that long; he wanted it now. The money, the freedom and the girl. All of it, particularly the girl. He wanted out, and he wanted her with him.

To hive away that amount of money in eighteen months had required application, nifty footwork and a convincing line in confidence and reassurance. Confidence certainly, though it never really had come down to reassurance, or rather the assurance had been implicit in Just's manner of a winner, and the evident prosperity which Teller Mostern was enjoying.

On the day of Just's defection, laboratory credit to the company stood at £90,000, the bank loan guaranteed by the Morar brothers was £100,000, and the travel agency were owed £120,000 and were not even pressing. The lines of credit were still good and the matter could have been taken a whole lot further.

But he could not wait. Marianne was his love and he wanted it now. He brought forward his final plan and two months after meeting her he put it into operation.

He flew to Zurich, listed them from the yellow pages, and interviewed chartered accountants. He did not select these alphabetically, but offered them up to Fate. He cut them into individual names and, for want of a hat, tipped them into a waste-paper basket.

First out was Herr Alex Hausser. He proved to be fifty years old and worked in a comfortable suite of offices, with a bookkeeper and two secretaries. Dauntingly respectable, he was simply not right for so informal an operation as Just had to propose.

The next was Dr Liebel, dark haired and in his forties, handsome in hanseatic fashion, and conveying an impression of amazing cleanliness. His nails were short and impeccably manicured, his haircut close and trim. His jowls were smooth as wax and his breath diffused the aura of an hygienic mouthwash.

'Michael Law,' said Just falsely, extending his hand.

'Now what I'd like to do is this: there is a certain sum of money in Holland which I aim to move from there. It must surface finally into an account in Switzerland, but I want it washed thoroughly on the way. I want not one but two total dead end cut-outs on its trail. Now, would handling such an operation be of interest to you?'

Liebel showed neither enthusiasm nor disinterest.

'All transactions concerning money are of interest, Mr Law. Each poses problems of technique which it is my profession to solve. In what currency are these funds held?'

'Dutch guilders.'

'And when would they become available for transfer?'

'First of April,' said Just.

'May I ask please, my services you require only *after* the transfer? That is to say, upon receipt of these monies into an account whose detail I shall give to you; or do you require me to ... to assist professionally in the liberation of these funds from their present holding?'

Just smiled.

'Post liberation. Upon receipt by you.'

'Provenance ex Nederlands. Which bank?'

'Banque Worms, The Hague.'

'Then there is no problem in act of transfer. Do you smoke, Mr Law?' asked the doctor, pushing forward a silver box.

'Not cigarettes.'

'Nor I. A dirty habit and bad for the health. Are you sporty, Mr Law?'

'Occasionally,' said Just.

'You look like a man in good condition of physique. Do you play tennis?'

'A little.'

'And I, a little. We shall play and you shall beat me, I think.'

'I doubt that, Dr Liebel,' Just said. 'I doubt that very much. But I think we can work together.'

'Yes. In such a ... "washing operation" as you say, it is best to choose a laundry which is as far away as possible. I would propose first the Cayman Islands. We transfer first to one of many such banks with important sounding names, but little premises and small staff. It is good as few people know as possible.'

Dr Liebel thought for a moment, then added a rider.

'In the event people should ask, these niggers are very unhelpful.'

'We're not supposed to use that word.'

'Is what they are,' he said.

'And then?'

'Keep away from Europe. In Andorra, Monaco, Leichtenstein, banking details are secret, but always someone is knowing someone who is playing golf with the manager. Out of Europe is better, I say. Curaçao is good.'

He spoke of continents and countries with the authority of a connoisseur.

'It is?' asked Just.

'Tax haven with liberal banking laws. For this it is best to use a company. Money comes in, money goes out. I have connection with one such. From there back to Switzerland. That is easy.'

Dr Liebel, sleek and deodorised, set his fingertips together. The gnome had spoken.

'How much will this cost?' Just asked.

'Each place is 5 per cent. Also my fee is 5 per cent.'

Just told him the price was acceptable and the accountant wrote in small neat capitals on the back of his card:

Krauser Holdings Limited
Account Number 117 AD 482
Federal Bank
Grand Cayman

'This is where you direct the transfer. You will telephone me, please, on the date it moves from Holland. To confirm, yes?'

Just said, 'There is really only one other question.'

'Yes, Mr Law,' Dr Liebel enquired politely. 'What is this?'

'How do I trust you?'

The accountant placed his plump pink hands neatly on the desk top.

'I tell you how it is in Switzerland,' he said. 'Our banking business is based 95 per cent on the money of foreign nationals. As citizens we are controlled by Swiss law. But operations that our clients are doing nearly always are illegal in their own country, and they have no recourse if something is going wrong. So, as everything that we are doing is unprotected and unlawful, our most essential tool is our honesty. We are dull and honest, Mr Law, and this reputation is precious to us. Without it we get no more work and then be poor. So you see honesty is necessary. I enjoy my work and my life. If I steal your money then I must go away and start again somewhere else, when here I am only one hour from skiing. Does this answer your question, Mr Law?'

'Elegantly,' said Just. 'I shall not ski against you either, Dr Liebel. You would certainly be faster.'

'Yes, I am heavier,' stated the accountant with complacency. 'This is an advantage, I think.'

He returned from Zurich by way of Paris.

He stayed at the Raphael where he was known and where, big boss spender attended by a corporate entourage, his casual manner of dress had come to be accepted.

That evening he dined at the Brasserie Lipp, alone and well. There was a pleasant sense of occasion about the meal, the private celebration of an epoch drawing to its close.

He had considered bringing Marianne with him on this trip, for by now she passed nights and weekends in his company – though their liaison remained secret – but he had chosen not to do so. With her an evening was delight but, while he made the final arrangements for his disappearance, he wanted nothing to divert his judgement or distract that serene analysis which unrolled through his mind in the course of a dinner alone.

For digestif he drank a single brandy, lit a cigar, then strolled back to his hotel through the night-time city. He retired and slept soundly.

Next morning he was five minutes early for his appointment with Dr Benoit in the Boulevard de Courcelles.

His offices were more luxurious than Dr Liebel's, containing a prettier secretary and separate waiting room, with broad hints of good taste suggested in the furnishing and pictures. The style of decor in both establishments was the same however: Professional, Successful. From examination of their rooms, it would have been impossible to divine what either man actually did for a living.

Similar also was their mode of dress. Both wore striped suits, soberly unostentatious, the Frenchman's marginally more modish in its cut.

Indeed, reflected Just as he was shown in to the consulting

room, these men performed the same role. Purveyors of topical skills, both were servitors to the Rich, expert and discreet.

'May I ask,' enquired Dr Benoit across a Louis XIII table, 'may I ask who recommended you to come to me?'

'A film star who prefers to remain anonymous,' lied Just.

'Ah yes, whose picture has recently received such magnificent critiques?'

'Exactly,' confirmed Just, with no idea who this might be, and watched the doctor jot a neat notation in a leather folder, then resume the scrutiny of his client's face.

'And what exactly has brought you to consider surgery?'

'Age,' said Just.

Casting a commercial, he would have chosen the man opposite to endorse a fine whisky or to sell cigars. Only a year or two older than Just, comfortably sleek, hair streaked by grey, he might have been an ambassador or a superior government official whose measured cadences indicated a fondness for his own voice.

'My job in medicine is to assist people to live *within* their skins, to accept and come to terms with themselves. Wherever possible I recommend them *not* to have surgery.'

A likely tale, thought Just as the winter sunlight gleamed on Dr Benoit's gold watch. He said, 'But I am dissatisfied with my skin. In the mirror when I see this lined and sagging face, I do not recognise it. It is not me at all, for inside I am twenty-seven years old.'

Unsmiling, Dr Benoit made a further note upon his pad. Did it read 'vanity' wondered Just, or was it a reminder to order flowers for his wife?

Three portraits hung upon the walls, a woman and two men, meticulously executed.

'Yours?' he asked.

'A hobby of mine.'

'A steady hand,' he observed, and the doctor taking this to be a compliment, acknowledged the remark with the slightest bow.

'You are what age, Mr Law?'

'Forty-seven,' said Just, 'and what I want is removal of these creases around the eyes and a general lifting. It would suit me if this could be done as soon as possible.'

'To be twenty-seven again, that is not possible. But it will give you the appearance of five to eight years less.'

'Also the nose,' said Just.

'But the nose is good.'

'Too long,' said Just. 'Too curved.'

'Perhaps. But I must inform you there is a clinical as well as an aesthetic effect. Remedial surgery frequently is followed by a period of elation, which then sometimes is succeeded by depression as we realise that internally we remain the same, with imperfections which no operation can remove. Also relationships within the family and with our associates can alter. The way they see you is changed. I must tell you that if I perform the operations which you suggest, you will not only look younger but also a very different and perhaps not recognisable man.'

Just held back a grin. Inside himself a little man – aged twenty-seven – cartwheeled and skipped in glee, then wildly laughed.

He said, 'I am at your disposition. What is the earliest date you can give me, doctor?'

That afternoon, he bought a suit and two silk shirts from the St Laurent Boutique. They were the first decent clothes he had purchased in more than two years, and he regretted keenly not being able to wear them from the shop. The box which contained them went into a luggage locker at the Gare du Nord, together with 100,000 francs in cash, the .32 revolver he had acquired in Soho, and an International Driving Licence which lacked a photograph for its owner, Mr Michael Law, had not yet entered the world.

But all was prepared and ready now for him to do so.

Twenty One

'Lucky', the mechanic in Lezat had called him; he had been lucky. Staring at the river, Just recalled the day before and Marianne's accident with the Ferrari.

The conclusion was inescapable: someone was trying to kill him. But who? There could be only one answer to that, the man who had been asking after him at the paper shop, the same man with bouffant hair who had photographed him on the way to the Colombe d'Or. He had not imagined that incident, despite what Marianne thought. That had not been paranoia; his instinct had been correct all along.

It fitted too well, the enquiries, the photograph . . . He no longer matched his description. Whoever had hired that man to track him down had wanted to be sure. Now they were.

This afternoon Marianne had wandered off somewhere but he did not fear for her. It was him they were after, him and the money.

He was glad she was not here. He needed an opportunity to think this through alone. He was on edge and tense in her company. He admitted this to himself; to the girl he gave no sign.

She could be remarkably unpleasant when she chose. Not intelligent, expressing her thoughts clumsily in limited jargon, nevertheless she had a guttersnipe's gift for repartee. Urchin face white and sharp with anger, her words could sting.

He pondered upon this as he sat in his overgrown bower above the pool. Often there was a separateness about her now, a moony detachment of manner. It was not hostility but a mood which excluded him, whose nature he could not determine.

He was confident that he could handle it. He was experienced in the whims and capricious vagaries of adolescent girls. He could treat them with tolerance and understanding and wait for them to pass. Brief storms in a summer; there was a certain price to be paid for everything.

It was a warm June morning yet Just, legs crossed and book resting upon his knee as he reclined in the Bognor Corporation deck-chair, wore a light suit in Prince of Wales check and a silk shirt open at the neck. Good clothes were an affectation which gave him pleasure, yet, though now overdressed by modern standards, he was not too warm. After the years in Belida, it took fierce sun to heat his blood.

A change might do the trick, he thought. Yes, that might solve it, but it must be circumspect. The gun was on him now. He had to be vigilant and alert to everything, especially the unexpected. Yes, a change, he thought, a move, but it needed to be worked out very carefully . . .

'I can't see HER,' Henry said.

He sat at the window with a pair of binoculars raised to his eyes.

'What's *he* doing?' asked Yvonne.

She was on a sofa in the centre of the shadowed room, for bright light troubled her eyes.

'I can see his shoulder and the back of his head, part of it. Then his foot, white shoes. He's reading a book.'

'He's always smart,' said Yvonne.

'Smart,' her husband repeated, as his mouth twisted bitterly. 'Yes, that's the word for it, I'd say. A smart Alec, that's what *he* is. A jumped up scheming nobody!'

'You don't *know*, dear,' Yvonne observed mildly, 'not for sure.'

'Ha! I do,' Henry answered with conviction. 'I can smell it a mile off. Oh yes, I know. *Always*.'

'But where is *she*?' Yvonne demanded. 'She's always with him.'

'She's not on the usual rock. I wasn't watching when they came down. She may be lying further in.'

'Naked,' said Yvonne. 'You can bet she's lying where *he* can see her. The little hussy.'

'Slut,' said Henry. 'She's no better than he is.'

Marianne, however, was not by the pool.

On the other side of the valley, she walked toward the bridge which spanned the river two hundred yards below the mills.

Well-built little schoolgirl in jeans and scuffed sneakers, droop-shouldered, she slouched homeward, kicking a pebble ahead of her down the slope. She carried a plastic bag which swung full and heavy in her listless hand. She had been collecting snails.

Just lay back, idle in his deck-chair and turned his face up to the sun. He felt the heat of summer seep into his skin. It warmed and cheered his being.

Someone wanted to kill him. Well, it was not the first time that had been the case. And this joker was no expert. To fix the steering on the car ... Really! Just's lip curled. What a method! The fellow had been watching late-night movies.

Still, he must be very careful. It would be best to get out. Everything indicated a sudden well-timed move. That would solve the problem of the girl as well. She was bored here. It was perfectly understandable; she needed a change. So did he.

He knew how to handle Marianne. Her tantrums, her occasional *longeurs*, were unimportant, he told himself. These shows of spirit were part and parcel of what captivated him; rogue quality, infinitely preferable to that dumb obedience which too often in the past had finally disqualified the object of his lust.

It was a question of *dressage* ...

Slitted against the sun, his half-closed eyes had been looking out across the pool into the forest on the further bank. With a sudden start he realised that he was staring at a face among the trees. The boy.

In the same instant he heard her footfall on the path behind him.

At the window Henry stiffened.

'It's HER.'

His hands tightened on the binoculars. Head and neck pecked forward, straining into the magnified circle of view. His breath came tight. Blotches of crimson discoloured his cheeks.

Marianne tossed the bag upon the ground and flopped down at his feet.

Just's heart was beating unpleasantly fast. He made the yawn of a waking man and controlled the slow ease of his lazy smile.

'What have you been up to?'

'Walking. I've got some shells.'

A spark of anger flared in him. Shells! At a thousand feet above sea-level! This was not stupidity but contempt; she was indifferent to whether he believed her lie.

She sprawled on the ground, mocking him with duplicity. Now she jumped up urgently to her feet.

'Cor. Got to go.'

His hand shot out and grabbed her wrist.

'No!'

She tugged away.

'Let me go, Bob. I must go to the lav.'

'Don't call me Bob. Here!'

Threshing in his grip, she cried out, dancing.

'Let me go, Mike. I got to go. Honest.'

'Here!' he ordered.

Her eyes widened as she understood his meaning. She twisted from him.

'No, Bob.' She coloured hotly.

'Here!' His hand pulled her down.

'No. Please, Bob. No. Let me go. Please!'

On a level with his, her eyes pleaded with him.

'Take them down.'

After a second her hand went to her belt. She shifted awkwardly, crouched captive in his grip.

'Please don't make me. Please!'

'Now.'

She cried. 'No. I *can't*. No!'

His left hand swung across and slapped her face. She gasped. A shudder ran through her. The next moment he heard the rattle on the leaves between her feet. Her eyes dropped away from his in shame and she moaned.

He held her there. Then, he dragged her forward. Losing her balance, she fell upon her knees. He paused to free himself and pulled her to his lap. She offered no resistance. Her mouth opened and she took him blindly. He twisted his fingers in her hair. He drew her head up and felt her lips clasp to keep him. He let go his hold and she clamped her slobbering mouth around him and sucked with perverse greed.

His blood was heavy. The taut wire tightened across his nerves, and his loins were already close to bursting.

His look had been down, at the blonde cascade spilled across his thighs, delicate rim of shell pink ear and swollen engorging cheek; now he raised his eyes and directed them across the river.

The boy had stepped out from his hiding place.

He was younger than Just had thought on the two occasions he had glimpsed him among the trees. He looked no more than seventeen years old, of medium height, with strong shoulders and stocky peasant's body yet his face was oddly delicate, fine featured and olive skinned beneath jet black curls.

Spanning the ravine, Just's eyes locked with his. He felt the surge start in him, the great wave swell and begin to topple.

The boy stood, as though hypnotised by Just's unblinking and exultant stare. He saw a flicker start in the man's face, the mouth sag and a spasm shake him as the white wave broke within and flung him forward, bending over the head in his lap so that, momentarily, the figure in the deck-chair and the girl who kneeled beside it became one.

The movement severed the look between them. When the man's head fell back against the chair, the eyes had closed and freed him. The face was turned away into shadow, but in the full blaze of the sun the greying hair had turned to white.

Just's eyes were shut. Again, he had been looking out across the river and had not turned to glance behind him. Again, he did not spot that flash of light in the window of the upper mill as Henry's binoculars caught the sun in a wink, suddenly extinguished. Again, the warning went unseen.

Twenty Two

In London it had been the 31st March, a Monday night and the eve of April's Fool.

In the bathroom of his Mayfair apartment Just shaved off his beard. Stripped to the waist his body was white now; no trace of tan remained but his stomach was hard and flat still. Swimming had kept his muscles firm.

No only did he see but actually felt himself change as he watched his face emerge. A sense of quickening and of rebirth and promise. His pulse shifted to a faster pace. His nerves sharpened.

Through the open door came the sound of music from the living room.

'I need to laugh ... And when the sun is out I got something I can laugh about ...'

The Beatles. He had first heard that number in New York, in Elaine's the night he had scored the money to start Belida. The Mersey sound had taken over the world. Then London swung and Fashion looked to Britain. In New York it was the Season of the Englishman. All had been on his side when the music played and that night his luck was running.

He gathered up the swatches of hair which clogged the basin, then refilled it with cold water and bent to plunge in his face. Holding his breath he opened his eyes in the milky light. Two years ago he had been able to last a minute and a half under the dazzling water below the coral reef.

AIYB—H

Soon he would be free again. He raised his head and dried his face.

He sat at the dressing-table where the tubes and jars of cosmetics were laid out and started to make up his face.

He put on a pan stick base in two tones, the darker to cover the palled skin of his jaw, moulding it into the paler shade upon his cheeks. He saw the shadows softening, the flesh becoming smooth and youthful as he masked the lines of age. He applied a blusher to his cheeks – suddenly healthy now – then dusted his face with powder.

He worked upon his appearance with fine attention to detail. In half an hour he was satisfied with the face reflected by the mirror. He replaced his shirt, ran his fingers through his hair and entered the living room.

At the tape player Marianne turned and stared, fascinated.

'Wow!'

'Well, what do you think?'

'Man, it's neat. Pretty classy, I'd say. Incredible.'

'Right. Let's go.'

He wore a trench coat, collar turned high and his chin tucked low as they crossed the pavement to the waiting taxi.

'Victoria,' he directed.

It was seven-thirty in the evening, the station quiet now after the commuting crowds' departure, its grimy glass roof arched above a resonant cavern of dead air and desolation.

The girl stood outside while he entered the booth, drew the curtain, slipped a tenpence in the slot. He composed his face ... FLASH, to a smile ... FLASH, of casual ease ... FLASH.

They waited it seemed, much longer than three minutes before the damp strip of photographs edged out along the slide. And for some reason it was here, whilst loitering in this deserted station, that for the first time in this crooked enterprise he experienced the furtive thrill of criminality.

From the station they took a taxi back to the apartment.

There, he said, 'Put the Beatles on again.'

'Golden Oldies? Can't I help you?'

'No. I shan't be long.'

In the bedroom he checked all his things for the next day and packed his case. By the time he had finished it was filled to overflowing and only with difficulty did he close the lid.

When he came back into the living room the air was thick with the bonfire smoke of marijuana. Her back to him she was dancing to the music, feet set motionless and her slender body shaking to the supple rhythm.

'I feel good ...

In a special way ...

I'm in love and it's a sunny day ...'

She giggled as he set his hands upon her waist; without turning she danced more wantonly, bending to shake and twitch her narrow rump into his groin, suddenly to straighten and pull away, elusive and demure as his jiving feet pursued and, separate, both stepped courtship on the beat till her movement slowing to a languid bump and grind he laid fingers to her waist, unloosed her belt and, still dancing, rasped slowly wide the zip, eased his hands around her buttocks and drew down her jeans ...

He picked her up and carried her in his arms to the bedroom, there to unwrap her twitching body, lose himself in her moist heat, drown in the impure depths of her sweet and tender wetness as he shared her quivering sigh and died too on her final expiring gasp.

It was better than it had ever been. She curled against him like a soft and trustful puppy. He was at peace, both extinguished and renewed.

'The breath of young girls restores the blood.' But the effect was more radical than that. It was better than ever. He felt an entirely new and different person, impressionable and hopeful, overflowing with excitement and delight. He felt reborn.

And he was not even dead yet.

He was up at first light, alert and wide awake to file his flight plan on the telephone and check the weather:

'London four octas; strato cumulus at 3000; wind 5000 feet 270°. Weather improving and South of England and Amsterdam is CAVOK.'

He made coffee, brought a cup to the room and shook her out of sleep as she groaned in protest.

'Get up! Move! There's villainy to do.'

Complaining bitterly she stumbled from the bed with exquisite pouting mouth and eyes blurred by sleep.

Without a beard his face looked unfamiliar in the mirror; without make-up just as old, but changed. He squeezed gum on to the fine hair netting of another beard and fitted it to his jaw, confronted again his too-usual self.

She dawdled in the kitchen only partly dressed as she made more coffee.

'Move!' he ordered. 'Wake up. Get straight.'

He handed her the strip of photographs and watched her put it in her pocket.

'What have you to do with that?'

'I remember,' she protested, sulking.

'What?'

'Give it to Roger in the French Pub.'

'At what time?'

'Twelve o'clock.'

'And if he's not there?'

'Go back at six.'

For a second he was irritated with her sloth, for he was keyed tight by excitement. Still, there was reason; he had more riding on this than she. Greater risk and more to do.

He telephoned a taxi.

She trailed behind him down the stairs.

'You know when to wait for my calls?'

'Sure I do.'

He put her in the cab. She pulled down the window.

'Good luck, Bob,' she said.

He kissed her and sent her off. He threw his flight bag and suitcase into the back of the Bentley and started.

It was a chill grey morning, a dull sky, the city streets uncrowded at this hour. He saw them with the same freshness of eye and sharp detail as a voyager returning after years of absence. Familiar yet strange. It was the last time he would pass this way, the last time he would drive this car which gave him so much pleasure.

There was not the faintest shadow of regret in the way he felt.

At the airport he left the car in the usual parking area. The attendant recognised him as he came out.

'Away for long, Mr Just?'

'Till tonight.'

'I'll see you then. I'm here till seven.'

Just pressed a pound note into his palm.

'I'll buy you a drink, Bill.'

'I thank you, squire. Be seeing you.'

Let us hope not, thought Just. Goodbye Bill, forever. Then he went by the Control Tower to tell them he was off and to check the weather.

The morning was appreciably brighter when he walked out on to the field, the wrack of clouds lifting and blue sky showing through.

Mr Benson, the Customs man, drove out to meet him at the plane.

'*Another* business trip,' he said. 'Where to this time?'

'Holland. This aircraft is chock full of invisible exports.'

'I wouldn't mind *your* job,' Mr Benson remarked.

'It always looks better from the outside,' Just told him.

He started up, measured the oil level and ran his checks, then taxied over to the pumps and filled up with duty-free petrol. He handed over his credit card; when the man came back with the receipt he helped him push the nose round.

In the plane again he switched on the master switch, started one and then the other engine. He ran them up to check the oil pressures then throttled back and switched on the radio:

'Tower. This is Foxtrot Tango. Do you read, over?'

The tower came back at once.

'Foxtrot Tango; reading you fine. Go ahead.'

'Foxtrot Tango; request taxi clearance.'

He released the brakes and eased the throttle forward till the plane began to move then cut back on power. At the holding point he set the handbrake, ran the port engine to 1800, checked for mag. drop, throttled back to 1500, checked the variable pitch, then back to idle at 1000. He repeated on the starboard engine, ran through the take-off checks, set the compass and fastened his harness. He called the Tower.

'Foxtrot Tango; request back track.'

He checked the empty sky, gunned an engine into the turn.

'Foxtrot Tango; ready for take-off.'

'Foxtrot Tango; clear take-off.'

He spanned his hand across the twin throttles and pushed them forward. The tarmac raced past below and became a blur as he gathered speed. In his hands he felt the aircraft tense, its wheels skim the earth. At 100 knots he pulled back on the control wheel and lifted off.

'Goodbye England,' he shouted to the speeding air. The clouds ripped in tatters from his wings and he soared up into azure light. He began to sing:

'I need to laugh ...
And when the sun is out
I got something I can laugh about ...'

He crossed London at 1500 feet then, clear of the control zone, went up to 3000 feet and flew straight and level on the compass.

The clouds were gone over the Channel. Far below the sea spread away in frozen wrinkles, a blue and shimmering symmetry of pattern.

Bearing 72°. 160 knots per hour.

The coast of Holland took form as a band of sepia haze.

He called Schipol on the approach frequency to report his position and request landing instructions. The controller's voice came back loud and clear in perfect English, telling him to come down to 1500 feet and report again over point Whisky. There the same clear voice cleared him for straight-in approach to the runway.

He was on the ground at 10.22. He parked and walked to Control where he filed his flight plan back to London and telephoned for refuelling. The truck was waiting for him when he got back to the plane.

Just went through Passport Control and Customs and officially entered Holland.

He travelled by taxi into Amsterdam. Over the last eighteen months he had come here several times to visit his money and talk to the bank. The last three occasions had been with Marianne, for to be seen with her in public in London was hazardous to his plan. Here they were anonymous and at ease in this waterborn ancient city whose canals were lined with gabled houses built by merchants, comfortably solid and well-to-do, and whose narrow lanes contained more dim and cosy bars than any place in the world.

This time, as always, he was struck by the youth of people in the street. It was no longer possible to identify nationality through dress. Here the majority were clothed, as Just, in jeans and sweaters. He approved, though today he was impatient to abandon this uncharacteristic mode of dress which he had worn for far too long.

He surveyed the view from the taxi window with a delighted grin. He felt liberated and extraordinarily well. Going straight never had suited him, he reflected, any more than jeans.

He paid off the taxi at the corner and walked up the one-way Keizersgracht, climbing the steps of 203 to enter the Algemene Bank Nederland.

The Dutch were much less secretive than the Swiss in the manner of their business. Mr Lubbers sat at his desk in an open plan annexe off the tellers' area. He saw Just and waved him over.

'Sit down, yes please. You had a good trip?'

'Grand. You like to fly?'

'Only in big planes. Even then not so much.'

Lubbers' blond hair was thinning. He was a young man and he had been in banking all his life. He said: 'I have all ready per your instruction on the telephone yesterday.'

He reached for a slim folder on his desk, opened it to expose a single document which he handed to his client.

'Yes. You sign here, please.'

Just did so.

'You will come with me,' said Mr Lubbers, rising and beckoning one of his colleagues.

He led Just downstairs to the vault where a guard stood aside from a cage door so Lubbers might unlock it and take his party through. There, the two bank officers moved to separate spy holes which contained the numbers of the paired locks. With professional curiosity, Just stepped in close and watched their fingers on the hidden dials. It would be a blind bitch to blag he thought, and noisy as hell, as the door swung open.

Lubbers stepped into the safe and returned with an aluminium suitcase which he handed to Just.

'You will check this.'

Just said, 'Mr Lubbers, I know you better than that.'

The banker made a pleased nod then led the way upstairs.

'I have asked our telephonist to call for you a taxi.'

'Thank you,' said Just.

Lubbers escorted him to the door and held out his hand.

'Goodbye, Mr Just.'

They shook hands and Just turned down the steps and crossed to the waiting taxi.

Only for three additional, not strictly necessary seconds did Lubbers watch the man in the trench coat cross the pavement and enter the cab, slinging the suitcase negligently in beside him.

The Dutch guilder was a free currency. It was not his business to ask why Just wanted to take away 1.66 million in a suitcase. But it was only human to be curious.

'Dam Square,' Just said to the driver.

He left the cab at the Royal Palace, then walked across the square to the Grand Hotel Krasnapolsky and took the taxi at the head of the line.

'Central Station,' he instructed.

He bought a ticket to The Hague. Suitcase in hand he walked through the tunnel to wait with twenty or thirty other passengers on platform 7A.

Aboard the train, alone in a first-class compartment, he watched the flat winter landscape slide by with satisfaction. The penultimate journey of Robert Just. Beyond the window flicked past the trim terraced houses of men who knew who they were and would remain so.

He studied the sky. Bright and blue, 20 per cent cloud, a heavier bank of shadow forming in the west below the sun. Weather was true to forecast.

At The Hague he took a taxi to Banque Worms. Mr Lense could not be found for a minute then came bustling in to the private room where Just had been shown.

He glanced at the case.

'Ah yes. This is the matter, yes?'

He touched a bell as Just swung the case onto the table and snapped it open.

Three tellers appeared to count the money. They set out the stacks of notes then dealt them between them, seated in line at the long table. Their deft fingers rifled through the bundles, passed and exchanged them, double and treble-checking, players in a game whose cards were all the same.

Mr Lense gave Just a sheet of paper.

'Our fee. Transfer and handling charge. These are shown on the receipt.'

Just nodded and signed.

Ten minutes later he walked out, the empty suitcase light in his hand. On the way to the station he filled it with forty newspapers. He took a taxi from the rank, throwing the case into the trunk.

'Schipol,' he said.

As they drove out of town he studied the wide expanse of sky spread out over the desolate frozen fields. A bank of haze hid the west but the weather held fine. So far the angels were holding off.

At the airport, Charlie, the Surinama customs man who had been there that morning was still at the private flying desk.

'You taking out anything then?' he asked.

Just held up the case.

'Ten kilos top grade fine Chinese brown.'

'Wrong way, Mr Just. Dat's what you bring *in*. What goes out of here is herawn.'

'Never had a head for dealing,' he said, and walked through. Apart from the customs officer the hall was empty. No one else was going out at that time. Charlie would recall the conversation later when they came asking. He would remember the aluminium suitcase.

It was 4 PM as he came out across the tarmac to the plane. The sun was down behind the band of haze which smeared the horizon on the west. The afternoon had ended.

Unlocking the door he stepped up into the chill cockpit. He belted the suitcase onto the seat beside him and glanced back to check that the bag he had brought from London was still in place.

He switched on and pressed the starter. The propellers turned painfully, kicked as the engines coughed and caught. He watched the needles on the twin oil gauges jerk up as the noise steadied and the motors ran smooth and sweet.

He put on his headphones and took up the microphone.

'Foxtrot Tango; to Tower. Request taxi clearance.'

The airfield was a desert sprinkled with snow, its pathways

dotted in coloured lights. In the distance, outside the main terminal, the high tailplanes of two jumbos reared against the failing sky.

He taxied into position behind a Sabena Caravelle at the holding point: he heard its captain ask permission, then watched it lumber on to the start line. The controller cleared it away and his own aircraft shook in the thunder of its afterburn as it barrelled away down the runway.

He gunned the motors and took the airplane into position, aiming the nose down the converging tracks of light.

'Foxtrot Tango; ready for take-off.'

Hand across the throttles, he thrust both forward. The plane quivered and gathered itself then shot forward to race down the path, a greyhound after Sabena's elephant.

The airspeed needle soared around the dial. The plane angled up and leaped toward the sky.

At maximum rate of climb he took her up on full power to 3000 feet. He set course on a bearing of 290°. He checked the fine lines which scored the map upon his knee and checked his watch. 16.27; it was a half-hour later than he had planned. Up here it was still day but below and ahead the sea was hidden under a bank of mist.

After one further glance at his map he switched over to automatic pilot and unfastened his seat belt.

He moved aft, then standing in the narrow aisle between the passenger seats, he undressed down to his briefs and socks. He unsnapped the locks of his London suitcase and started to unpack.

He took out first a waterproof compass which he strapped to his wrist before picking up the rubber trousers of a wetsuit. When he was lying down in the aisle a view framed between his feet of cockpit controls and the sky beyond and the small movements of the stick in automatic hands.

On his bedroom floor in Farm Street he had timed putting on the trousers at a minute forty, then calculated twice that. Supine in the confined space between the seats of the plane it took longer. On his feet again, the jacket was easier. Zipping it up he moved forward, carrying the hood and fins and the waterproof float bag which contained his clothes. He set these ready.

He eased himself stiffly into the pilot's seat and checked his course against the map. He throttled back the airspeed and put on half-flap.

Then he stood up again, moved back and arranged the two suitcases, one empty now and the other filled only with newspapers. Bracing himself against the hull he undid the door. The catch clicked open and an icy blast of air knifed into the cabin. He put his foot against the door and forced it open. The plane lurched and the floor angled as a frozen gale howled through the gap, then the automatic pilot caught it and levelled out. His hold on the seat relaxed. Swiftly he shoved the cases into the void. Withdrawing his foot, the door slammed shut in the slipstream. He did not refasten its lock.

Before returning to the pilot's seat he passed a careful glance over the cabin. He saw nothing untoward, nothing he had forgotten.

He sat down. He donned fins and helmet. Setting clumsy heels on the bar he switched out the automatic pilot and took control.

Height 3000 feet. Airspeed 110. The sky was clear. Below stretched an endless floor of level cloud.

He checked course and watch, pressed the start button on the timing hand and began the countdown. He eased forward the stick and started to descend. Four minutes later he entered the cloud layer, losing all vision. He took her down to 600 feet before levelling out, still in the same opaque cocoon of sombre grey. It was evening here and the menace of see-nothing night. No sign of the sea.

He consulted map and watch, every few seconds glancing at the instruments to check that he was maintaining height and still flying straight and level. Up, down, sideways, from the windows all directions looked the same.

Well ... he thought, his mouth dry. On his watch the hand was coming up to time. He looked once more carefully at the map then set it aside.

He pressed the control wheel forward. Swirling up at him the cloud shifted and eddied, shredding past. Straining his eyes he peered ahead down the delusive tunnel.

Two hundred feet. He was losing height as slowly as he could, yet the descent was terrifying. Suddenly the darkness thickened. His hands twitched back on the stick. At the same instant he saw the sea.

It looked horrible. Black, cold and ghastly. The dark waves flecked with spume in a winter wind. Fear flooded him at the thought of what he had to do. For five full seconds he knew he could not make it.

He took a deep breath. He eased the airspeed back to 110, applied full-flap and took the plane down to skim the waves. He was hyper-alert now, tensed on the controls, sensible to the slightest shift of flight. He came down as low as he dared and kept there rushing perilously above the water for dangerously too long.

Ninety-five was stalling speed. He throttled back till he was on the line. He glanced back momentarily to check the position of the door. Then he cut the engines.

Good-bye, Just. Cross your fingers, he said aloud. Here's hoping and pray to God.

She held for endless seconds, clinging bravely to the air with the heart failed, sensing and fighting the clasp of death. Then she staggered, stumbled on the lack of speed, tilted and pitched forward.

The horizon reared. The waves leaped up to meet him. At 90 mph the little plane slammed into the solid surface of the sea.

Twenty Three

'No, we shall not have Henry and Yvonne to dinner,' said Just.

The day was blazing hot. Summer was fully here now. The fireflies had perished with the cherry blossom. In the mountains the nights were cool but throughout every day the sun reigned high and hot in a brilliant sky.

'But I've already asked them,' said Marianne, 'for Friday.'

From the bower where he sat in the deck-chair, with the girl curled at his feet wearing a bikini, he looked down over the rock-pool. Much less water was coming down the chute now; away from the turbulence below the fall the surface was still and clear. Two dragonflies had made this place their territory. Each day he watched them patrol straight and level up the current, hovering on shimmering crystal wings, at the last moment before they reached the waterfall banking and swooping downwind to their starting points, from there to beat up again on parallel course as they hunted for surface insects in the same grid pattern as aircraft conduct a sight and radar search.

'Why? What for?' he demanded in irritation, bringing back his mind from other, more serious considerations.

'Why did you see them anyway?'

'I had to see them.'

'Why?'

'The electric fire in the bedroom's packed in. They've promised us another.'

'Why did you ask them to dinner?'

'I sort of had to. They asked us for a drink this evening.'

He fought to control his bad humour.

'I told you. I don't want to become friends. Once we do they'll be round our necks the entire time.'

She promised, 'I'll see they don't become friends.'

'Anyway, what are you going to cook for them?' Just asked, and she answered, 'Snails.' Her face was expressionless.

Just went up to have drinks at the old couple's that evening with great reluctance. It seemed ridiculous. He had not gone through all that trouble and retired here for this. He had just spent two years acting. It was absurd to find himself still doing things he did not want to do and seeing people he did not want to see. With one and a half million Swiss francs hidden here, and an assassin roaming the area with a contract to kill him, the situation was grotesque.

He did not mind being rude. He did not care if he offended them. But Marianne had accepted their invitation and it seemed important to her that they should go. He went to please her.

'Poor old things,' she remarked as they climbed the steep path to the upper mill. 'They're really cut off here. It's nice of you to come.'

'No deed of Christian charity goes unpunished,' observed Just as he trudged up the path behind her.

For poor expatriates in the South of France, Sunday afternoons are celebrated on Tuesday. The newspapers are second hand.

The Observer and *The Sunday Times* were always dropped in by Brigadier Groves on his weekly trip down to the English library in Nice to change his books. Henry and Yvonne always had a roast that day, even during the worst times, and a bottle of wine with lunch, and then Nescafé while they read the papers.

Yvonne tended to nap these days, but Henry read them all with concentrated attention. Apart from a few letters this was the only contact with Home. What he read did not make him nostalgic; it made him livid. Eighty per cent of the stories moved him to rage. Yet to spend a Tuesday without the Sunday papers was wretched.

Yesterday they had settled down after lunch and Yvonne's head was already nodding over the Magazine section when she was startled out of her wits by a harsh discordant cry. Jerking awake, she saw her husband reared into the page, his face white, clenching the edges of the Business section in his fists.

For several seconds Henry gazed wildly at the text. Then he rushed forward and thrust the paper under her nose.

Woken so abruptly, Yvonne could make neither head nor tail of what she was supposed to be looking at. Henry's finger jabbed at a photograph.

'Well?'

Yvonne saw a bearded man with long hair stepping into a Bentley.

'That!'

A close-up of the same bearded man. Yvonne felt at a loss. She had no idea what she was supposed to say. She glanced at Henry doubtfully and, meeting his fierce demanding stare, back to the headlines of the print for inspiration:

IN SUCCESS, DOWNFALL CHAMPAGNE COMPANY WAS A DEBT-RIDDEN HOUSE OF CARDS.

BENTLEY, PRIVATE PLANE AND THE DEATH OF A HIGH FLYER.

'Well?'

Yvonne felt weak and helpless.

'I don't know what you mean, dear.'

'You don't know what I *mean*? Those don't remind you of anyone?'

She looked at the photographs in desperation.

'No, dear. Honestly they don't.'

Henry's hands crushed the paper.

'I'd recognise those shifty eyes anywhere. And look at the way he stands getting into the car.'

Yvonne strained to see resemblance.

'Yes, well ... I *think* I see what you mean.'

Yvonne sent him to fetch a magnifying glass. They spent all afternoon studying the photographs; reading the article; poring over the photographs again, and re-reading the article.

At the end Yvonne still was not sure. But Henry was ninety-nine per cent convinced it was.

Yet it seemed impossible for it said in the paper that he was dead.

Just sat where he was placed and accepted the glass of sweet sherry he was given.

The rapport between Marianne and the old couple surprised him. Manners were not her forte yet the three of them began an animated conversation immediately.

He had noticed the English papers beside the chair when he sat down. Up to a month ago he had bought and studied them daily but, after the report of his death and the plane's wreckage being found, which he had read while still in the nursing home in Paris, there had been nothing.

Music, they were discussing. He was amazed at her interest in songs popular twenty and thirty years before she was born.

'You mean you've got these sounds recorded on *seventy-eights*,' she exclaimed. 'Wow, that's *something*!'

Twittering like birds, the old pair led her off ceremoniously to view the collection. It was natural for him to pick up the top-most paper. How badly the Business section was mauled, he noticed. The by-lines hit him the instant he turned the page.

'WE HAD ABSOLUTE CONFIDENCE' SAYS LORD MORAR.

HOW IT WAS DONE

He started.

'The what ...' he asked, 'I'm sorry ... the what?'

He had no idea what Yvonne had called to him from across the room where the three of them crouched at a cupboard.

'I'm so sorry, I was reading. But there's absolutely no reason why you should. I'll buy a new fire.'

'My dear man, the extravagance,' said Henry.

'Why on earth *should* you? There's a nearly new gas one which *belongs* to your place. We'll put it back tomorrow. A much better one than the electric.'

Henry had not seen the action made. He had been with the others sorting through records in dusty sleeves, and he had seen no reaction pass on his face when Just read the article and he thought then for the first time that he was wrong.

Even after that, though he watched covertly from where they were he had not seen Just's action. Certainly Just had asked if he might take the papers but, 'We haven't read them yet ourselves,' Henry objected.

He had seen Just rise from the chair and take out a cigar, uncap and light it, wander to the window and back to the table. And then, kneeling with the records scattered all around them on the floor, Henry called out to help himself to another drink and had seen him pour it.

And then the girl was asking could she tape this, borrow and return it when they came to dinner on Friday. Then they were all standing and talking together and Just was saying they were going out to dinner and all at once 'Goodnight. Goodnight' everyone was saying and then the door closed and the two of them were alone.

When Henry checked the newspapers he did not believe it at first. It was inconceivable that he should not have seen the action done. He went through them again. The Business section was definitely missing.

His face pinched sharp.

'It's gone! He took it!'

Such a strange mix of fear and triumph were in his voice.

'He did it. It's HIM all right. The *swine*. I was *right*, Yvonne. I told you so!'

Twenty Four

The plane dropped dead from a height of twenty feet, belly flat onto the water. The forward velocity was 90 mph. It felt like coming down onto solid concrete.

It struck, bounced away in a final breaking leap and then the trailing tail was grabbed by the sea so the plane pivoted in its sudden grasp and slammed into the waves.

The pilot did not know what happened then. The impact rammed the breath out of him. The safety harness cut off his blood. There was the noise of the world falling apart then black over him like a hood.

He could have been out only for seconds at most yet it was like coming to after a long and restful sleep. He was still in his seat and the plane canted at a dead angle, flopping in the waves.

Just felt so relaxed and detached from what was happening that he could happily have sat there for ever. Nothing mattered. Then a flicker of memory stirred in his brain: he was in the middle of something.

One wing was broken and the plane lay slantwise in the water. The floor tilted. Forcing himself to move he unbuckled his harness. He clambered up the slope toward the door. It was tight shut, the catch jammed. He put his finned foot to it and kicked out with his heel, feeling it yield and the sea wash in around his ankles.

Outside was broken water whipped by the wind and the swirl of wreckage. It was tempting to remain within the plane in that small safe place which he knew. But his home was breaking up;

each lurch between the waves brought the crash of something smashing and giving way. His movements were sluggish. It was as if he were drugged.

He sat on the tilted edge of the door and dropped out the float bag tied on a cord to his waist. He slid down into the water. A wave punched him in the eyes. The cold bit at his face and bare hands, then, as he pushed carefully through the flotsam there was the miserable seepage of chill water into his wetsuit.

A wing slapped the surface, threshing spray, then towered above his head to swat him. He kicked out with his fins and thrust away.

As soon as he was clear he turned to look back. The plane flapped and wallowed like a bird shot, downed but not yet dead. It cracked his heart to see it.

He raised his wrist and the compass needle danced before his eyes. Taking a deep breath he arched his body and dived.

Ten feet down it was quiet; silence and the slow heave of the ocean. He held his hand out and saw the luminous arrow steady, turned till it lay on North then took his course and went up at an angle. At the surface he rolled into a crawl stroke and did not glance back.

When he paused after a few minutes to check his direction there was no sign of the plane. He was alone in a small soaked capsule of awful night, dismayed to find he had swerved thirty degrees off course.

He went down to take another bearing and struck off strongly.

Just had always been a good swimmer and he was in fair physical condition. In setting up this operation the danger looked to lie in the actual crash, how she hit and whether she dug her nose in and went over. Those ten seconds after impact when all the hounds of hell tore loose in the cabin and anything could happen. The swim to shore had looked the least of it, the postlude.

But it was seven years since Just had dived in a Northern sea, it was the first of April in the English Channel and a short sea pitching him between its crests. It was later than he had planned and the tide was now running against him.

He slid low in the water, his head down, four strokes to a breath, face rolling to snatch air, four strokes to a breath, towing the float bag, four strokes to a breath in a steady monotonous rhythm with the muscles warming and settling to the count. Four strokes to a breath. Four strokes to a breath. After a while all thought went away and the pace became mindless, a steady crawl straight as a Roman road across the hills and valleys of the sea.

He had been going for over an hour before he sensed that the noise had changed. Below the slap and groaning of the ocean was another sound. The mechanical thud of a pulse beat. He brought his face up and trod water, looking about him terrified. There were no stars, no moon, nothing around him but liquid crests of foaming waves. Yet now he could feel the thumping in his whole body, the shockwaves going through him so near it was.

Then a red star swayed out of the night and suddenly the bright run of portholes were rushing past like a train thrusting aside the water and surging by. He was lifted and flung on his back, glissading down a rollercoaster slope which itself was rushing across the sea, twisting as he fell to somersault and dive, to go somewhere it was calm.

Which, fifteen feet down, it was, the dulling churn of the propellers receding into a cavern of silence. He stayed there and rested till his breath ran out. He came up for air then dived again to take his course. On the surface he kicked off again, the same regular crawl toward the invisible shore of France.

Half an hour later he paused to rest and check his watch. It was 11 PM. Still the same clammy womb around him, sea and sky the same and darkness everywhere. He pressed on.

Again it was his body which sensed the change in its primeval fishy origin perhaps, or else the density of its own liquid mass which echoed the shift and hurry at the sea's edge, as the depth shallowed and the waves shortened to dash upon the shore. He trod water, looking ahead, and distinguished the low line of the coast and a rocky beach chewed by white water.

He came on carefully, at the last moment flicked forward to ride the wave and career in, braking hard, and grabbed a slimy rock as the sea sucked him back where he belonged. He scrambled up, dragging his float bag, his hands grasping on seaweed. He crawled across sharp stones, reached a rim of driftwood and dead vegetation and sank to rest. He lay there only for a minute then undid the float bag and took out a towel, dry and comforting to the touch. He peeled off the rubber suit and rubbed himself vigorously and felt the heat quicken to the skin. He took out jeans, slightly damp, two sweaters, socks and shoes, and dressed in them quickly. He felt tired but only with that pleasant muscular fatigue which succeeds a day of skiing or an afternoon of tennis, best part yet to come, with the mind clear and body sated and at rest, the evening ahead and promise flavouring the air.

Waterproof bag containing his diving suit slung over the shoulder, he tramped toward a line of trees. He had thrown away the map, knowing it would be useless. He could be anywhere on a ten-mile stretch of coast. The sky was overcast but pale, either from a hidden moon or some nearby town reflecting from the cloud layer.

Coming out of the trees he saw fence posts. Ducking between the wires he found himself on a road. Left or right? He could be north or south of any one of three small ports. He set off toward the lighter section of the sky.

A car whirled past, ignoring his outstretched thumb; after a few minutes another passed, equally ungenerous or cautious of this soliciting nightwalker. And then the rackety noise of an ancient truck which passed him slowly, washing him in yellow light, and drew to a stop thirty yards up the road.

'*Vous avez des ennuis?*'

'No. Not so. You are going to town?'

The driver studied him.

'*C'est une drole d'heure de faire l'autostop.*'

'Slow and unsuccessful I agree,' said Just. 'I am going to the station. Can you drop me?'

'*Ça ne me derange pas trop*,' the man admitted.

Just jumped up and slammed the rusty door.

The driver was a peasant, he reckoned in the uncertain glow from the dashboard, at any rate not a talker; a man who took people as they were however wet and slick their hair or maybe just not noticeable in this light. They clattered between dark fields, then below sparse lights on the hideous outskirts of a town. Just asked:

'From the station, is it possible to go to Paris tonight?'

'There is always the last train,' the driver answered, 'for those who must.'

In the provincial station was that special feeling of cold night-time desolation as he waited on an empty platform. It depressed Just's spirits not at all. In this bleak chill was the very tumult of a birth: Michael Law was struggling toward the light of day. The train roared in and sighed to a hissing stop. He mounted and before he was seated it jerked away, pulling him through the night.

The occasional villages showed few lights. Outside was farming country, early to bed and rising with the beasts.

He had bought a second-class ticket, desiring to raise no curiosity as to how this ill-dressed stranger with but a single article of luggage should choose to travel first. The entire train had looked empty. In the compartment it smelled of stale and welcome heat. His jeans dried. He took off one sweater. The bad part was over now. He had got away with it. From here on was pure pleasure.

He felt wide awake, his muscles relaxed and warm, as after sex. He had never comprehended '*le petit mort*', the time which follows love. For him it had always been like this, all tension burned away and the mind's horizon vast and luminous with expectation.

The suburbs of Paris found him ready to go dancing. It was 2 AM and the bars still open. He was in the mood to drink and cruise, find casual company in the dubious world. He had foreseen this hectic urge which possessed him, as all criminals, after a daring venture was safely done and neither the Law's hand nor the finger of Death had crooked him; he had foreseen and planned for it. At the bottom of the grip which he retrieved from locker 17 in the Gare du Nord – stuffing in its place the rubber float bag – were two sleeping pills. He could not risk the unexpected, some inadvertence and a raided club finding him between identities with no documents or name and a tale which did not bear examination.

Outside the station was a whole street of dismal transient hotels. He chose the second, without reason for all looked the same and all certainly had this same grim concierge in her frowsty lair guarding the board of hook-hung keys.

She took one down and gave it him, requiring the money in advance.

'*Cinquante trois. Cinquème étage. Sur le droit.*'

All the cogs and antique machinery of the elevator were exposed, filmed with dust on oil. Carrying his bag he entered the rickety cage, pressed the button, lurched and shuddered upward.

His room was close and gloomy, its sepia wallpaper marked with stains. Unaffected by these dismal surroundings he checked the contents of his recovered bag.

He opened the window, forced up the metal bar and threw wide the shutter.

The night was thick with light saturating the sky from bright raucous streets. Its rooftops arranged in tiers and layers, the city of Paris stretched far as the eye could see and further, over squares and boulevards and gardens and then the river and the Left Bank and St Germain and Montparnasse and then Sceaux and Villejuif and the teeming suburbs of a vast unknowing and uncaring metropolis.

He was not in the womb still. Buffeted by the waves this unborn child had clawed his way toward the light and now reposed in seemless safety waiting to be born.

He closed the windows, took his sleeping pills and slept.

He woke with a headache and a blurred confusion as to where he was. He stared blankly at the tracery of cracks across the ceiling. His body ached as though beaten with rods.

He rang for coffee. A slatternly girl had slouched in and dumped his tray before he remembered he had been told to eat and drink nothing.

His skull was stuffed with cotton wool. He felt awful.

He left the hotel and in the street found a taxi and had it drive him to the clinic in Avenue Foch. He started to recover somewhat in the lobby. The entrance to Dr Get-Young-Again's magical parlour was a happy composite of Private Hotel and Nursing Home. The guests who came here were rich, one knew, and none had anything *really* wrong with them, nothing which 25,000 francs could not smooth out in a painless dreaming hour. The crisp nurse was reassuring in her smile.

'You are so early, Mr Law. I am desolated but your room is not ready yet.'

It was clumsy of him not to have realised this. In such five star-establishments the hour of check-out is fashionably late.

'Under the circumstances I cannot propose to you a coffee. In half an hour your room will be prepared.'

Just said, 'I'll take a walk.'

The avenue was bordered by trees growing from spacious pavements and, set well back from these, elegantly proportioned apartment blocks were guarded by uniformed doormen. He passed a nursemaid leading two small brisk girls to school, buttoned up and scarved in the weak spring sun. Here was the order of the well-to-do; in this, one of the lit places of the world, he sensed the serenity of their solid presence.

At the corner stood an automobile showroom. And as he looked through the plate-glass window and glimpsed the squat white body on fat tyres and the brutal bulk of the motor rammed up behind the cockpit he fell head over heels in love.

He lingered at the window, eyes on the emblem of a prancing horse. He had to buy that car.

It was exactly the sort of thing he had determined he would not do. He would *not* be tempted by those flashy toys and vanity and show which so often in the past had caused him enemies and led to trouble. He would not. And yet, he reasoned, when that adult infant Michael Law should first draw breath it would be as well if he were correctly outfitted for the world in which he was so soon to play a part, not burdened by possession yet not destitute of style – for that was the closest word for those tribal symbols whose ownership announced: 'Don't fuck with me. I'm rich. Respect!'

So it was not indulgence; it was merely provident. He entered to ask the price of the young salesman with the tweed suit and the one-of-us manner.

'Registered twenty-four months ago and thirty thousand kilometres on the clock. Sixty thousand francs, but this is not a car for anyone.'

'I'll have it,' Just said. 'I will pay for it now in cash and you will take care of the documentation and I shall pick it up in two days.'

'If that suits you,' said the young man without hint of surprise that such a sum should be produced from a leather grip by a man wearing jeans so very creased they looked as though he had taken a bath in them.

Just left the showroom with health and spirits fully recovered, in good morale for the hours which lay ahead. In his childhood no one had promised him anything, but he had learned the habit of offering presents to himself.

He checked into the nursing home and retired immediately to bed.

A half-hour later he was shot intravenously with premedication. Then Doctor Benoit passed on a bland and hazy visit.

When they came to get him he was thinking of Belida, of the fine time before the sky split and the angels let it come down. He was warm, languorous from the dope and remembering the beach and days with little playmates on the boat.

They slid him on a stretcher and wheeled him out. The ceiling of the corridor slipped by with the same detached clarity of detail found in that bright slowed world under the coral reef. Then a door and white figures shifting at the rim of his vision and Dr Benoit's voice murmuring out of the milky light commanding him to count . . . to count . . . and struggling to remember what came after five as the moment faded into black.

At 5.30 PM that same afternoon, Michael Law, born to adulthood, opened his bruised eyes on the first dawn of a new world.

Two days later he checked into the Crillon wearing a nose shield which masked him like a Moslem wife. Marianne joined him there, flying by way of Rome and Athens to confuse her trail in the event of any possible connection. Furnished with the passport which she brought him, Michael Law was complete. Born an orphan, he was a man with no antecedents. The child had no parents and a drowned man as his godfather. He was a newcomer to the world, who possessed nothing except a Ferrari, an eighteen-year-old mistress and rather over 600,000 dollars of stolen money.

Twenty Five

The morning after drinks with the old couple. Marianne was gone when Just awoke. He had slept badly and rose late. Whilst shaving he was irritated by the awkward position of the mirror. Its height was designed for a midget. 'Designed'; that word could hardly be applied to this bathroom. Cracked walls and stained tub on rusty feet, the place had been put together with second-hand materials at minimum cost. Indeed the shabbiness and discomfort of the whole house was outstanding.

What on earth were they doing here? *He* doing here?

A shift of colour in the view caught his attention through the window.

The dark water of the rockpool had turned to white. A sea of foam seethed slowly down the river. Marianne stood naked beneath the waterfall shampooing her hair.

In the bedroom he dressed, today even more carefully than usual, but was obliged to return to this only mirror to do his tie.

He regarded his reflection with detachment, studying the bronzed firm face, long hair one would have said prematurely grey, the casual stance in expensive clothes. The image was of a total stranger who bore no relation to the man inside. He felt chilly and grown old.

He did not go to the rockpool or tell her he was leaving. He went from the house, took the Ferrari and drove away. He had need of solitude to ponder. The man in the mirror had looked convincing. The boy in the paraffin truck stopped at the light sensed a pang of envy wondering who the driver was and what you had to do to own that car.

Its accoutrements became him but he had always been an interloper, an outsider to the world of thoughtless privilege. He had aped the manner of the rich, their ease and certainty and their disdain. He had fashioned a style superior to their own and used it to dupe and to exploit them. He had left them baffled and betrayed, punished and robbed blind.

For what? Just asked himself.

For a slouched and sulky adolescent. For a resentful schoolgirl whose body excited him to frenzy. For a lean-hipped slut driving him to madness by her indifference and, worst of all, conscious of her power.

He joined the autoroute and raced down the outside lane at 180 KPH with hands alert on the wheel and mind absent planning some way to tackle her duplicity.

'Man, sex with you is so *heavy*, such a major *scene*,' she had once said.

For her it was not so, was but a casual function, lightly done. She was neither vain nor greedy, he reflected, without ambition and indifferent to wealth. There was no detectable motive to her life which he could employ to discipline and control her. Satisfying her whim to buy the mills had pleased her – but for no longer or more deeply than the delight he had observed when she swam, stoned, beneath two dragonflies in the brilliant glare. Now that she owned it, the possession of the property seemed to mean nothing to her.

He had always understood his girls completely and, doing so, had been able to indulge and humour them. But there was a side to this one which eluded him, a steely spirit concealed within the puppy flesh. And its denial to him was leading him into problems. He found himself cast in a role which he did not care for. In the mirror he had looked at an ageing fool with the sham face of a younger man.

He slammed into low gear and braked behind an overtaking

car, then stamped savagely on the accelerator, swerving through the gap and gunning away with the motor howling and his nerves stung raw by the torment of her imagined lovers.

She knew it. And that was his great mistake of course, he had let his feelings show. Now she was excited by his anger. She teased his jealousy to the brink of violence.

He lipped the hill above Cannes and raced down the long curve behind the bay.

'*Nous voulons un roastbeef*,' said Yvonne. '*Un très bon*.'

'For how many persons?' the butcher in Lezat enquired.

'For two,' Yvonne answered.

The man trimmed it of fat. It was wrapped and handed them and she arranged it carefully in her string bag. When they were in the street Henry said, 'Now a chocolate cake!'

The display in the Patisserie was extensive: apple and apricot tarts, bons bons and elaborate confections tiered in icing. They had bought the chocolate cake at Christmas and knew it was superb but Yvonne was wistful for meringues, fluffy with whipped cream.

'We'll have both,' Henry announced.

'Both!'

She was aghast at the extravagance.

'Certainly. Chocolate cake *and* meringues. And after you've been to the hairdresser we'll buy champagne.'

'Champagne!'

'Certainly,' Henry said as a rare smile softened his harsh face, 'Champagne is a capital idea for this evening.'

At the end of the afternoon the bathers came off Tahiti beach in pairs and small groups and the old *plagiste* who had worked for Felix for years gathered up the mattresses and carried them in piles of six or eight draped over his shoulder to stack them away under cover for the night.

By that time Just was perfectly clear about what he had to do.

Under the beach shower he washed off the sand and oil which clung to his body. When he stepped out from the cold water and dried himself his skin felt tight and pleasantly burned from the day in the sun. He dressed in the changing room behind the restaurant.

On the walk to where his car was parked among the others beneath the split cane roof which shadowed the parking area he attracted no attention as the only man in suit and tie. At St Tropez nothing was eccentric.

He motored back slowly to the little port in a long line of cars on the country road. The solid column wound into town and the narrow streets closed around them.

He stopped on the cobbled slope down to the port to allow a Porsche to pull out from the kerb then slipped the Ferrari into the empty place. It was a good omen: for twenty summers it had been impossible to discover parking space in town.

Senequier was already crowded but he found a table on the terrace and ordered a campari tonic which took a long time coming.

The sun was low above the hills on the other side of the bay. It was six o'clock and the evening parade had begun. The cafés were filled with people; cars crossing the harbour square moved slower than at walking pace through the dense throng of pedestrians. None of the drivers were impatient for none were going anywhere. They were there to see and to be seen, to show off themselves and their vehicles and to attract. At pavement tables groups discussed the evening's plans, seeming not to watch for it would be crass to be seen avid or impressed. Just noticed a girl swerving toward him with a brilliant smile of recognition. He raised his face and returned her look as she pushed her way between the tables, at the last moment veering past crying, '*Comment allez-vous* you-all?' in broad Southern accent to a party of young Americans behind him.

Along the harbour front big yachts were moored tightly with less than a metre of water between them and in many cases rubbing fenders with their neighbours. In their normal lives their owners and occupants would have been horrified by such proximity. Yet, at this hour, at this place, such was the decree.

The canopied sterns of the yachts closed off the seaward side of the square. They were arranged with tables and chairs where the guests talked and laughed and accepted drinks served by white-coated stewards, the music playing and fresh ice chinking in the glass.

These decks formed a series of raised terraces giving onto the square, terraces which were both balconies and stages, for the people who lounged there playing backgammon or conversing with cigarette and glass in hand were at the same time spectators and performers of the pageant.

A vintage Rolls pushed through the mob on the quay attended by a trick cyclist, clown to a king. Two kings, young, plump and sleek. For an uneasy moment Just thought he saw the Morar brothers braying from within.

Whatever drive it was which motivated all these people, which impelled them here at this season to an obscure fishing port where they costumed themselves in faded jeans, boxing shorts or safari uniforms, as once at Versailles they had dressed as nymphs and shepherds, its force could be felt keen and tangible in the air. A high electricity had built up in the tight-pressed crowd with all this strut and show and fine display and Just felt his own blood quicken to the blatant promise of the evening.

These were the best people here now in early summer. Best, not in any moral sense but the brilliance of their cast. Later, in August, no one came to St Tropez, absolutely nobody – except the hundreds of thousands who knew no better.

Just turned his attention from the spectacle and raised his empty glass to the waiter for another drink.

At this same time in the upper mill Henry and Yvonne were dressing for dinner.

The roast was in the oven. Cork drawn, the claret 'breathed' in the temperature of the room. A bottle of champagne chilled in an ice-bucket upon an upturned tea chest.

In her bedroom Yvonne inclined to the mirror and studied her reflection. With a fingertip she rubbed away a smudge of blue eye shadow which smeared her cheek. She pulled back her lips in a vivid smile and inspected her teeth. Then she stood up. She opened her bedroom door, straightened her back and drew herself to her full height, chin up. At a slow gracious pace she moved down the corridor and into the living room where her husband was waiting.

Henry wore a dinner jacket. Holding the champagne bottle he used a fork to lever off the wire around its neck.

The cork flew off with a bang. The wine splashed into glasses.

'You look enchanting,' he said as he handed one to Yvonne.

'And so do you dear. Madly elegant.'

Now at the start of their evening, Henry and Yvonne raised their champagne glasses in a solemn toast.

It was 11 PM when Just turned onto the autoroute at Le Muy, coming from St Tropez. The night was brilliant with stars and a quarter-moon hung over the range of mountains toward the sea.

He drove fast and well. He had dined lightly, drinking only two camparis and a half-bottle of wine. He felt alert and wide-awake. And he felt about a million times better than when he had come past here this morning.

He knew how he was going to handle everything.

He had passed the whole day going through all of it, piece by piece, the girl and the matter of the man who was trying to kill him. The last did not make sense, he had decided. Assuming it was the Morar brothers who had hired someone to track him down, the last thing they wanted was his sudden death. That would mean their money was lost forever, for only he could lead them to it. No, they did not want to kill him but, rather, to scare him into flight, thereby betraying its location. They were trying to outsmart him. Well, that was dumb of them; guile was his trade, not theirs. They were unpractised in that skill, whilst it had been his profession, his life. If that was the name of the game, they had made a bad mistake for he was more adept at it than they.

It had to be that, Just thought. No professional hitman would have advertised his presence as this one had, spent so long and bungled the attempt. They were trying to scare him into a move, to make him run. So . . . he would not disappoint them. He would do just that, but it would be done by his strategy, not theirs . . .

Just heard the scream of its jets only a split second before he saw it – the lean white airplane hurtled across the road only a hundred yards in front of him, tilted like a falling dart into the forest.

Instinctively he braked hard, yanking back on the wheel and waiting for the crash . . . which did not come. The trees ended and a runway opened up on his right.

He read the sign 'Aerodrome de Mandelieu', his foot easing on the brake, and without deliberation he swerved to where the exit road led off.

An old Beechcraft, floodlit and painted yellow, surmounted a column by open gates. He turned in to coast down a road hemmed by street lamps and wire netting. Beyond was the outline shape of hangars dark against the sky, a pen of light aircraft. He saw a Cessna and a Hughes helicopter as he passed, headed for the illuminated administration building.

He parked the Ferrari among a half-dozen cars outside. As

soon as he entered he could see through the plate-glass wall onto the tarmac where the Lear jet was taxiing up to the apron and coming to a stop. The slender plane was all white with a broad black stripe running along its length, and the thin nose of a shark in place of whose fins were the raked nacelles of the jets.

As Just watched a man descended from the cockpit. He wore a dark business suit and swung a briefcase in his hand as he walked toward the building in that fine mood which comes, however often-experienced, at the end of a flight and a safe landing. As he entered the glass door and turned toward the area marked 'Offices Administratifs' Just said: 'That is the most beautiful plane I have ever seen in my life.'

'Yours for half a million dollars,' answered the man gaily, pleased at the compliment.

The words were out of Just's mouth without a second thought: 'I'll buy it.'

Candles burned upon the table. From the shadowed background the music played, at the end of each disc a pause as the old player coped with the changeover, a click ... and then the rich tenor of Richard Tauber ... the voice of Howard Keel ... music from Oklahoma and Annie Get Your Gun ... the time when they had been young and rather rich and all the future stretched out ahead.

Henry and Yvonne dined formally, elaborately and well. There was champagne with the prawn cocktail, St Emilion which accompanied the roast; after chocolate cake and meringues just a taste of cheese to finish up the claret.

'I believe I'll never eat again,' Yvonne announced.

'Better leave a little room,' her husband cautioned. 'After all they have invited us to dinner tomorrow.'

Yvonne giggled.

'I do believe I'm tiddly,' she said.

Henry winked, and the gesture in that papery ancient face was horrible.

All shall be well, thought Just as he drove down the hill toward the mill at one AM with the moon down beyond the ridge now and the night darker. All is seasonal. All can be restored. He would close up the house, pack money, baggage, girl into the Lear jet and take to the airlanes of the world. To pay for it was exactly the stimulus he required. He was too young to retire. There would always be another option and a fresh beginning.

The thought of the new plane put him in fine good humour. The Cessna and the Bentley Continental had gone in the passing of Robert Just but, unlike that worn, unique and one-eyed teddy bear whose loss had left him forever bereft, the toys of adulthood are all replaceable.

Now, reborn as Michael Law, he was a rich man. Also thanks to Dr Benoit's ministrations at the delivery, he was five years younger. The idea of it made him feel he had stolen a march on life and put the knock on Father Time himself. The windows of the lower mill were black but upstairs a light still shone in the old couple's house.

It was very dark down at the bottom of the valley. The dense foliage of the steep banks soaked up the starlight into sombre gloom. The spire of rock which reared behind the house was bleached by the unseen moon. He saw the mountain lean. For a moment he had the dizzy fancy that it swayed and was about to topple forward and extinguish him.

He let himself into the house. The room was dark, and growing chill, the fire out. He went upstairs. Her door was ajar and somehow the light within was different from that dim and cosy glow which showed when the electric fire burned. Harsher and more blue.

Indeed that new Calor heater was the thing which he saw as

he drew abreast of the door and first looked in. Then he saw the bed. And his mind grasped back to the image of the new stove, clung desperately to the humdrum remembrance that he had said he would fetch it down from the upper mill and had not, that it looked heavy and she and the old couple had been obliged to hump it down themselves. That he had said he would and had not. And then his mind's frantic evasion cracked. There was no thought but only feeling, only that massive shock in the gut and icy fire seeping into his limbs, a wave of weakness drenching him as he looked at the two figures coupled on the bed.

The boy lay upon his back. The girl squatted on his groin, crouched and resting on her hands. She drove down on him inside her, rocked forward to withdraw. With a grunt she drove down hard again. And then she felt Just's hand upon her back. The boy's eyes flared in alarm. He tried to sit up but Just's hand on the girl's spine pressed them together. And in that second of time when, held down by him, they saw the man, they saw that he, as well, was naked.

Much later, the boy dismissed, Just lay with her alone.

She slept upon his breast, a sweated curl stuck to her cheek, her adorable lips parted with exhaustion. Used, abased, subjected and won over, she was his now entirely. Slut schoolgirl, waif and innocent, his joy, his girlhood, his creature and his slave. His love.

The door was shut upon the world, the window closed. His body was languorous with heat. His face wore the lineaments of satisfied desire.

The man's eyelids drooped upon his cheek, half-opened drowsily on the ceiling to a map of cracks shaping the blurred vision of a further landscape lit by the fevered pallor of the Calor flame ... and dimming into sleep.

Just's eyes closed for the last time.

Twenty Six

The lizard lived under a stone by the front door, at the angle where the crumbling steps started down toward the river.

He had slept there undisturbed throughout the winter and, at first, when the man and the girl moved into the mill he had watched them cautiously from the darkness of his hiding place and ventured out for food only when they were gone.

Then as spring became summer and the days lengthened and the sun rose higher and hotter in the sky the lizard had grown bolder and studied the man and the girl as they passed in and out of the house while he lay with his grey body flattened to the stone ready to flick back into his hole at the first sign of danger.

After a time he saw that they offered him no threat and he lay there through the summer and watched them in their comings and goings with his bright hooded eyes and came to know their habits.

Now the morning sun reached that corner of the house at 8 AM to warm his rock and the lizard came out then and basked with his ears keyed for the faint sounds from inside which told him that the girl was up.

Presently he would hear the handle turn and see her come out, pushing the door open with her knee as she balanced in her hands a box of trash. The door was heavy and stiff on its hinges, making the girl's movement awkward, and often the box would tilt and a few scraps scatter down on the two metres of paved stone outside the door which was the lizard's kingdom. The worst of this she would pick up and return to the box but his landscape remained baited. Immediately she was gone the first flies would come. This morning the sun was hot and higher than usual. It was late and the lizard was hungry. His domain was all of stone and barren. There was nothing there to lure his prey.

The lizard lay with ears tuned to the silence in the house.

He had lain there a long time, immobile and at one with the grey stone, before he heard the first human movement of the day. But it came from the path above. His eyes swivelled up. An old woman was descending the steps toward the lower mill. She walked carefully, with high exaggerated steps picking her cautious way. The lizard's eyes followed her to the door. She rapped twice, timidly. She leaned forward and set her ear to the woodwork. Then she knocked again. Louder this time, and longer.

A third time she banged. Listened. She set her hand to the door, pulled it open and went in.

The lizard's eyes switched back to his estate but his ears followed her footsteps on the stone floor and heard the tap of her shoe on the first step of the stair.

'Mr Law! Marianne! I say!'

The footsteps receded up the stairs.

A fly wavered at the far corner of his territory. The lizard's eyes darted to it. The fly landed and began to crawl across the stone. Then suddenly a clatter and commotion from within, rat-tat-tatting down the spiral stairs, clatter across the floor and the door flung wide, whacking into the wall.

Yvonne came flying out, scarf slipped down and sparse hair flapping with her ungainly haste, scrabbling in desperate urgency up the path, mouth wide and ... the lizard had not moved till then. He had tensed ready when the door slammed open and that dishevelled harridan rushed out ...

... SCREECHING ...

On that terrible noise the lizard flicked into his hole as the crazed figure stumbled up the hill shrieking.

'Henry! The doctor! Call the doctor! Quickly! It's both of them!'

Upon the crumpled bed Just and Marianne sprawled in shit and vomit. In the sour breathless air they lay in the discarded attitudes of death and both their naked bodies were brightly coloured blue.

Twenty Seven

The story was announced on the front page of Nice Matin:

'*DOUBLE ASPHYXIE ACCIDENTELLE DANS UN MOULIN A LEZAT*'

The reader was referred to page three for the story.

There was a photograph of Henry and Yvonne captioned: 'The English couple who discovered the body'.

'Of course that's not strictly true,' said Henry, 'the papers always get everything wrong. It was you, dear, who discovered the body.'

'Go on, dear,' urged Yvonne. 'Read it out.'

'*ENGLISH LOCATAIRE SUCCUMBS. HIS LITTLE FRIEND IS IN COMA.*'

Yvonne sniffed.

'Friend!'

Henry read: 'An asphyxiation accident has cost the life, in the night of Thursday to Friday, of Mr Michael Philip Law. 47 years, English tourist. His young friend Marianne Gladys Brent, 18 years, equally *intoxiquée* ...'

Henry paused.

'*Intoxiquée*? That's intoxicated – but it doesn't make sense.'

'Perhaps it means "poisoned",' Yvonne suggested.

'Go on anyway.'

'... equally *intoxiquée*, has still not regained consciousness at the hospital of La Fontonne where she was transported in all urgency. No improvement in her condition has been constated and the doctors at her bedside will not prognosticate. Mr Law and his friend descended to the Coast in the month of April where they rented the mill from M Henri and Mme Yvonne Wilkinson. During their prolonged stay they became so impressioned by our Coast that Mr Law purchased the property where he met his death.

On Thursday, after an agreeable day on the beach and dinner in a restaurant the unlucky pair returned to their house and retired to bed.

On Friday, toward midday, Mme Wilkinson rendered visit on her friends. There being no response to her knocks, she penetrated into the building and discovered the inanimate bodies of Mr Law and his friend in their bedroom. Comprehending immediately that the air of the room was rarefied Mme Wilkinson opened the windows and gave the alert. Shortly afterwards, Dr Bocca, specialist and president of Red Cross at Cannes, joined the efforts of the Sapeurs Pompiers who were already in place. Mouth-to-mouth, cardiac massage, injections, oxygen mask, all were attempted, but in vain. Mr Law had succumbed. However, after long efforts, the rescuers *suprirent* ... I'm not sure how to translate that to you, exactly.'

Yvonne said: 'It doesn't matter. Go on.'

'... A breath of life in Miss Brent who was immediately transported (while artificial respiration continued) to the hospital La Fontonne. Yesterday evening the condition of the young woman, who had still not recovered consciousness, was causing profound anxiety.

The Gendarmerie of Lezat has been able to determine the cause of this asphyxiation. After going to their room the couple set in action a portable gas heater. When the door of the room was closed the combustion of this heater absorbed the oxygen in the surrounding air and carbon dioxide filled the room. The two were overtaken by the poisoned atmosphere and Mr Law perished without waking. His death has thrown the neighbourhood into consternation and the M and Mme Wilkinson are receiving medical care in their distress.'

Twenty Eight

It is an ill wind that blows nobody any good, but then John Quinlan, *Daily Chronicle's* stringer in Cannes, was about as close to being a nobody as anyone could get who, in his bouts of sobriety, still worked for a national daily paper.

It was he who had copied to London the local story about an English couple who had come by a fatal accident in the hills. It was he who was landed with its follow-up which involved being dressed, shaved and coherent at 10 AM at Nice airport to meet Marianne's parents on the first connecting flight from London.

Quinlan found the assignment acutely embarrassing. Their grief did not distress him for he was a journalist, professionally distanced from the pain of others, but it was the first time Mr and Mrs Brent had ever been abroad. They travelled on emergency passports issued the previous afternoon and were so clearly incapable of recovering their luggage or changing currency or looking after themselves in any way that he was obliged to perform these functions for them as might a courier to some embarrassing cut-price package tours. Three people of Quinlan's acquaintance passed while he was so engaged, people who knew him only as the sophisticate *raconteur* of the Blue Bar and Carlton Terrace, the intimate of film stars and crony of lesser royalty. That he should be spotted scurrying to serve a couple so unsuitably dressed, instructed by them in such loud and common accents, was, he found, profoundly upsetting.

He drove them to the hospital at Antibes and waited while they visited their daughter, who was still in a coma. Afterwards he acted as interpreter in their discussion with her doctors. From there he took them to lunch, though he chose a restaurant which would certainly not be frequented by anyone he knew.

The Brents had been very upset by the shock of Marianne's appearance and the vagueness and foreignness of the physicians attending her, who had been unable or unwilling to give any prognosis on when, or if, she would recover consciousness. In the restaurant, after drinks, wine and the reassurance of the food, they relaxed sufficiently to answer questions which Quinlan himself only now felt well enough to ask.

They had no idea their daughter was in France, they said. She had gone on holiday for the summer. They had believed she was hiking around Europe with a girlfriend. She knew how to look after herself. She was no-one's fool, was Marianne. Like a bad penny, they had known she would turn up in time. But what of this man, Quinlan asked and checked his note, this Michael Phillip Law who had perished in the accident, had she not informed them she was with him? The Brents stared blankly back. This was the first mention they had heard of Michael Phillip Law. They had no idea who he might be. It was a puzzlement.

Quinlan rid himself of the couple that afternoon only by driving them to Nice, installing them in a hotel and explaining he had work to do but certainly would call for them next morning if not later that very day. They clung to him with pathetic friendliness, abroad was for them a place of unknown terrors.

Quinlan felt enervated. Having extricated himself he went to the Negresco, gave the hall porter the hundred francs which he slipped him every week for information on the hotel guest list, then installed himself in the bar for a large restoring brandy. In these opulent and familiar surroundings he soon revived. Ordering a second brandy he called for the telephone and rang the British Consul, a man with whom he sometimes played golf. It was monstrous, he complained, that he should be left holding the baby in this fashion. The Brents were not his responsibility. He had done a day as nursemaid, tomorrow the Consul must send his girl to escort them to the hospital and make any arrangements which might prove necessary. Out of the question, he was told, the police had picked up three English hairies on a drugs raid in Juan. One of them had turned out to be the son of an MP. The girl was fully occupied in trying to get him bail. Then what of the man who was dead, Quinlan asked, had he no relatives flying down for the funeral who could be of help? Well, it was very odd, the Consul said, he had telexed details of Law's passport to the Foreign Office in order that they might trace next of kin. He had just heard back. There was no record of such a man in London. It seemed the passport was a forgery.

Quinlan rang off then, ordered another drink and pondered. As the man said, it was certainly very odd. It looked as though what had started as an insignificant human interest story might be turning into something else. Quinlan had a dinner invitation and the prospect of further work that day was distasteful, yet his senses were not so completely atrophied by three years of retirement living among the fleshpots that he could not recognise the smell of news.

An hour and a half later he was at the mill in a thoroughly bad temper over the difficulty he had experienced in finding his way there.

He knocked, introduced himself to Henry and Yvonne, and was warmly welcomed. They served him tea and talked willingly, retelling at considerable length the circumstances in which they had discovered the accident but were of no help in his cautious enquiries concerning the identity of the victim. The couple had stayed there since the spring. No mail had come to the house nor, so far as they knew, had they received any visitors.

After wasting a couple of hours with them, Quinlan asked if he might look over the place where the man and girl had lived.

It was dusk by now. They led him down through the overgrown garden and showed off the house with pride and pleasure. He concealed his surprise at the shoddy nature of the accommodation and exclaimed in gratifying wonder at the splendid mill room with its flagstone floor and massive beams.

They took him back to their own place and he prepared to depart. On the way out he paused. Would they mind, he asked, if he came back next day with a photographer? They were delighted; of course they would love it. But was there enough light, he wondered aloud; might he take one further glance over the lower mill as he left, just to check the power supply and points? He would not dream of incommoding them further ... if they would only lend him a torch he would leave it where they would find it in the morning. How kind.

Alone this time, he made the descent again. The undergrowth pricked and caught at his trouser legs. What a deserted God-forsaken spot this was, Quinlan thought. If someone wanted to hide out he could scarcely find a place more isolated and concealed. But who might he have been, this dead man who was not called Michael Law?

The house was chill. The huge room was bleak and empty, its shadows harsh in the thin light of an overhead bulb. From outside came the low roar of the waterfall. The ashes of a long-dead fire lay scattered in the grate. No trace remained in the mill-room of the couple who once had lived here. He climbed the stairs. He glanced through the clothes hung in the girl's cupboard then went down the passage to the bedroom where the man had died.

Suits and shirts were neatly hung in place. Paris labels, and everything almost new. The soles on three pairs of shoes were scarcely marked. There was nothing old or worn and no bric-a-brac, none of the odds and ends or litter which a person accumulates in the normal course of living, no old letters, credit cards, address book, keys, cheque stubs. He had been a man sparsely, even minimally, equipped.

He examined the contents of a massive rickety chest of drawers which stood beside the bed. He found handkerchiefs, socks, a copy of *Time* magazine folded back at the Milestones page. He read,

> 'DIED. Franklin Lewis Maxwell, 42, self-proclaimed President of Belida, Windward Islands; of cancer. Seizing power in a coup two years ago, Maxwell instituted a reign of terror, ruthlessly eliminating all opposition before nationalising foreign investment, destroying tourism and crippling the island's economy to a point where it will take years to recover.

Who had marked that paragraph, he wondered, and what had the information meant to him? The answer would never be known. He tossed the magazine upon the chest, watched it land and slide, hit the wall and drop behind. He heard it check, the chink of metal . . . fall. He leaned, peered down. Dust and darkness; he could see nothing.

Quinlan lay down upon the bed where the unknown man last had slept. Turning his head upon the pillow, he squinted along the crack between chest and wall. Something was jammed there, resting on the ledge formed by the wooden crosspiece. He stretched in his fingers – then snatched back his hand in shock at the cold kiss of steel.

He could hear the beating of his heart, a noise in his ears like surf which could have been the river or the roar of his own blood. He wrapped his handkerchief around his hand and reached in again. He gripped the object at the very extremity of its muzzle and drew it slowly out toward him.

He laid the gun upon the sheet with infinite gentleness and studied it, his mind racing in conjecture. So who had he been, this fugitive hidden in a lonely mill, a man on the run without identity or possessions? A man afraid, who slept at night a gun within reach beside his bed? Who? The definitive answer had to lie here, in the fingerprints marked upon this deadly and unlawful instrument.

Quinlan was filled with a great joy as he looked at the gun. He wondered what had brought the man to die here, what force had driven him. He thought of the route which he had followed himself to reach this coast, and the fear and humiliation and the ageing. He thought of the concealments, all the evasions, and of the shabby compromise which had obliged him to accept this job as alternative to redundancy and to nothing. An uncharacteristic flicker of gratitude roused for a moment in his heart at what the dead man had given him. Inadequate; a has-been; a soak. I'll show them now, he thought.

At an altitude of 30,000 feet the British Airways Trident flew down the valley of the Rhône. From it, in the cloudless air, the river line was clearly visible with, beside it, the black ribbon of the autoroute down which Just and Marianne had driven months before in the Ferrari on their journey to the South.

The plane passed high above Avignon, coming to the sea and turning left, steadily losing height as it followed the coast toward its landfall at Nice.

The Morar brothers were passengers on this plane and so were Inspector Mallinson and Sergeant Byrne of the Fraud Squad at Scotland Yard. These two pairs, both with the same objective, were not seated together as the Morars travelled First. They did not come face to face until they descended at the airport. For the Morars, well-laced with free champagne, their stomachs lined by pre-packed delicacies, it was an unpleasant experience, this encounter with the policeman who had caused them so much trouble by his investigation into theirs and Just's affairs and who was responsible for the criminal prosecution which shortly would bring them into court for violation of the laws which govern British Currency Exchange Control.

Flash bulbs spluttered in their faces. A man pressed forward ... 'Quinlan ... *Daily Chronicle*'.

'No comment,' said Lord Morar, pushing past. 'No comment ...'

A police Citroen waited for Inspector Mallinson and Sergeant Byrne, a chauffeur-driven limousine for the Morars which, obeying the speed limit, reached the hospital at Antibes second by some fifteen minutes.

Though the police officers were allowed in immediately to view the unconscious Marianne whilst the Morars did not manage to penetrate further than the reception area despite the insistence of their lawyer, both groups advanced their enquiries by precisely the same amount: Nothing.

The woman on duty that afternoon in hospital reception left work seven hundred francs richer than she had come. By the hand of their lawyer the Morars bribed her to be informed when Marianne recovered consciousness. Earlier that same day a Dr Liebel from Zurich had asked to be apprised of the same information, putting down two hundred francs where the Englishmen gave five. But then the Morars were accustomed to pay too much for everything.

The English police, the Morar brothers and Marianne's parents, all remained on the Coast awaiting her recovery.

During the three weeks that she remained in a coma the story achieved bold prominence in the European press. It was disclosed that the man who had died in the name of Michael Law was an impostor and a thief. The manner of his embezzlement was revealed and the sum disclosed which he had with him in a suitcase at the start of that journey which led him between three countries through a fake death to a real.

Considerable interest was aroused in the whereabouts of the missing money. Just's movements were plotted and retraced. From Belida to London to Amsterdam to France his trail was laid bare. A part of that journey was reconstructed, a further part inferred. On television and in the papers the story was expanded and retold with speculation and informed conjecture.

The police, the parties concerned, the public, all awaited the revelation which would follow upon Marianne's returning to consciousness.

During the period whilst all this went on, Henry and Yvonne became firm friends with the Brents, Marianne's parents, who stayed with them. The old couple lived in the spotlight of celebrity. In town where they were known, they were regarded with a certain awe. They dressed in their cleanest clothes and always looked their best for they received many visitors, the manner of all uniformly solicitous and polite. Their photographs appeared in all the papers and they were interviewed on television.

Far from being distressed or made nervous by so much attention, they adored every vibrant moment. Both of them were thrilled. They could not sleep with excitement. At night, when they were alone, joy possessed them. There was Justice in the world. They had proved it and found Fame.

Even after she recovered from the coma Marianne remained for many weeks in hospital at La Fontonne, not well enough to be moved.

Three days after she woke, Inspector Mallinson and Sergeant Byrne returned to England. On the same day, but this time on a different plane, the Morar brothers also flew back to London to resume consultation with the lawyers preparing a defence for their forthcoming trial.

After a further week brought no improvement to his daughter's sad condition, her father returned, through necessity, to his job in London. Her mother remained with Henry and Yvonne and visited her in hospital every day.

Since coming out of the coma Marianne had not recognised her parents. Her state was tragic. The brain damage she had suffered was irreversible, her amnesia total. Her memory and power of speech were gone.

At first a flurry of excitement followed her return to consciousness but, after that, few further stories appeared about the case. The stolen funds had disappeared with the death of Just. Even if Marianne knew the answer – which was far from sure – the secret of its whereabouts was lost forever in the barren wilderness of her disordered mind.

Days passed. New events happened in the world. The papers carried news of other matters and, as time went by, public interest died.

By all except a very few Just was entirely forgotten. He was a man without morals who had lived according to his lights. More than most he had struggled to direct the course of his existence. He had sought delight and suffered pain, experienced advances and reversals of fortune and known both penury and wealth, but he had never stayed ahead. Now the angels who watched over him had finished their sport with Robert Just.

But even his passing contained one last and hidden irony.

In the several official investigations of his fraud, which involved the police forces of France, Britain and the Netherlands, and in their consequent reports, in the wide coverage the subject received on television, in the enquiries which lawyers conducted on behalf of the deceived creditors and in the countless thousands of words written about the case in magazines, Sunday supplements and daily newspapers over a period of weeks, the one question which was never raised by anyone was whether Just's death had been anything except an accident. The alternative occurred to nobody.

Twenty Nine

Marianne's mother ran a dress shop in Willesden.

In France she was allowed to visit her daughter for an hour every day and for the rest of the time she felt foreign and uncomfortable. Nice though the old couple were to her, Mrs Brent was restless and ill at ease.

'Of course you're *welcome*,' Yvonne told her one day as she had before. 'Welcome to stay absolutely as long as you like, but really it's *absurd* for you to make this sacrifice. The poor sweet, even when she comes out of hospital she'll need building up. How can you manage to look after her in London when both of you work? Now what would be *much* more sensible would be for you to fly back to England and sort out all these *ghastly* problems at the shop you've told us about and *we'll* look after Marianne till she goes home to you. She'll stay with us. The air, the sun, this splendid climate . . . it'll be so much more healthy than dusty old London.'

Mrs Brent, who loved her daughter, was dubious about this arrangement though, in a way, it did make sense.

'What you must try to understand,' Henry added in his gentle voice, 'is that at our age one tends to feel redundant, sadly useless. It's a privilege to have this opportunity. We have so much here. And this beautiful place *belongs* to Marianne now, anyway. We *want* to be of help.'

Yvonne said, 'When you come to fetch her, Mrs Brent, I promise you won't recognise the little girl. She'll be the very *picture* of health, a real Bisto baby. Henry's right, it'll be our privilege. And I was *trained* as a nurse. In the WRENS, you know ...'

And so it was arranged.

Today the living room of the upper mill did not look the same.

For one thing, the furniture had been properly repaired and vases of cut flowers stood on the bureau and the table. With the many friends who dropped in to visit now, Henry and Yvonne had been obliged to make the place look its best. It meant a lot more work, of course, but a woman from the village came in for three hours a day and that was a great help.

In truth, Yvonne thought this afternoon, the place really was looking superb. They had even had a mason come to do some work outside.

Dressed in a new summer frock, alone in the house, she was preparing a slap-up tea for three.

She set a table in the garden where there had been a lawn, painstakingly maintained, which now was a paved terrace shaded by an awning from the bright heat of the afternoon sun.

A difference was noticeable in Yvonne as well. She looked younger. She hummed cheerfully as she worked.

Little water flowed down the river now. The cascade had shrunk to a trickle into the rockpool and ferns sprouted where the torrent had roared. On this secluded terrace which overlooked the property the noise was no more than a murmur.

A taxi horn sounded on the road below.

Yvonne hurried indoors for a plate of cucumber sandwiches which were keeping cool and moist until the last second before arrival. Seting them down, she stepped back to admire the effect. Covered by a lace cloth the table was elaborately arranged. There were willow pattern plates and the good silver. There was a crystal dish of meringues swollen with cream and a pedestal stand for the chocolate cake. The feast was displayed in the diffused light below the canopy with backdrop of the leafy valley in the lull of a summer's afternoon.

Like an advertisement, thought Yvonne with a thrill of pride. It looked like a colour photograph in a glossy magazine.

Two figures came up the path from the road. She smoothed down her skirt and turned to greet them.

It is the obligation of the gentlewoman to show no shock, to allow no dismay or setback, loss nor horror, to crack the bright brave smile. *Noblesse oblige.* Yet, when she first saw Marianne, Yvonne's expression wavered, faltered and almost fell.

Henry had been prepared for this. He fielded the stumbled second with a hearty cry. 'I say, how smashing! What a simply *ripping* tea! I say, how you've *slaved*!'

Gripping the girl firmly at the elbow he led her across the terrace and settled her into a chair.

Yvonne stared in dismay.

Marianne had been a very pretty girl. All the features which had made her so were still in evidence, but now the relationship one to another was altered. The landscape of the face was brutally rearranged and the effect was horrible. Blank eyes stared from a dead, sagged face. The jaw hung slack. A rope of spittle suspended from the drooling mouth.

'Now, the most *marvellous* idea,' Henry cried, '*so* hot it was in the taxi. Positively stifling. *So* hot, and we've been playing a little game, the two of us, haven't we, dear?'

He appealed excitedly to Marianne as if the very force of his enthusiasm might draw some spark of response from the leaden figure slumped in the chair.

But Marianne did not move. Her dead gaze strayed across the valley. Henry chattered on undaunted.

'We were imagining, the two of us, what we *most* wanted in the whole wide world. And what it is ... you'll never guess.'

'I'm *sure* I shan't,' said Yvonne, recovering her normal manner. 'Whatever can it be?'

'*Iced tea!*' Henry announced in triumph.

'Iced tea?'

Yvonne looked quite confused.

'*Yes!* In great big glasses with ice and mint in it.'

'But ...'

'Of course we've got mint,' Henry said with a trace of impatience. 'It's growing just behind the house.'

'But how ...'

'You crush it, and you put ice ... come, I'll show you, dear.'

In the kitchen Yvonne set the kettle on to boil while Henry waded into the brambles and wrenched up handfuls of the herb, ignoring the thorns which tore his bare ankles above the short Marks and Spencer socks.

Yvonne was at the sink attempting to extract ice cubes from their tray when Henry returned and said quite loudly, 'It will be all right.'

Yvonne glanced outside and whispered, 'Are you sure?'

'She's an idiot, a cabbage, a stupid useless lump of flesh.'

In the same furtive tone, Yvonne asked, 'What did the doctor say?'

'Her memory *may* come back. This place may do it ...' his eyes narrowed, 'or a shock perhaps.'

She threw him a quick frightened glance.

'But you don't *know* it is here.'

Henry's nails ripped at the leaves. His face was sharp, white with hate.

'Of course it is! We'll get it out of the little bitch and if we don't, so what? Once this place is ours again we've got all the time in the world to search.'

A bowl of roses stood upon the table. Yvonne watched a bee clamber from a flower's furry throat.

'Henry,' she asked in a voice which trembled, 'isn't it terribly wicked?'

'*Wicked?*' He sounded outraged. 'Wicked? With people like *that*?'

She whispered, 'It mustn't be another fire.'

'Fire?' Henry repeated and she was frightened for he sounded so very angry. 'It wasn't a *fire*, you idiot, it was a Calor heater and entirely their own fault. The fools should have known without being told to open a window. I'll tell you how to deal with the little slut. You can trust *me*, can't you?'

'Yes,' Yvonne said, chastened, 'I know I'm silly sometimes. Yes Henry, of course I trust you. You're the only one I can.'

They returned to the terrace with crystal glasses of iced tea on a silver tray. Marianne sat in the same collapsed attitude with vacant face. Urged by Henry she had started to eat but now the sandwich lay mashed in her listless hand. A slice of chewed tomato had dribbled from her mouth to stain the crisp white shirt.

Henry picked up a napkin from the table and wiped Marianne's lips and chin. It was done without embarrassment, as though the gesture were the most natural thing in the world. He said, 'It's going to be a *lovely* summer. Brigadier Markham has got the most *adorable* rabbits. "Giants of Flanders" they're called and they're simply *immense*. Huge cuddly bundles. He's said we can go to see them.'

He set a glass in the girl's hand. Even as he drew back it slid from Marianne's grasp, fell and shattered on the ground.

Yvonne let out a little cry but Henry stifled his annoyance.

'Tch Tch! What a butterfingers. Aren't we such a clumsy muggins? Never mind.'

He got up to fetch a cloth.

The girl seemed unaware of the accident. Neither crash nor disturbance had penetrated the cottonwool cavern of her mind.

With the dull eyes of an idiot she gazed out over the valley in profile to Yvonne who watched her now in hypnotic fascination. No word came. Deprived of her husband's presence she had absolutely no idea what to say.

Time seemed to stretch. The fibres which held her together began to fray and come apart and an awful sense of helplessness crept over Yvonne and then she heard a funny noise.

Water was splashing through the chair. She stared in horror at the puddle spreading below where the girl sat. With a moan she leapt up and ran to find Henry.

Even now the girl did not shift position, slouched in the awful dumped stance of the defective. Catatonic, she continued to stare out over the garden and the river and the lower mill where the money was hidden and where she had lived with Just.

Yet, if you had been there at that particular moment on that sunlit terrace in the summer afternoon, yourself unseen and watching very carefully, an outsider, a stranger and observer to the scene, you might have noticed something else.

The slack mouth tightened and Marianne's lips twitched in a terribly strange smile.

It was over in the instant. No one was present to notice it. No one saw. Yet, had you been there and remarked that smile, you would not have said this girl was an imbecile.

No, you would not have thought that at all.